BOOKS BY DAN JENKINS

SEMI-TOUGH

SEMI-TOUGH

DAN JENKINS

New York   *1972*   ATHENEUM

A portion of this book has appeared in PLAYBOY *magazine.*

Copyright © 1972 by Dan Jenkins
All rights reserved
Library of Congress catalog card number 72–78289
Published simultaneously in Canada by McClelland and Stewart Ltd.
Manufactured in the United States of America by
Kingsport Press, Inc., Kingsport, Tennessee
Designed by Kathleen Carey
First Printing July 1972
Second Printing September 1972

Once more for June and the dumplings,
who surrender their time

CONTENTS

PART ONE

Good Old Pals

I could halfway fall in love,
For part of a lonely night,
With a semi-pretty woman in my arms.
　　　—from "Nuthin' Much to Want,"
　　　a song by Elroy Blunt

I GUESS BY NOW THERE CAN'T be too many people any-where who haven't heard about Billy Clyde Puckett, the humminest sumbitch that ever carried a football. Maybe you could find some Communist chinks someplace who don't know about me, but surely everybody in America does if they happen to keep up with pro football, which is what I think everybody in America does. That, and jack around with somebody else's wife or husband.

Anyhow, Billy Clyde Puckett turns out to be me, the book writer who is writing this book about his life and his loves and his true experiences in what you call your violent world of professional football.

I happen to be writing it in my spare time between running over a whole pile of niggers in the National Foot-ball League.

And let me get something straight right away which bothers me. Just because I may happen to say nigger doesn't mean that I'm some kind of racist. One of the big troubles with the world of modern times, I think, is that somebody is always getting hot because somebody else says nigger instead of nee-grow.

Because of this very thing I said nigger just now to get your attention. It seems to have a certain shock value. But

I don't think nigger in my heart. Not the way some people do when they mean a nigger is a lazy sumbitch who won't block or tackle or wash dishes fast enough.

It's just a word, anyway. Nigger, I mean. It's just a word that some dumb-ass plantation owner made up one time by accident when he tried to pronounce nee-grow.

I say nigger sometimes in jest, and most of the time I'll say it to a nigger who understands what I mean. On our team, in fact, we even have a play—a deep pass pattern—which some of us call Niggers Go Long.

I also use a few words like hebe and spick and some other things which might not necessarily flatter a person's name and address, but actually this is how a lot of studs talk in the National Football League.

We're fairly honest. We might call a spook a spook, unless he's a spick.

What I'm getting at is that a football player is a football player and nothing else as far as we're concerned. Now if a nigger doesn't want to be a nigger in real life, that's something else. But I sure know several who can block and tackle themselves pretty damn white.

My best buddy Shake Tiller and me decided a long time ago about this racial question. We decided that nobody can help being what he is, whether it turns out to be black as a cup of coffee at a truck stop, or a white Southern dumb-ass like most of our parents. A man makes himself a man by whatever he does with himself, and in pro football that means busting his ass for his team.

So Shake and me joke about this racial business. Like me and Shake have this thing that we say to people at luncheons or banquets when they come up to ask for our autographs and grill us about what it's like to play pro football.

"Aw, we don't like it so much," Shake or me will say. "Mainly, we just like to take showers with niggers."

A few years ago when Shake and me first came up to the New York Giants—back there before we turned the Giants into a winner—I remember that there were some racial problems going on around the league.

Seemed like everybody was some kind of a holdout. There were salary arguments and pension disputes and a lot of courtroom business, and if it wasn't the white stud quarterback who wanted another two million dollars, it was the spook flanker.

These were days when there were more hell-raising agents in the dressing rooms than there was tape.

This was back when the owners and coaches had a saying they lived by. They said a team with seven spooks could make the play-offs and a team with nine spooks could get to the Super Bowl. But a team with ten spooks or more probably couldn't beat Denver.

Back then the newspapers were full of some crap about the Giants being overdue for some racial turmoil because they had slowly become a squad with almost as many spooks as Catholics. This was when Shake Tiller made his first big impression on the team even though he was a rookie.

Everybody knew Shake could catch balls and give the Giants a deep threat like they'd never had before. But everybody didn't know Shake had a big old heart in him about like a grapefruit that went around feeling things in regard to the world in general.

It was up at Yankee Stadium one day after practice that Shake made this talk to the squad which, I think, helped us to become a well-knit unit. Shake brought the racial turmoil out in the open where the Giants could all look at it.

Shake stood up on a bench in the dressing room and said, "I think we got some shit we need to talk about, man to man."

I recall that Puddin Patterson from Grambling, our best offensive guard, was flopped out on the floor picking at his toenails, and when Shake said that, Puddin belched real loud.

"Puddin's with me," Shake said. "Anybody else?"

Nobody said anything, but T. J. Lambert, our big old defensive end from Tennessee, hiked his leg and made a noise like a watermelon being dropped on concrete out of a four-story building.

When everbody stopped laughing, Shake got into his talk.

"I think a man has a right to be whatever he wants to be," Shake said. "By that I mean if we've got any niggers who'd rather be spicks, then I say we ought to buy 'em some sombreros and guitars. On the other hand, if we've got any hebes who'd rather be chinks, then I say that's all right, too. But I also think a nigger can be a nigger if he wants to."

Shake said, "There's only one thing. If a nigger's gonna be a nigger, then he better be able to block."

Puddin Patterson butted in and said, "Say, baby, that don't seem fair. Cat don't have to block if he's tired, does he?"

Everybody laughed again.

Shake smiled himself and he said, "That's right, Puddin. You don't have to block anybody at all, but you know yourself that a sumbitch who don't block or tackle is nothing but a nigger hebe spick with a little A-rab thrown in. By the way. We got any A-rabs around here?"

Puddin said, "T. J. Lambert smells like one—with a goat under each arm."

As far as I know, T. J. Lambert is about the meanest sumbitch that ever lived, much less stunk. He's about six feet five and weighs about two sixty without a towel wrapped around his freckled belly. I'd guess he takes a shower about every five days and some people say that this alone is what makes T. J. so mean.

They say that when T. J. was in college at Tennessee he kept a mad dog chained up in his room in the dorm and used to feed it live cats. They say that instead of going down the hall to the toilet T. J. had a habit of taking a dump in his closet. And when it got to smelling so bad in his room that even T. J. would notice it, they say he would throw a bunch of newspapers in the closet and set fire to the whole mess.

I would never say to T. J.'s face that he smelled like anything other than perfume because I think a man who can live with a mad dog and a closet load of dump can be expected to bust up some furniture every now and then.

We say the T. J. stands for Torn Jock because that's

what T. J. does to anybody who carries a football in his general direction. He tears their jock off. Actually the T. J. stands for Teddy James but you'd sooner call T. J. an A-rab than his real name.

When Puddin Patterson said T. J. smelled like an A-rab that day in the dressing room, T. J. walked over to where Puddin was laying on the floor and cut another one that sounded kind of like a washing machine that was breaking down.

I guess I could tell stories about T. J. Lambert for as long as somebody would listen but I think certain things ought to be personal.

However, I think I ought to explain about T. J.'s ability to fart. Now that I've brought it up, in other words.

He sure can fart is what I'm getting at. And he can do it in as many different tones as you can imagine. And almost any time he wants to.

You can go up to T. J. and say, "Give me a long slow one," and T. J. can give you a long slow one, right away. You can ask him to give you a short sweet one and T. J. can lay it right on you.

As a matter of fact, T. J. has always claimed that he can fart in a lot of different colors, too, but of course I don't know anyone who ever cared enough to check up on it.

When T. J. went over and cut one at Puddin for calling him an A-rab, Puddin looked up and grinned, "Say, baby, was that one purple-pink with a little touch of green?"

And T. J. said, "Naw, it was light brown, the color that some niggers are, if they're lucky."

Puddin only laughed and said, "Sure would like to see me a nigger some day to find out if that's true."

While I'm on the subject of T. J.'s exceptional talent, I can't resist telling about his wedding night when he and his wife, Donna Lou, got married. He likes to tell it on himself, so I can't get into any terrible trouble with him.

It seems that when T. J. and Donna Lou got married they checked into a motel in Knoxville, and one of the first things T. J. wanted to do was play a little trick on his bride.

So when Donna Lou was in the bathroom changing into her nightgown, T. J. got naked and laid down on the bed and spread out his big old pink legs with his ass facing the bathroom door.

"I was gonna give her my Class A boomer," T. J. says. "When she come out of the bathroom, I was gonna cut one that would jar the window shades, and then for the rest of our married life there wouldn't be no trouble about me fartin' around the house. You never know whether a woman likes that kind of thing."

What happened of course was that Donna Lou came out of the bathroom and for the only time in his life, old T. J.'s talent betrayed him. Instead of farting, he shit all over the bed.

When Donna Lou gets drunk enough these days, she enjoys telling the story herself and she refers to T. J. as "old Rudolph Valentino over there." At which point T. J. is liable to unleash his Class A boomer.

But I've gotten away from Shake Tiller's talk to the squad.

My buddy said, "You studs don't have to listen to me because I'm only a rookie, and I'm what a lot of you spooks might think of as a red neck with a terminal case of the dumb-ass, but this team will wind up in trouble if we don't talk about it.

"So far as I can tell, we've got a real good bunch of ass holes around here and some stud athletes, both black and white. That's really all that matters. I want to get it straight that me and Billy C. there don't give a fuck what color any sumbitch is if he wants to win.

"There's no way I can prove to any of you spooks that I'm not a Southern dumb-ass because you don't know me so well yet. But I'll tell you this. The trouble with the world is not that a nigger can't get *in* a restaurant somewhere. The trouble is that a nigger can't get thrown *out*."

About right then, Puddin Patterson said, "Baby, you 'bout to make some sense."

"Well, I'm not up here to talk about the world," Shake said. "All I want to make clear is, a nigger who plays football can whitewash himself by knocking down more sumbitches than knock him down. And when he knocks down enough, he'll look around one day and find out he's rich and famous. Then he can go buy a Cadillac and a big house and start fucking up a good white neighborhood—or whatever it is you guys like to do."

Shake grinned in order to let everybody know that was a joke. The spooks, I mean. Some did and some didn't.

A couple of them just kept on standing around with their arms folded, staring down at the floor. As if they were listening to an assistant coach who was reminding them they had to quit stealing socks and sweatsuits.

Puddin Patterson said, "Say, baby, you don't have no idea what it's like to be black, you dig? So how come you standin' up there layin' out all this jive?"

Some spook voice from the back of the room said, "Tell me somethin' *about* it."

And another spook voice said, "Two, four, six, eight. Texas gonna integrate."

Shake answered Puddin. "All I'm talking about is trying to be a good football team. Is that what we're here for?"

Puddin said, "We doin' a job, baby. You catch them balls and I'll block them folks. Ain't nothin' else to it."

From somewhere again in the back of the room, a spook voice said, "Say, Puddin. You know what a Texan is?"

Puddin half-turned around.

He laughed and said to the room, "Cat done told me it was a Mexican on his way to Oklahoma."

Shake laughed.

"Here's all I mean. If any of us get the red ass about something, then we ought to talk it over among ourselves without any goddamn agitators or business agents telling somebody he ought to be a flanker instead of a guard. Or he ought to be doing more hair spray commercials."

Shake looked down at Puddin.

"I'm gonna catch the football and run like a nigger,

Puddin. You gonna block yourself white?"

Puddin didn't say anything.

"I can't help it because the Old Skipper up there put some niggers in the world, Puddin," said Shake. "I guess if we all had our choice we'd be rich, white, handsome and able to tap-dance. What I *can* help, though, is acting like I don't know any of you are *here*."

"We here, baby," somebody said.

Shake said, "To tell you the truth, I'm not eaten up with any goddamn hundred years of guilt about you sumbitches. You're just guys to me. And athletes. We've got to trust each other and be honest. And get drunk together, and get fucked together. That's the only way we can win together."

Shake paused a minute and stared at Puddin.

"Are we gonna win together?" Shake said.

Puddin slowly smiled and said:

"You want to know somethin', baby? I believe a cat could hang around with you and get hisself some white pussy."

There was honest laughter all around.

After a minute Shake said, "I just don't think a team has to have the kind of trouble that some other teams have had between spooks and everybody else. I just think we all ought to work to have a winner and if there's anybody around here who doesn't want to do that, then he can move his ass down the road."

Puddin said, "Everybody wants that, baby, but you sound like you think that if we don't win, it's gonna be the cats that fucked it up. You dig that?"

Shake grinned and said, "That's because we all know how lazy you folks are. Shit, we all know you'll quit a stream after two catfish. Right?"

Shake said he didn't have much else to say. He just wanted to bring it all out instead of keeping it buried, about feelings and all, and who everybody was, seeing as how most niggers were darker than whites.

Puddin finally said, "Say, I been thinkin' what movie star I want to be after I done took rich and blocked myself white. I believe I'll try bein' that cool Robert Redford cat. He looks like he could get hisself some good wool if he put his mind on it."

Shake said, "And I think I'll be that Sidney Poitier cat so I can cut all of your asses with white chicks."

I am white, of course. That's only important when you consider that I run with the football.

I'm white, stand about six two—just under—and weigh about two eighteen. If you're interested in what else I look like, my nose is slightly bent from catching a few licks and I've got about seventeen hundred dollars worth of teeth in my mouth that I wasn't born with.

There are those who say I have a warm smile and don't look mean off the field. My eyes are what you call your hazel, I guess. I don't tan so good in the summer. Just turn sort of light khaki.

I've got some shaggy hair that covers up most of my ears and hangs down in back, just below the bottom of my helmet. Barbara Jane Bookman says I can't keep my hair combed with a yard rake. It's dark brown. My hair, I mean. Not Barbara Jane.

I'm a neat dresser on game days. I keep my socks pulled up and I don't wear my hip pads on the outside of my jersey. I don't wear wrist bands or elbow pads, and I don't jack a lot of tape around on my low-quarter shoes.

The reason it's important that I'm white and play running back is that most of the great runners in history have been spooks. It used to be said that if a white stud came along who was as strong as Jim Brown and as quick as Gale Sayers, he could get richer than the Mafia playing football. I suppose I'm just about that person.

Old Billy Clyde's salary is up there in big figures now, and if you lump three years together, it's a real asstickler. I don't mean to sound like I'm bragging but I've been told to talk about myself in this book so that the casual followers of the game as well as the non-football readers would know something about me. That's what I'm doing in all honesty.

It turns out that I was a total All-America back in my college of TCU in Fort Worth, Texas. And so was my good buddy Shake Tiller, who has written the pilot film on split ends.

My running comes natural is the only way I can explain it. It seems that when I get a football in my arms I have a tendency to not get tackled so easy. I can't truly make it very clear about my life-chosen craft. But what I'm getting at is that even today after five years in the NFL when our quarterback, Hose Manning, squats back of the center and hollers out a play like, "Red, Curfew, Fifty-three, Sureside, hut, hut, hut," then what I mean is, if I get the ball, I have a serious tendency to turn into some kind of Red fuckin' Grange.

That almost takes care of me. Except that what I was leading up to is that I have carved out a special place for myself in football history by being a white pisser.

Shake Tiller has said that if I was black I would not be thought of so much as any kind of hell and it would hurt me in the pocketbook. He's probably right. I wish that I was black sometimes, not because it would make me any faster, but because a lot of my buddies on the Giants are spooks who don't really enjoy being spooks. I don't think I'd let the world jack me around so much if I was a spook, but then I can't actually say.

This has just reminded me of the first time me and Shake ever realized, deep down, that spooks weren't so bad. It was when we were freshmen at Paschal High and we were showering one afternoon after practice with some spooks.

Where we grew up, you never came in contact very often with many cats. Only at track meets, or in ball games, and never very many even then. You never said much to any of them, except, "Good lick," or something like that.

In Fort Worth the spooks all lived somewhere other than where your friends did. They certainly hung out at different drive-ins. I suppose we grew up thinking that a spook who could mow the lawn or get a job caddying had a better deal than most spooks could expect.

Something like that.

Anyhow, me and Shake were showering one afternoon and these cats came into the squad shower room with us. We just nodded to each other. We didn't know their names, only that they got bused in and played basketball pretty good.

If anybody had asked us—a couple of fifteen-year-old smart-asses—what their names were, we'd have probably said they were Isiah T. Washington and Clarence Er-Ah Teague.

After a few minutes, Shake said, loud enough for the spooks to hear, "Hey, Billy C., we been under this sprinkler for a long time and there ain't no smoke come off these Indians yet."

I said, "I guess that means we can't get contaminated or anything."

We were grinning.

One of the spooks looked over at us and said to his buddy, "Coach he say he promise this soap wash this grease right off me. Shit."

The other one said, "Yeah, Coach he say to scrub hod. I say er-uh I scrubbin' hod as I kin."

And they laughed.

Nobody said anything else.

We turned out to be pretty good pals with those two cats before we got out of high school. One of them had a hell of a fallaway jump shot.

I think it's fair for me to say that me and Shake never had anything against a spook of any kind—except for the ones which raised so much hell on the TV news. Everybody hates any shit-ass that raises so much crap

on TV that it knocks off your favorite show because a network thinks it has to do a special on all the hell that's
being raised.

A spook that didn't raise any hell was O.K. with us,
we thought.

And that's really no joke that you hear. They can solid
fuckin' dance, I'll tell you that. Nearly every one.

I have been so carried away trying to begin this book
that I've forgotten to tell anybody why I'm writing it, or
how it is getting itself written. I guess I ought to explain
it so it will give me a semi-clear conscience with my
teammates.

The main reason I'm writing the book is because I got
talked into it by an old newspaper friend in Texas. His
name is Jim Tom Pinch and if you've ever poked through
a garbage can in Fort Worth, you may have seen his
daily column, "Pinch's Palaver."

Jim Tom persuaded me that it might be good for a pro
football stud to have a book which might have a healthy
influence on kids. He also said he would help me with it.

People keep saying that kids are the hope of the world,
and maybe even Texas. If that's true—and they're not all
a bunch of vagrants—then I suppose I'm doing something
worthwhile. Not to get too serious about it, but it might
be true what Jim Tom says. That my ideas on football
and relationships between athletes could help change the
minds of several little old Southern motherfuckers whose
families have taught them to hate niggers, hebes, Catholics and whores.

The other reason for the book is that I happened to

scare up a publisher in New York who was enthusiastic
enough about it to give me a whole lot of what you call
your up-front whip-out. Which is a shitpot full of cash, is
what it is.

I hope the publishing company of LaGuerre & Koming
won't mind me mentioning their generosity. All I did was,
I asked Shake Tiller if he knew a book publisher that
liked to win Nobel prizes. He told me LaGuerre & Koming had published a lot of great authors, so I phoned them
up. I asked them for the editor they had with the most
hyphens in his name.

I got hold of a real nice fellow who drew up the deal
in exchange for nothing more than an autographed football and a promise.

I'm sure I don't need to be telling anybody this. It just
helped me to say it out loud, because of the team.

How I am writing the book is sort of funny, I think.

What I'm doing right now is sitting on my ass in me
and Shake's palatial suite here at the Beverly Stars Hotel
in Beverly Hills, California. I'm just sitting here on a
sofa with my feet propped up on a coffee table. I've
got a glass of young Scotch in front of me and this little
tape recorder that Barbara Jane Bookman gave me.

Everybody agreed that if the book was going to get
written at all, I would just have to talk into this tape
recorder ever chance I got and say whatever was on my
mind.

I asked Jim Tom Pinch who I would be talking to, and
he said, "The world in general, your massive public, and
your friendly neighborhood typist."

So that's what I'm in the midst of, World. Hello, World. How you? I only hope the final version isn't too embarrassing for anybody.

Right now, Shake is down at one of the swimming pools reading the newspapers about us, or reading a book. He does a lot of reading, which is why it was easy for him to tell me about a book publisher. In our apartment on Sixty-fifth and First Avenue in New York there are enough books to support the Fifty-ninth Street Bridge if it ever starts to sag. Shake reads just about everything he can, whether it's politics, novels or something interesting.

Barbara Jane is down at the pool with him. She's usually wherever we are and has been since about the fifth grade. We're all best friends, only better than that. Really close. Except it's a little different with Shake and Barbara Jane. They're about half in love.

So, anyhow, here I am writing my book. But don't get to feeling too sorry for me because Shake and Barb are hung up in what you call your romance, and I'm only the cruise director. I happen to be in the pleasant company right now of the lovely Miss Cissy Walford, who has been on the traveling squad for a number of weeks.

The lovely Miss Cissy Walford is starting to blush as I speak her name.

She's sprawled out comfortably across the room from me with a vodka tonic and a movie magazine. She has her legs draped over the arm of a big chair and she's wearing a pair of those expensive, crotch-tight, thigh-grabbing pants that must be made out of skin and she also has what obviously is a whole bunch of dandy lungs underneath a silk blouse.

I guess I don't really need to point out that Miss Cissy Walford is some kind of good-looking, or she wouldn't be with old Billy Clyde. She's right up there in the majors with Barbara Jane Bookman on looks and Barbara Jane, of course, is so damned pretty it makes your eyes blur.

The only thing wrong with Cissy Walford is that she's about half-Eastern. She's got one of those lispy, semi-stutter, fake-British accents that can really piss you off.

She's from out on Long Island somewhere with a mamma and daddy who think Princeton still plays good football. They say things like they'd like to "go get a lob for dinner," meaning a goddamned lobster, and her fuckin' daddy wouldn't pick up a thirty-dollar lunch tab if he owned Wall Street, which he does.

Her daddy can put you into some kind of a snore with stories about his golf game, or how he once played in a pro-am with Lee Trevino. He also goes on and on about where you can get a really good meal in New York and they are always places where nobody has gone in ten years except people from Des Moines or Cleveland.

Barbara Jane says Cissy went to school somewhere like Briardale in Westchester County and majored in Bloomingdale's and minored in Bonwit Teller. Those are stores where women go in New York.

Well, Cissy likes hanging around with old Billy Clyde, so I guess she can't be all bad. To tell you the truth, I think she's deep down a pretty good wool and if it weren't for the fact that she's such a self-centered, spoiled bitch with that nitwit accent and her shitheel parents, I'd probably marry her.

She just threw a pillow at me.

Missed, though. Kid never did have an arm.

Now I think I'd better get down to why we're all out here in California. The fact is that the New York Giants have got themselves a little old date this coming Sunday in the Super Bowl against none other than the dog-ass New York Jets.

This is some kind of joke back in New York, of course.

Here are two New York teams in the Super Bowl, finally, and the game's being played in Los Angeles.

Naturally, Commissioner Bob Cameron has been taking a lot of kidding about this. There are those who say it wouldn't have happened if Pete Rozelle was still the commissioner instead of becoming a United States Senator.

I don't know about that. I don't think it's any more unusual for two New York teams to be playing the big game out in California than it was for the Dallas Cowboys and the Dallas Chiefs (the old Kansas City Chiefs) to play last year's Super Bowl down in Mexico City. Rozelle arranged that, just before he got elected to the Senate.

Commissioner Cameron seems O.K. is all I'm trying to say, even though he sort of lucked into the job as a compromise candidate of the owners on the forty-eighth ballot.

I think Commissioner Cameron deserves most of the

credit for straightening out the Las Vegas situation. Wasn't it Commissioner Cameron who brought in the new owners to take over the Las Vegas Blackjacks (the old San Diego Chargers) after it came out that the franchise was somehow owned by Angie and Tony Mastrioni, who also happened to own the Jets?

Commissioner Cameron ruled that nobody can own two pro teams, even if they're Italian.

And wasn't it Commissioner Cameron—back when he was Rozelle's assistant—who helped the Maras sell the Giants for twenty-five million to DDD and F so the ad agency could keep us in New York instead of Bermuda?

That was a big thing. The Maras would have moved the Giants to Bermuda or Honolulu just as sure as hell if Commissioner Cameron hadn't found a buyer who would pay the price. I think the Giants should have stayed in New York. I don't think New York would be the same without all the spooks and hebes and criminals and pro football teams which make it such a colorful city.

All I'm trying to say is that Bob Cameron is a good old boy, as far as I'm concerned, and besides everything else, he and Shake and me have chased some wool together.

Shake just stopped in to get a book and take it back down to the pool. He said T. J. Lambert was down there raising hell and it was kind of funny. He said T. J. had just run a bunch of hebes into their cabanas by putting his hand between the cheeks of his ass and asking a little old lady hebe, "Anybody got a hook I can pry this loose with?"

Shake said a lot of people at the pool had been asking him and T. J. and some others for their autographs and that T. J. had been writing some interesting things down.

He said T. J. wrote on a magazine that a little boy had given him, "Hope your old Daddy stays rich and you get yourself lots of cock when you grow up. Yours truly. Torn Jock Lambert."

Shake said T. J. went over to the pool office where the telephone and the P.A. system are and got on the microphone. He said T. J. made an announcement to everybody at the pool.

He said T. J. announced: "Telephone call for whatever Jew can get here first."

Shake also said there was a whole stack of semi-starlets down there that I ought to see.

I said I'd just as soon get some more writing done and contemplate some of the atrocities I might perform on Cissy Walford.

"Have you mentioned that we're gonna kick the shit out of the dog-ass Jets?" Shake asked.

"That's a foregone conclusion," I said.

"Put in there that I went on record as saying I would play the greatest game of my life," said Shake.

"Put in there that I'll probably catch two or three balls behind Dreamer Tatum and at least once I'll dough-pop him on his black ass," he said.

One thing my buddy Shake has never lacked any great amount of is confidence. I don't think anybody has ever truly embarrassed Dreamer Tatum, at least not in all the films I've seen. And I've never heard of anybody bringing him any bodily harm.

Dreamer Tatum is a roverback for the dog-ass Jets, which means that he plays a combination cornerback and linebacker and sometimes covers deep pass routes. He got his name Dreamer in college at USC because he put guys to sleep when he hit them.

I'll tell you. Dreamer Tatum is a stud sumbitch on the football field. He's the only defensive specialist who ever won the Heisman Trophy. That's a trophy that's supposed to go to the best college player every year—and almost never does. Seeing as how me and Shake never won it.

But Dreamer deserved the Heisman the year he got it, which was really an upset over those fuckers who vote in the East and Midwest. And besides that, he's been All-Pro for all three years that he's been with the dog-ass Jets.

Dreamer Tatum is what we call a pisser. I mean that sumbitch will make your helmet ring when he puts it on you. He's about the best proof I know of that a spook can go around on a football field without any keep-off signs on him.

All you can see in most any film of the dog-ass Jets is Dreamer Tatum sticking some poor sumbitch in the gizzle when the poor sumbitch has tried to run a sweep.

All of a sudden the blockers go South and there's Dreamer knocking some poor sumbitch on his butt.

Me and Shake were talking about Dreamer the other day, and I asked my buddy how in the hell Dreamer could keep making plays like that, over and over.

"Wants to," said Shake.

We don't know Dreamer so well. Shit, he lives out in Long Island somewhere, like most of the dog-ass Jets, and of course most of the Giants live in Manhattan or Greenwich or Scarsdale.

You never see many of the dog-ass Jets around the city, even in the off-season, unless you want to go to a bunch of bars where off-duty vice-squad cops hang out.

We know Dreamer well enough to say hidy but that's about all. He moves up every now and then and falls into a classy place like P. J. Clarke's, which is where we go a lot. Usually it's when Dreamer is with some real estate or insurance phony who only wants to be seen with him.

I hear Dreamer's really a good spook when he's not making somebody's hat ring, but my only thoughts about him right now is that he's on the other side from me in this game and that means we're at war.

It's actually sort of like the Giants and dog-ass Jets have never played each other before. All of those exhibitions we've played up in New Haven every August don't mean a damn thing.

Hell, this season nobody's first units even got in the ball game up there. Last year we only played the first half. And the year before we only played the first quarter.

The thing about exhibition games is that they ought to be for rookies, and then if the fans are dumb enough to pay to see them, they know what they're getting. All of the owners swear they have to play these fake games to stay in business but that's a pile of crap. They don't have to play seven of the sumbitches. I really agree with the spooks on this.

I really think the day will come when the veterans won't play in any of these games unless they're scheduled in Paris, Rome, London and Madrid.

Up in New Haven last August before our exhibition with the dog-ass Jets, I exchanged a few words with Dreamer when we were out on the field warming up. After we'd said hidy, I told Dreamer I didn't think he was apt to see much of my ass in the game.

"I'm about to think me up a hamstring." I smiled.

Dreamer said, "Oh, you got it, baby. I can see it hurtin' on you right now. You ought to see this hip-pointer I got. Oooo, it hurt. I may have to limp over and get into my street duds before them cats ever hit that anthem."

"Need some help?" I said.

"No, I believe I can jog," Dreamer said.

We talked on for a minute or so. I told Dreamer that I had noticed that our entire first unit offense either had suddenly come down with the flu or muscle spasms. He told me it was the same with the dog-ass Jets.

"Seems like New Haven's just an unlucky town for us," I said.

"There's lots of others, too," said Dreamer. "Until mid-September anyhow."

Well, of course, the Super Bowl isn't any exhibition game, and I don't know anybody on either team who wouldn't play Sunday with four or five broken ribs.

As you might suspect, the newspapers are building it up about what's liable to happen when I run at Dreamer, or when Shake runs a route at him. Yesterday a guy in the LA *Times* quoted Dreamer as saying we were good in "an inferior league" and that playing the Jets would finally prove how good we really were.

The *Times* writer quoted Dreamer as saying, "I hope the Giants have got their hats on Sunday because we want to welcome 'em to pro football."

You try not to get upset by anything you read, of course. Most of it is bullshit. But you read it. Any football player who claims he doesn't read the papers or the magazines about himself or his team is telling about as much truth, like Shake says, as a President or Senator.

Anyhow, Shake answered Dreamer in the papers this morning, and we all had a good laugh, even Cissy Walford who doesn't understand any of it.

The paper quoted Shake as saying, "I just found out that Dreamer Tatum's real name is Obert Kimberly Tatum. The only Obert I ever knew was so dumb he couldn't figure out a ball-point pen. And the only Kimberly I ever knew was an interior decorator. So now that I know Dreamer's straight name, I've got to wonder if he's the little bit of hell he's supposed to be."

The writer asked Shake if he planned to run his routes differently in Dreamer's direction.

"I might put a couple of new dance steps on him," Shake said.

The writer pointed out to Shake that Dreamer seems to read a fake better than any athlete he ever saw.

"Tell me that after he quits spinnin' like a top on Sunday," said Shake.

I mentioned to my friend this morning, "Old buddy, you keep talking like that in the papers and Dreamer's liable to take it out on me. You'll be sitting out there at split end with someplace to hide, but I've got to run right at his onery soul."

Shake smirked.

"Eat his ass up is all you're gonna do, Billy C.," he said.

Cissy Walford asked if the two of us were actually, terribly, very, intensely concerned.

"Shit," said Shake.

I think I'd better knock off for a while now. We've got to go to practice over at UCLA in Westwood where the Giants are practicing. After that I've got an interview at the Beverly Hills Hotel with some kind of high-rent bitch from a women's magazine. On the phone she said she wanted to do "a full take-out" on me, and then print it in the spring if we won the game.

She said she wanted to "rap with me" about the "underside" of the athlete's mind.

I also have to go with Shake over to a TV studio. And then all of us have to go over to the Beverly Wilshire Hotel for a Super Bowl cocktail party that the magazine *Sports Illustrated* is giving.

Players really hate to go to shit like that party but our owners insist we show up. They think it's good that we mix it up from time to time with some of those big money spenders from the East who hang around parties like that.

There's never anybody at those things but a bunch of freeloading writers who get high school drunk and a bunch of Madison Avenue types who get even drunker and tell you how they've always been with the Giants win, lose or draw.

There's also some talk between Barbara Jane Bookman and Cissy Walford about going to Ugo's for dinner. Cissy wants to go because she thinks there might be some movie stars there to look at. Ugo's is where everybody out here goes now that they don't go to La Scala or Matteo's.

Ugo's is all right with me. At least we'll get a good table from lovable old Ugo, as much as me and Shake have hit that phony fuckin' wop in the palm when he was a captain waiter at La Scala and Matteo's and the Isle of Sauce.

I hope there'll be some heavyweights at Ugo's. Not for Cissy to be thrilled by, but for her to dazzle with her own self. When we go out on the town, Cissy has a habit of not wearing much except a lot of jeweled belts and necklaces, some little old panty bottoms and a variety of suede and rawhide boots.

Barbara Jane calls it her "whip me, whip me" outfits.

Anyway, this is Billy Clyde Puckett signing off for now. Tranquillity Base here. Shake Tiller and Billy C. Puckett have landed at the Super Bowl.

Ten four.

Barbara Jane said last night that she had listened to my first tape on the book while we were at practice. Barb said she hoped Jim Tom Pinch would give me a little help on the grammar, here and there, and maybe take out what somebody might consider to be "excessive vulgarities."

I told Barb I had never heard or seen anything vulgar in my life, and I certainly wouldn't allow anything vulgar in my book.

I also said I wasn't so sure Jim Tom was any great student of the English language, seeing as how he was just a sports writer for the Fort Worth *Light & Shopper*.

Excuse me for introducing you as a character in the book, Jim Tom, but since you're the collaborator it won't hurt to give you a little credit and let the world know something about you.

You can take out anything you think's semi-libelous, anyhow.

"Jim Tom's a neat guy," said Barb. "He'll do a good job, if the Old Skipper's willing and the Scotch don't rise."

I said Jim Tom didn't have anything to do but type up the tapes and not lose the manuscript at Reba's Lounge. I said if he changed very much of what I spoke he'd get his arm broken and he'd never play the Olivetti again.

I'd like to say right here that it's a damn shame Jim Tom can't be out here for the Super Bowl. He could sure help me observe some things for the book.

The reason Jim Tom's not here is because of that piece of Kotex he works for, the Fort Worth *Light & Shopper*. He only has a three-man staff, including himself. And the other two, from what I hear, are what you call your undependables. There's a desk man named Big-un Darley who eats cold green peas out of a can, and one other writer named Jerry Toby who, according to Jim Tom, spends most of his time trying to shake down the local bowling proprietors.

On the phone the other day Jim Tom said, "Sure like to join you out there, Stud, but the Super Bowl happens to fall right in the middle of a very important event here at home. The Fourth Annual Fort Worth *Light & Shopper* High School Basketball Festival."

I said I didn't see how anything could be more important than one or two old boys from Fort Worth being in the Super Bowl. Or one of the paper's famous columnists writing a book about it.

"Our editor doesn't know about the book," Jim Tom said. "He only likes books about religion and soil conservation, anyhow. I'm gonna stick some soil conservation up his ass if this sumbitch sells any copies. The main thing, though, is that I've got to keep the official box scores and present the trophies at the festival."

"I suppose teams are coming from all over," I said. "It's all very exciting, I'm sure."

Jim Tom said, "Aw, you bet. We got the Itasca Wampus Cats coming in, and the Hutto Hippoes, and the El Campo Rice Birds."

I said, "How about Coleman's Fighting Blue Cats?"

He said, "How about Trent's Gorillas and the Port Lavaca Sandcrabs?"

"Sounds action-packed," I said. "Can the Sandcrabs handle the Cuero Gobblers?"

Jim Tom said, "Yeah. They got more niggers."

I said, "Hey, you red necks down there better watch your language. Don't you know the Democrats can have you shot for saying nigger in public?"

Jim Tom said he knew all about language, otherwise he wouldn't be writing a book. Anyhow, he said, I probably hadn't seen a basketball game lately, had I?

I said I hoped not.

"It's not like you may remember it, stud," he said. "There's not much defense or strategy. The high schools are like the NBA now. You've heard what a game in the NBA is, haven't you?"

What was the joke, I asked.

Jim Tom laughed and said, "Ever twenty-four seconds ten niggers jump up in the air."

Then he said, "Listen, Paschal's got one now you'd really like. Astronaut Jones. Is that a good name? Last spring he won the hundred-yard dash in the city meet and when he crossed the finish line he released a small parachute from the back of his shorts. Funniest thing you ever saw."

"Does he put the ball in the air?" I asked.

"Hey, stud," said Jim Tom. "Does a bear shit in the woods?"

I chuckled.

"He crosses midcourt," said Jim Tom, "and down at the press table you can hear him holler, 'Tryin' one.' Then he fires. And he can hit. Schoom. *Two*. He say *two*."

"Tryin' one," I mimicked.

Jim Tom said, "He'll say, 'Tryin' one,' and when the ball's about halfway there and he knows it's in, he'll say, 'Yawl come on back now.' Is he great?"

"Tryin' one," I said.

"Astronaut Jones," said Jim Tom.

I offered to pay Jim Tom's way out to the Coast and cover all his expenses, including hookers, in case he didn't choose to bring along his fat wife, Earlene. But Jim Tom said the paper still wouldn't let him come. And he couldn't trust Big-un and Jerry Toby anyway.

He said, "Big-un would drink himself a lot of that Colorado Kool-Aid and go to sleep in the middle of a double overtime between Paschal and Port Lavaca."

I said, "Does Big-un like his Coors?"

"Oh, he'll drink that Colorado Kool-Aid," said Jim Tom. "He don't like it any more than he likes gettin' fed and fucked before sundown."

I don't actually know very much about the newspaper business, other than what little I've heard Jim Tom complain about over the years. All I know is, he's got a fairly rotten job for a hundred and fifty a week and a by-line.

As I understand Jim Tom's job, his workday goes like this. He has to get up at five o'clock every morning, stop at the post office and get the mail, tear all the stories off the wire machine, write his column, write two or three other stories, write all the headlines, answer the phone, rewrite whatever Jerry Toby turns in, make up the pages of the sports section because Big-un Darley is drunk, and then go out in the afternoon to a high school or to TCU and try to find something else to write about the next day.

One of the reasons it would be nice for this book to make some money is that it would help my friendly neighborhood typist get his pockets on the outside of some extra cash.

That would sure make Earlene happy, and take some heat off a good old boy. Maybe he can buy Earlene a new shower-head, or whatever the hell it is that fat wives want for their homes.

Earlene's maiden name was Padgett. She's one of those bitches who couldn't wait to get fat right after she got married.

The best way I can describe Earlene Padgett is to say that she was a semi-fleshy clerk at the bank who had a nice ass that stuck out when she danced. She seemed to be a swinger at one time. At least she drank her share of whisky and said "piss" a lot. And over-all she had that racy kind of look that most men like.

Barbara Jane once called her an eye-shadow junkie.

But about ten seconds after Jim Tom married her, Earlene went out and got herself some fat arms, a big butt and turned dumber than a fundamentalist preacher.

Are you there, Jim Tom? Mad Dog One to Mad Dog

Two. Come in, Mad Dog Two. Sorry I had to gloss it over there about your marriage. Just felt kindhearted, I guess.

Maybe you'll be divorced and fired before the book comes out, and then it won't make a shit what we say about your wonderful wife and your wonderful editor.

At the risk of embarrassing my collaborator, I've got to say that he's a stud when it comes to knowing about football. He can tell you when a zone secondary bleeds and when it gushes. He knows a counterkey for the cornerback on the triple option.

I don't suppose he's ever written much that would dazzle the literary geniuses at *Sports Illustrated*. But then he doesn't write so often about a lovable snow goose or kite-flying in Dark Harbor, Maine.

As Jim Tom says, "In Fort Worth I don't get many chances to do my Grantland Rice number. If I could make my column read like a grocery ad, I'd be the biggest thing in town."

He's managed to sell a few stories to some small magazines but *Sports Illustrated* keeps turning down his suggestions. One of their turndowns made him so hot once that he sent them what I thought was a funny telegram.

It said something like:

"If you folks ever decide to stop being a slick cookbook for the two-yacht family I will consider an assignment."

I reminded Barbara Jane that anybody who knows how many touchdowns I've scored and how many yards I've gained from high school through five years in pro ball has got to be a better book writer than some Eastern dumb-ass who thinks football ended when Vince Lombardi went to the big power sweep in the sky.

"How old is Jim Tom now?" Barb asked.

"I think he must be about thirty-two," I said. "That's his body. His soul of course is over a hundred."

Barb said, "Let's see. Thirty-two. Yeah, that's right. He was about four years ahead of us in Paschal and TCU."

"Good guy," I said.

She said, "I suppose he still makes it with every waitress and secretary in town."

"They think he's a celebrity," I said. "They're overwhelmed by his checkered sports coats, his cigarette holder, the premature gray in his hair and the fact that they think he's single."

I asked Barb to give me a little better book review than the fact that it sounded excessively vulgar, which it wasn't.

She smiled and said, "Remember those magazines called *Climax,* or something, that you guys used to hand me under the table in the fifth grade? With the color photographs of people in Denmark doing some swell things to each other? I'll level with you. It's better than that."

I said she was a real inspiration.

As for last night, there isn't much to say about what happened except that it was semi-exhausting. We all went to the *Sports Illustrated* party. Most of the Giants went but none of the Jets. The Jets are all still hot at the magazine because none of them made a cover during the regular season. Not even Dreamer Tatum.

Maybe that would make me mad, too. Me and Shake have both been on their cover several times in the past, starting with TCU. And I'm not even counting the one they did of the two of us when we were All-America our senior year and dough-popped Arkansas thirty-seven to twenty-one. I don't count that one because as far as I could tell, it wasn't us. It was a painting, I think.

Shake said he thought the cover looked like some kind of polka-dot linoleum that was all twisted around a goal post with birds circling.

What was primarily funny about the party was this nitwit who was fairly drunk and got into a conversation with Shake.

I never knew who he was. Just one of those striped-tie, Ivy League, midtown, semi-lockjaw, Eastern mother-fuckers you run into.

For one thing, he turned out to be a dog-ass Jet fan, and that was a dead giveaway right there that he wasn't too heavy to anybody outside of Queens.

Everybody knows the Giants are Manhattan's team, which means New York City. And like Shake says, Queens is in Russia, except with less glamour.

Anyhow, this nitwit comes up to Shake and first off he wants to know how Shake is going to feel on Sunday when Dreamer Tatum shuts him out on catching balls.

Shake thought at first that the nitwit was joking, like some of our friends do. You know. We've got some pals who are always saying things to me like, "There's old Number Twenty-four, we'll never forget him." And my number of course is Twenty-three. Things like that.

But the guy was serious. And his voice had a bit of a belligerent tone, seeing as how he had put a whole pile of gin down his neck.

"Marvin (Shake) Tiller," the guy said, sort of loud. "Big deal."

Shake just stood there with a young Scotch in his hand, grinning, and brushing his red-blond hair up on his forehead when it would fall down, like it does.

The conversation, as Barbara Jane and I have tried to remember it for the book, went something like this.

"Marvin (Shake) Tiller," the guy said. "Hero."

"That's me," said Shake.

"Tell me something, hero. Have you ever thought what you'd be doing if you didn't make a lot of dough playing a kid's game?" the guy said.

"Once or twice," Shake said.

"And what did you decide, hero?" said the nitwit.

"Oh, I thought I might get into conglomerates," Shake said.

"Conglomerates, huh?"

"Yeah, big ones," Shake said.

"Great big conglomerates," said the nitwit.

"Just a whole bunch of 'em," Shake said.

"Conglomerates of what, may I ask?"

Shake said, "Well, my idea was that I'd have some great big conglomerates of money."

The nitwit stared at us all.

He said, "Of course, that's a joke."

"Yeah, that's what bothers me," Shake said. "All these ideas I have about business only make people laugh."

We all kind of stood there awkwardly for a moment and tasted our drinks.

The nitwit said, "Well, it's good to know that a hero like yourself has given some thought to his future."

"I have done that, sir," Shake said.

"No you haven't," he said. "You haven't done a goddamn thing but catch passes."

"Only the ones they threw me," Shake said.

"Just run out there and catch the goddamn passes," the guy gestured. "Big football deal. The Giants, for Christ's sake."

"Yes, sir, most of the passes I catch are for the Giants," said Shake.

"If it weren't for pro football most of you heroes would be running a goddamn gas station somewhere. Tulsa or somewhere," the guy said.

"That's fairly close to it," Shake grinned.

"It is, huh?"

"Yeah, fairly close," Shake said.

"But not quite?"

"No, just fairly close," said Shake.

"And just how close is fairly close, hero?" the guy asked.

"I don't know exactly. I've been there, too. Fairly Close was the home of Martha Nell Burch," said Shake.

"Oh, that's cute," the drunk said.

"No, it's Fairly Close is actually what it is. Right out there near Not Quite. Good cattle country," said Shake.

"Jesus Christ," said the guy.

"He came around there some," Shake said.

"Jesus, you're an ass hole, you know that?"

"Yeah, but that was later," said Shake. "Back in Fairly Close all of her friends and Martha Nell Burch just thought I was a rascal, more or less."

The nitwit was getting dark pink in the face and kind of weaving back and forth.

"You're all wise guys, is that it? Big football deals. Holy fucking Moses, these goddamn football types," he said.

The guy made an effort to belch an excuse me toward Barbara Jane and Cissy. For the language.

But Shake was talking.

"Never saw Moses around much," Shake was saying. "Just Martha Nell Burch and her friends. Most of 'em were in the 4-H Club. Some people said you had to seek your fun elsewhere than in Fairly Close. That's what some people said."

"Ought to be running a gas station or something," the nitwit said.

"Of course, some people didn't know Martha Nell Burch as well as I did," said Shake.

"I don't know what the hell you're talking about now," the guy said.

"That's what I've been meaning to ask you," Shake said. "What the hell am I talking about?"

"I don't have any goddamn idea," he said.

"Now, you see there?" said Shake.

"What?" said the guy.

"What you just said," Shake laughed.

"What's that?"

"You just said you didn't have any idea about something and here I've just been trying to explain to you about Martha Nell Burch," said Shake.

"Martha Nell who? Where the hell is she? Christ, get her in here. Is she a hooker? I got a lot of dough. Is she a spade? Goddamn I love a good-looking spade hooker." The guy spilled part of his drink.

And Shake said, "Martha Nell Burch is anything she wants to be."

"Get her in here. Jesus, I'd rather spend my time with a good hooker than a goddamn football hero," said the guy.

"Well, that's the sad part. She wanted to be here but she phoned up to say that her cattle are sick," Shake said.

"You're full of shit," said the guy.

"No, sir. That's the cattle. They're all full of it, so Martha Nell says we'll have to wait a while before we can kill 'em and eat 'em," Shake said.

"Huh?"

"That's what you do with cattle. You kill 'em and eat 'em. That's called good government," Shake said.

"Jesus Christ," said the guy, turning up his drink.

Shake looked around and said, "Does anybody know if I'm finished? Billy C., am I all done here? Barb?"

Barbara Jane said she thought that about summed it all up. I agreed. I told the man that stud athletes like us had to get to bed pretty early. Cissy Walford just kept staring at Shake and frowning.

"Well, hero," the nitwit said. "I just hope you can make more sense in the LA Coliseum on Sunday than you did here tonight."

"Will you be there?" Shake asked.

"Hell, I didn't come all the way out to California to stand around with this bunch of drunks from New York."

"New York? Is there anybody here from New York?" Shake said.

"Greatest goddamn city in the world, New York," the guy said.

"That's sure what all the folks in London say," said Shake.

"New York's where it's at," the drunk said.

"I think you're right. That's where it was, anyhow. At least it was there the last time I saw it. We had it hidden pretty good. You don't have any with you, do you? No, I guess not."

Shake raised his eyebrows at us.

"Hell of a city, New York," the guy said.

Shake said, "Nobody ever called it Wanatchapee, Wisconsin."

"I'm from Noooo York City, hero. Home of the New York Jets," he said.

"Dog-ass Jets," Shake said.

"Goddamn live town, New York," said the guy.

"They tell me the Bronx is up and the Battery's down. You know anything about that?" Shake giggled.

"Center of every goddamn thing there is, almost," the drunk said.

"There's a broken heart for every light, too, somebody said," Shake went on.

"They give you this southern California bullshit. Hollywood, for Christ's sake. Bunch of goddamn weirdos in their swimming pools," said the nitwit.

"I'll sure take New York over a bunch of weirdos," Shake said. "The thing about weirdos is, you don't know who their families are."

"Listen, hero," the guy said, looking serious and squinting.

"Yeah," Shake said.

"Knock off the crap. You want to know something. You're a good-looking son of a bitch," he said.

Shake laughed sort of clumsily.

"You're a lippy son of a bitch but you're a good-looking son of a bitch," he said to Shake.

"You got me then," Shake said. "Sure did."

"No, it's all right. We're just talking a lot of crap here, right? You're O.K. You're an ass hole but you're O.K.," the drunk said.

"That's, uh, that's really keen," said Shake.

"You're going to get your cock knocked off Sunday but you're a good-looking son of a bitch," he said.

And he weaved a little.

"Good thing my wife's not here. She'd be after you like a goddamn starving hooker," he said.

"Now I wouldn't talk like that about old Hazel," Shake said. "She's one of the finest ladies that ever played paddle tennis."

"The wife's name is Dorothy, hero. And you're goddamn lucky you don't know her," said the guy.

"I don't see how you can talk about Alice that way," Shake said.

"Alice who?"

"Hey, sir. Listen. We've really got to be going," Shake said.

Shake took Barbara Jane's arm and started backing off. I did the same with Cissy Walford.

"All the best, hero," the nitwit said. "Watch out for your cock on Sunday."

"Been a real pleasure, sir," Shake winked.

"Get out of here, football deal, ass-hole hero," the guy said.

"You say hello to old Grace now," said Shake.

"Dorothy, you prick," said the guy.

"You say hello to old Dorothy, too," said Shake.

"Fuck the New York Giants," the nitwit said.

Shake laughed and said, "God love America."

And we left.

I'm afraid we made a bit of a spectacle of ourselves at Ugo's later on. We started making up stories about Martha Nell Burch in the middle of our lemon veal and fettucini.

We decided that if she had gone to TCU, she would have come from Floydada with big lungs and skinny calves and a lot of chewing gum.

She would have had Amelia Simcox for a friend, Barbara Jane said, and in their sophomore year they would have screwed the whole varsity three-deep chart.

Shake said she probably would have fallen hopelessly

in love with Bubba Littleton, who was our equivalent of T. J. Lambert.

Bubba Littleton was a second-string tackle from Odessa who once went one whole semester without bathing, shaving, combing his hair or brushing his teeth. He did it to get back at Honey Jean Lester for breaking up with him. Shake said Bubba smelled like Albania.

Bubba Littleton couldn't top T. J. Lambert for sheer, all-out filth but he had his moments.

Shake brought up the time we all went out on a varsity picnic at Lake Worth and Bubba got caught by his date, Honey Jean Lester, while he was beating off underneath the dock.

Honey had walked out on the dock looking to see if Bubba was among the water skiers. But when she accidentally glanced down between some cracks in the boards, there was Bubba in the shallow water and the shade staring at some lovelies on the beach for inspiration —and flogging away.

At dinner Shake imitated Honey Jean Lester hollering at Bubba.

"Bubba Littleton! You done grossed me out for the last time."

When we got back to our palatial suite at the Beverly Stars Hotel, Shake and Barbara Jane were feeling romantic so they excused themselves.

First, though, Barbara Jane gave me a kiss and explained to Cissy Walford that she and Shake had to go study Sunday's game plan.

She said to Cissy, "Don't you and Billy C. do any foolin' around now."

I turned on the TV and tried to look at a fag cowboy for a while with Cissy Walford's dandy lungs resting on my arm. I tried to look at the TV while she looked at me.

It won't hurt anything, I guess, to say that old Billy Clyde finished off the evening by doing his manly duty.

I've got to say, however, that I could have done it a little better if Cissy hadn't asked me a question in the middle of some serious goings-on.

"I don't understand something," Cissy said. "Is Martha Nell Burch a real person or what?"

I want to say that I got woke up this morning by Cissy Walford handing me the telephone through her long yellow hair. She stretched and blinked her mile-long eyelashes and seemed to be saying that there was a man on the phone who wanted to know if I had heard his imitation of a cricket.

"Sumbitch." I smiled. "Elroy Blunt."

That's who it was.

When I first knew Elroy Blunt he was a semi-talented defensive back. In those days he certainly didn't have his handlebar mustache and his hair like Prince Valiant. Elroy had played ball when I first got to know him at Memphis State, and me and Shake met him at the East-West Shrine Game and the Hulu Bowl and the Coaches' All-America Game and the College All-Star Game, all of which is the post-season circuit that senior studs travel on.

Elroy played one season with the Steelers after that. But then he quit. He was always jacking around with a guitar anyhow, trying to pick and sing and write country songs. And he had finally made it pretty big.

Elroy, of course, was crazy. And he was no more predictable than what I hear about bad wives. Elroy Blunt was apt to call you up from Portugal or somewhere just to say he had set a new headache record.

On the telephone for a minute or two, of course, I didn't hear anything but cricket sounds.

Then Elroy said, "Clyde, this here's your favorite cousin, Bernice Lovejowl, and I just been busted in Paraguay for going down on the mayor. I need two thousand to scoop up and bail out."

I giggled a hello.

"Clyde," Elroy said. "I'd first off like an explanation about that lovely sound of young wool that answered the electric telephone at this early hour."

I explained that it was the utterly fantastic Cissy Walford.

"Who might that be?" Elroy said.

"That's the American name she chose," I said. "In reality, she's a gotch-eyed, hump-backed, clapped-up Cambodian hooker who stopped over to help me work a pornographic jigsaw puzzle."

Cissy pinched my thigh until it almost bled.

Elroy said, "Well, I'd like to sing that little jewel a tune."

I gave Cissy the phone and leaned over so I could listen in. Elroy proceeded to sing a medley of his biggies.

He sang "I'm Just a Bug on the Windshield of Life" and then he sang "Eight Killed at the Intersection" and then he sang "Slept All Day in the Lobby."

"That's incredibly marvelous," said Cissy.

She listened to Elroy for a moment and squealed and handed me the phone.

"He wanted to know whether I liked Hershey bars, running water or vibrators the best," she said.

I told Elroy it was good to know he hadn't changed.

"Clyde," he said. "Son, I have called you up on a matter of important business."

I said yeah.

"Clyde," he said, "I would like to know if you studs are gonna win that big old sports event on Sunday."

I said, "We are if the Pope ain't a nigger."

Elroy said, "Now, Clyde, you know what I mean. I want to know for sure if you folks think you can handle them other folks. Hell, you've seen all them old films and all. Son, I just know you must have seen something in them films that'll help my confidence. I got to have my confidence helped before I go runnin' off to bet Mamma and Papa and Sister Marvene and the kids and the trailer rent and all."

"They're a good team," I said.

"Aw, shit, Clyde. That don't tell me nothing. I know they're a good team. Hell, everybody's a good team," he said.

I asked him what the price was now, just out of curiosity.

Elroy said, "They come three and a half but it's down

to pick because one of their niggers got hurt or something."

I said, "Those dog-asses don't have anybody hurt."

"Well, then, the New York Jews done bet it down to pick," Elroy said.

"They did open three and a half, didn't they?" I said, mostly to myself.

"Just as if it was Texas playin' Oklahoma," he said.

"Looks to me like a Super Bowl ought to be considered even," I said.

"It's even now. Them Jews done bet it down," he said.

"But they opened up on top," I said.

"Well, hell yeah," Elroy said. "Clyde, they been in this old Super Bowl before. Two or three times. But you ain't. That's why I got to know something."

"We haven't found out much," I said.

Elroy said, "Clyde, that's a lot of cheap shit and you and me both know it. All I want to know, son, is which one of them old defensive backs of theirs is a fag or has the clap or can't cover the outs. You know what I mean."

I said, "Gambling is sinful."

"Clyde, I got to know somethin'," Elroy said. "Now looky here. I want to bet my chest and lungs and kidneys and my future heart transplant on this thing. I got me some old Jet fans that want to give me three, four, five and six and I'm just about to lap it up. But I got to know a thing or two. You gonna get 'em?"

"I want to hear some more singing," I said.

Elroy whooped and said, "Clyde, I'm gonna let you be the first to listen to my new golden record."

I tilted the phone over toward Cissy, who was getting tangled up on my body. We heard Elroy sing "I'd Give a Dollar for a Dime to Put in This Machine and Play the Song That Brings You Back to Me."

It was pretty good.

"Don't that mother knock your dicks in the dirt?" Elroy said.

I laughed a yes.

Then I asked Elroy where on Earth he was calling from, and he said he thought he was in Atlanta but then it might be Seattle.

"Why don't you look out the window and find out?" I said.

"There ain't nothin' out the window but a cruel world, Clyde. There's ambulances and fire engines and insurance salesmen and data computers and all kinds of things out there," he said.

"Probably some police, too," I said.

"Naw," said Elroy. "There ain't none of them. Didn't you hear? The niggers got 'em all fired."

I said, "The police might be wearing plain clothes."

"Hell, no," Elroy said. "If there was any cops around they'd be wearin' their blue. You know how they like that blue. I'm gonna write me a song about the cops one of these days. I'm gonna call it 'Blue.' "

I told Elroy I had to get up and go to a squad meeting pretty soon.

"Clyde, listen," he said. "There's one other thing. Old Elroy Blunt is gonna be out there day after tomorrow."

"Oh, shit," I said.

"Sure enough gonna be there," he said. "Got me a big old house rented for the weekend in Bel Air. I'm bringin' in more pounds of barbecue and Scotch and them funny little old cigarettes than you have ever dreamed about, and I am also bringin' me an ensemble of horny little old debutantes that I'm sure you and your pals will want to say hello to."

I said, "Elroy, this isn't exactly a party weekend for us."

Elroy said, "You tell old Shake and T. J. about it. Saturday night's gonna be the night."

"That's the night before the game," I said. "No way you'll see any of us that night."

"We'll start early," Elroy said. "Now, Clyde, I know you well enough to know that you don't sit around and draw circles and X's the night before a game."

"I don't intentionally destroy myself either," I said.

"Ain't no destroy, Clyde. Just some barbecue and a couple of drinks, and some little old debutantes. It'll help you relax. You'll still grab your ten or twelve hours. You tell old Shake and T. J. now, you hear?" he said.

"Yeah, O.K.," I said. "Now I got to get moving."

"Clyde," said Elroy. "Just tell me what you think about all them old Jet linebackers and corners. Can you run on 'em at all?"

"We'll run," I said.

"Serious? Can you?" he said.

"I think we'll get outside, away from Dreamer," I said.

"Can you really?" he said.

I said, "Yeah, that dog-ass Buford on the other side

don't show me a lot of want-to."

"And what about old Dream Street his own self?" he said.

"He cheats," I said.

"Goddamn holy fornicate Christmas bundle of fried chicken!" Elroy hollered. "I just done won me a new air-o-plane. You lure them sumbitches up tight with the sweep and the slant, and then you go wide at Dreamer and option his black ass with the halfback pass to old Marvin Tiller! Shithouse mouse, we'll have their dog-asses on Sunday!"

"Say good-bye to my little old Cambodian friend," I said.

Elroy Blunt sang something semi-filthy to Cissy Walford and we hung up.

She said, "Was that important what you told him about the game? About being able to run away from the Dog-Asses?"

I pulled Cissy over on top of me and spoke into her long, yellow hair.

"Could be," I said. "Except for one thing. The danged old football's just not round. That sumbitch'll bounce funny on you."

Your special delivery letter arrived today, Jim Tom, and I just can't resist sharing it with the general population.

It says:

I-Slot, Fake Sweep, on two:
Any time you want to start sending me some

tapes, I'm ready to try to make you sound like you got out of a sixth-grade spelling test with a D—. Remember to keep an eye out for detail. Try to re-call the color of the wool you're chewing.

The Fort Worth *Light & Shopper,* a newspaper noted for its relentless crusades, found City Council-man C. T. Badger double-parked yesterday in front of the Mutual Savings & Loan building and ran sequence pictures of the automobile on Page One.

Earlene the Blimp wants to know if our book is going to make us rich enough to buy a Volks camper so we can take some wonderful trips to Benbrook Lake.

After the first edition closed this morning, I went to breakfast at the Picadilly Cafeteria and watched Big-un pour cream gravy on his cantaloupe.

I hope your book has a lot of dirty words in it, a couple of rapes on the first few pages, some pirates, dope smugglers, Indians, a revolution, a gaggle of orgies, and a heroine who's oversexed, deaf and dumb, and whose father owns a liquor store.

By the way, I have a title if you haven't thought of one. I think you ought to call it *If Niggers Are Tough, How Come You Never See One on a Motor-cycle?*

Earlene wants me home early tonight because she plans to fix her famous pinto bean pie. I hope so. It's a whole lot better than her famous can of sal-mon, jar of salad dressing and box of Premium crackers.

We thank thee, Lord, for this food for the nour-
ishment of our bodies.

I can face it if I stop by Reba's first and feel
around on Crazy Iris or Earth Mother Fudge.

Crazy Iris is a nasty little bubble-gummer who
works for Mid-Plains Oil Supply and makes a man
want to run away with her and rob filling stations.
Earth Mother Fudge knows quite a bit about jour-
nalism from the point of view of a spade hooker
with lungs like shoulder pads on a lineman.

Enclosed is a copy of a recent "Palaver" in which
you seem to turn out being greater than Bronko
Grange or Doak Rockne.

Stay with the tape recorder. Fuck the game.
Games have a way of ruining a perfectly good week.

Tryin' one,
Astronaut Jones

We all giggled at your letter, Jim Tom. But we talked
about what a shame it was that your columns aren't ever
as funny as you talk or write letters. Shake said it was the
paper's fault.

"Football is serious," he said. "If you let a man start
getting funny about football, the next thing you know
he'll start getting funny about your department stores
and your tire dealers, and then where would your newspaper be?"

Puddin Patterson stopped by our palatial suite a
while ago to sit down and laugh.

Puddin was wearing a T-shirt, shorts and shower slippers, and Cissy Walford had never seen anybody that big out of street clothes. Puddin is six feet eight and goes about two seventy.

Cissy looked at Puddin and quietly said, "Oh, wow!"

Puddin asked if I had realized that T. J. Lambert broke his all-time chili cheeseburger record this morning at the squad meeting.

I didn't know it.

Puddin pointed out that T. J. must have stayed out all night somewhere and came straight to the meeting with eight chili cheeseburgers from Tommy's Drive-In over on Beverly and Rampart.

"Eight of 'em," said Puddin. "And he inhaled ever one of them cats before we got through fifteen minutes of film."

The phone just rang and it was Commissioner Cameron, who said he was calling up both team captains to wish us luck and also to remind us that both teams are expected to be at a Friday luncheon at the Century Plaza.

At the Friday luncheon, I'm told, everybody on the two teams is supposed to meet a lot of governors and retired generals and movie stars and get a bunch of gifts, like watches and rings and blankets.

I may have neglected to mention that I'm the Giants' captain.

Commissioner Cameron said he had already called up the dog-ass Jets' captain, which is Andy Odom, who is not a bad tight end.

"Did you remind him that his ass is in deep water on Sunday?" I said.

Commissioner Cameron laughed.

He's a good old boy who's really helped all the players in the league get a lot of money out of their owners, most of whom are a pack of spoiled rich kids who give you bad stock tips.

Commissioner Cameron also likes a cocktail now and then, which I think is good. And besides that, it may not hurt to mention that on certain occasions around New York, Commissioner Cameron has been known to turn up in places like our apartment when word had circulated that some stewardi and light hooks had come over for an all-skate.

I asked the Commissioner if he'd got any good wool lately.

THE PHONE RANG AGAIN A WHILE ago but I didn't get around to answering it because it happened that at the time I was in the pleasant process of pulling Cissy Walford's wool down over my ears like a helmet.

I'VE BEEN THINKING THAT TRYING to write a book during the week of the biggest week in my life is probably less fun than being next-to-last on a high school gang-fuck.

There are parts of it which I don't mind because it helps me relax and take my mind off Dreamer Tatum. These are parts which I think of as being amusing.

It's the other parts that are a pain in the ass. All of the explaining you have to do. Things that Jim Tom says the publishing company, LaGuerre & Koming, will insist on being in the book. A lot of background stuff.

You better not be shitting me, Jim Tom.

I've been at it for over an hour now, telling all about last night and this morning. And I've just realized that I haven't ever begun to tell about people like our coach, Shoat Cooper, or the rest of the team, or in any depth about Shake Tiller or Barbara Jane.

Shake's in his bedroom of our palatial suite, either taking a nap or reading another book that some Russian wrote about God. And Barbara Jane has gone off to have some drinks with some advertising people.

That's another thing. I've forgotten to mention that Barbara Jane models for a lot of commercials on TV and on signboards. In the world of modeling she's a stud, is all she is. Probably everybody has seen her who has ever watched TV or driven a car. She's the girl on the signboards—right now, in fact—smoking those Kentuckians, those long skinny cigarettes. And she's the Pacific Basin Airlines girl looking back over her shoulder with just the bikini bottoms on, strolling along Waikiki in Hawaii.

About a year ago she was the girl on TV who did those funny imitations of a vampire bat, trying to get some kids to eat the right breakfast cereal. And she was also the girl on TV they dressed up like Cleopatra and put in a Volkswagen floating on a barge down the Nile.

DDD and F did all those.

Barb remembers having quite a time making that airline commercial in Hawaii, mainly because of Burt Danby, who's the head of Doff, Danby, Dendle and Frederickson. Ever since Burt Danby thinks he discovered Barbara Jane he's been trying to nail her.

Barb says she had to run a whole lot better than I ever did against the Cardinals or Eagles to keep from getting blitzed by Burt over in Hawaii when we weren't around.

He still tries, now and then. But Shake and me never get hot about it.

I think everybody in New York has been in love with Barbara Jane at one time or another. She's had every known swipe taken at her, but of course she doesn't love anybody but Shake Tiller—and maybe me.

Barb came up to New York when we did, just after
we had signed with the Giants. We were all really happy
to have been chosen by fate to wind up in the big city.

The Giants had told me ahead of time that they were
going to draft me. They had the second choice in the
first round. I had said that I wouldn't sign unless they
drafted Shake Tiller also. We were determined to play
for the same team, even if we had to go to the Canadian
League. I was taken first, of course, being a "white
runner."

The Giants worked it out that Dallas, which had the
third choice in the first round, drafted Shake for them.
I think they had to give up three or four players and
some future draft choices to get Dallas to do that.

Anyhow, that's how Shake and me became New York
Giants.

Barb hadn't given any thoughts at all to becoming a
model when we moved to New York. She immediately
got a job at CBS as a secretary. She just strolled into the
CBS sports department one day and one of their pro-
ducers saw her and said, "If you can make coffee, you're
hired."

She could have walked into any building in Rockefeller
Center and done the same thing. Barb is just so pretty
she sometimes frightens people.

Her main job at CBS seemed to be going to lunch for
about four hours every day, to places like Mike
Manuche's on Fifty-second Street, which is a restaurant
with a lot of sports paintings on the walls where Giant
fans go to discuss trades.

It was in Manuche's one day that Burt Danby saw Barb for the first time and decided she ought to be a model. I've heard her say that this was her introduction to the hip ways of New York. Burt spotted her, walked over to the table, unzipped his fly, looked down at his crotch, and said, "Now, sir. Would you please stand up, give us your name, and tell us what you do?"

When Barb roared laughing, Burt knew he'd found a good chick. He turned her over to his creative department at DDD and F and said, "I want her to be big, big, big."

In those days, even though Burt learned that Barb belonged to us, he high-played her all around town. He would always be thinking up reasons why the two of them had to have dinner or cocktails.

I think he just likes to turn up at all of his joints with a winner on his arm. He likes to put on velvet jackets, hot-comb his hair, hang a bunch of gold shit around his neck —dogtags and animal heads and the like—and prance into Elaine's up on Eighty-eighth and Second Avenue with a Hall of Famer in his company.

Burt takes considerable pride in being able to get a table anywhere he wants one, even Elaine's, where movie stars and archdukes and shoe company presidents and a grand assortment of born-rich fools have been known to stand in line for hours.

Barb doesn't mind going along occasionally, even now. Especially if me and Shake are out of town. It gives her something to do, and of course everybody likes front row center.

"He's harmless," she says. "And he's actually kind of sweet."

To which Shake says, "He wears Gucci underwear."

Well, I can joke about my employer, but I'll tell you how strong he is. One night he took Barb and Shake and me up to Elaine's and the narrow front room up there was packed as usual with all of the semi-artists and spoiled rich pricks who sit there and stare at each other's dates and clothes.

Seeing Burt was there and needed a table instantly, Elaine herself personally cleared out a bevy of brooding poets and eye-shadow junkies so we could sit down.

Burt leaped for the chair with his back against the wall, banged his fist on the table, and said, "Isn't this the *super*-est place in the whole world? *Broadway,* I'll lick you yet."

So anyhow Barb's off with Burt Danby now and some other advertising nitwits, and Shake is either asleep or reading, and who I basically have on my mind is Shoat Cooper.

I'll tell you something. The great miracle of our age is that the Giants are in the Super Bowl with Shoat Cooper for a head coach. Him being the coach was a stroke of genius on the part of Burt Danby, by the way.

When me and Shake were drafted, the head coach was Doyt Elkins, of course, who had originally been hired by the Maras, the old organization. I thought Doyt was a pretty good coach, considering that he only communicated with the players by memo.

We could have done all right with Doyt. But he went to the Cowboys and took the whole staff with him, except for the head scout, which was none other than Shoat Cooper.

Burt Danby didn't even look for anybody else. He said the press liked Shoat because they got drunk together. Besides, Burt said, he was sick of coaches who made the game so mysterious.

When Burt announced that Shoat had the job at a press conference, he said, "God, I'm just so up to *here* with zig-outs and *fly* patterns. I mean, the way they all talk, they just practically make me do a total *face-down* in the old salad. Shoat Cooper keeps its simple. And take it from an old advertising cock that if no one knows what you're *saying,* you couldn't sell welfare in Harlem."

What Burt didn't add was that Shoat Cooper came cheap.

I'm not sure where to begin to describe the country sumbitch.

Shoat's big. He doesn't have much hair left. He looks like he's got about twelve six-packs of Pearl in his belly. And he's always looking around for somewhere to spit.

He's got a slow, deep, country voice. A husky kind of voice, like somebody who just woke up, or like a deputy sheriff talking to a spook who forgot to park his pickup truck between the white lines.

I don't think I've ever seen Shoat act like he's excited.

The one time back during the regular season when we were behind, which was at a halftime when the Redskins had us down by thirty to fourteen on some lucky passes, Shoat Cooper just acted like nothing was any different.

When we all walked into the locker room at Yankee Stadium and slammed our hats down, there was Shoat on a little stool in front of the blackboard, looking down at the floor.

Everybody was bitching and moaning for a few minutes, those that hadn't peed yet or done various things. Finally we plunked down and got quiet and looked at him.

Shoat sat there, chewing on a toothpick, and then he got around to telling us about the first half.

"Well, defense," he groaned slowly. "Seemed to me like you all just kind of stood around and let 'em eat the apple off your head."

Then he spit.

Nobody said anything back for a minute or so and then Puddin Patterson said, "They stuntin', Coach. On Blast and Cutback, that fuckin' Seventy-six is comin' from somewhere and I can't get a piece of him."

Shoat said hmmmmm.

Puddin said, "I believe we can catch 'em, coach. We gonna roll like a big wheel this half."

Shoat said, "Well, we ain't gonna catch nobody unless our defense gets together and decides that they ain't gonna let 'em piss another drop."

Shoat said for the defense to go down to the other end of the locker room and get their problems worked out.

T. J. Lambert drew himself up and said, "Awright, defense. We got to screw our navels to the ground now and get them tootie fruities."

The defense moved away as T. J. hiked his leg and cut a big one.

Puddin Patterson said, "Coach, where that Seventy-six comin' from?"

Shoat looked at the floor for a while and then he said, "I tell you what let's do, Puddin. Let's you just go out there this half and concentrate on tryin' to hit ever sumbitch that's wearin' a different colored shirt."

Shoat's idea for the second half was for Hose Manning to throw a couple of new patterns in the third quarter, get something else on the scoreboard, and then "outgut" the Redskins in the last quarter.

He would always go back to the running game if you gave him half a chance.

"If you run the football up somebody's ass," Shoat says, "then it's them that has to get their hands dirty tryin' to pull it out."

Early in that second half against the Redskins, Hose Manning hit Shake for fifty-five yards on a fly, and that brought us up to thirty to twenty-one. T. J. recovered a fumble right after that and Hose kicked a field goal to make it thirty to twenty-four. But after that, we didn't do anything but run old Billy Clyde.

I carried the ball twenty-two times in the fourth quarter, and scored two sixes, and we finally won it, thirty-eight to thirty.

I was a heavy-breathing sumbitch on the sideline toward the end, but Shoat Cooper put his arm around my shoulder pads and said, "Stud hoss, I ought to buy you a rubber dolly. That was pure dee football out there."

* * *

Shoat Cooper had been a great player in the NFL himself. The old-timers will tell you that there weren't many linebackers any better. Maybe Tommy Nobis was. Or Dick Butkus.

But Shoat in his day was some kind of pisser, they say. They say he craved action so much he would beat his head on the locker room wall until they let him loose for the kickoff.

Shoat came out of Arkansas, like his name suggests. He was from Possum Grape and played ball at the University of Arkansas, where the freshman team is called Shoats.

But they say that's not where he got his name, Shoat. Growing up, I hear, Shoat just looked like a baby pig, or a shoat, so somebody started calling him Shoat.

I guess he might smile when we win Sunday. But in the three years he's been our coach, he hasn't.

You would think that Shoat might have smiled once or twice during our regular season since we're undefeated and untied and already have a diamond ring cinched for winning the National Conference.

We won that, incidentally, by dough-popping the LA Rams thirty-three to thirty-one. I scored three sixes.

But all that old Shoat has said all along is, "A football team with one more game to win ain't no better off than a tired old farmer with one more pig to slop."

As the head coach of the New York Giants I guess the best thing you can say about Shoat is that he doesn't fuck us around. Maybe there's something to that. Maybe a team of pros can just get together and do the job, like we would have done last year if a lot of us hadn't been injured and gone seven-seven.

Shake says this is true, and Shake is semi-intellectual about the game.

Shake says, "Winning is a happy accident of getting a bunch of guys together who want to."

Shake has studied it a lot and he says that coaches are not so important in the pros. He says they're important in college because there are those who can outsmart the others and outrecruit the others.

"But in the pros," he says, "there are studs on every team, and anybody can beat anybody else on a certain Sunday. It's all a matter of which team don't have the rag on."

Shake says that in the pros the teams that win are the ones that stay mentally tough.

When my old buddy talks like this, I tell him he sounds about half like a Darrell Royal or somebody.

Shake says hustle ain't nothing but acting like a gorilla.

"That's the part that's fun," he says. "Hitting people and getting hit and rolling around on the carpet is easy. The hard part is making yourself do something right— at the right minute."

He says, "When you get twenty-two studs who find losing a football game the most distasteful thing in the world, then you got yourself a winner. Hell, everybody wants to win, or says they do. But *not wanting to lose* is what it's all about."

Shake talked like this at our meeting this morning.

"We're just not gonna *accept* a loss to those dog-asses," he said.

"There'll be a minute out there Sunday," he said, "when one of us will do something better than he's ever done it before, and we'll win. One of us will do it because we'll *all* be tryin'."

All Shoat Cooper said at the meeting was that we'd stress the kicking game in workout this afternoon at UCLA, and then pose for some photographs with some starlets.

They better not let T. J. Lambert get too close to those starlets.

Hi, there, friends and neighbors. This is old Billy Clyde Puckett back from practice and showered and shaved and dolled up in his white-on-white-on-white, seeing as how I'm out in California.

Shake and Barbara Jane and Cissy have gone on off to dinner with Puddin Patterson and his wife, Rosalie. They all wanted to go hear somebody sing while they tried to eat but I said I didn't like anybody's singing but Elroy Blunt. And anyway, I wanted to write some more.

I said to call me later and I would go join them somewhere for half a dozen young Scotches.

I got my burgers and fries and my coffee here in our palatial suite and I'm finally going to get it off my mind about Marvin (Shake) Tiller.

Well, now, I presume that most everybody is aware that Shake Tiller is the greatest ball-catching end there ever was.

He hasn't been anything but All-Pro since we came up. I guess he catches eighty or ninety balls a year, and this makes a pretty good quarterback out of Hose Manning, who I think is the best since Joe Namath and Sonny Jurgensen hung it up.

Even the dumbest of the sports writers—and there aren't many smart ones—says Shake is probably better than Hutson or Alworth or any of those studs we've heard about in history.

The thing which makes Shake so great, aside from his hands and his speed and his moves, is that he runs a route so good. If he's supposed to go seven and a half yards down and four and a half yards out, then Shake runs seven and a half yards down and four and a half yards out.

Nobody knows it but not many receivers can do this.

Shake of course is a good-looking dude. He's got this red-blond hair that's thick and flops around. He's got a sort of dimpled chin and lots of good white teeth and some green-blue eyes that Barbara Jane says have an evil sparkle. His expression makes him look most often like he knows deep down everything there is to know, but naturally he doesn't.

He's trim like split ends are supposed to be, which is kind of like country club lifeguards. And his voice is soft and cool. As long as I've known him, which is forever, I've never been able to figure out his voice. He has this way of making things sound like you never know if he's truly serious. Even when he's serious.

The main thing is, Shake is my good buddy for a lifetime, and I really guess that he's my family since I never actually had another one worth mentioning.

Not that I'm complaining about it.

I couldn't have had more fun growing up. Between Shake's parents and Barbara Jane's, and an uncle named Kenneth, I had plenty of folks concerned about me.

Not that it matters any, but I guess you could say that I was from a broke fuckin' home. My daddy ran off before I ever knew him. He was a tool dresser in the oil field, and I guess a fairly good bad-check artist.

My mamma was a waitress and maybe a couple of other things, and she ran off, too. Which left me with Uncle Kenneth, who was not much more than a golf hustler, a pool shark and a pretty good gin rummy stud.

Anyhow, kids grow up. And once they get to be fourteen, it's out of everybody's hands about what might happen to them except their juvenile delinquent friends.

I was lucky that I had Uncle Kenneth to take me to all the football games I wanted to see, and to teach me how to run the six ball in snooker and that the best thing to do in gin was hit the silk when you got ten or under.

Uncle Kenneth always told me, "If you like sports and know how to gamble, then you'll always be interested in something and you won't come to no real harm."

Me and Shake never had anything but good times. I can't think of anything that ever happened to us that we didn't think was funny, even some bad things. Really bad things, and not just losing the city championship once.

Well, what's worse than somebody dying?

It was really terrible one time but Shake's real mother —not his mother now, but his real one—got killed in a car wreck when we were about sixteen.

She didn't die right away, where she got hit by a car-load of drunk priests, but about three days later in the hospital. She died one night just after Shake and me had left her room and gone to the cold drink machine.

We knew she was likely to die, though. She never had got conscious from the wreck, and Shake's dad, Marvin, Sr., a really good old boy, had prepared us for the worst.

But what I'm getting at is that after Shake had sort of put his arm around his dad and strolled off down the hall with him, and after he had hugged his grandmother and his aunt while Barbara Jane and I just stood around, Shake came back and told everybody he just had to cut out. Move it on.

The three of us left and didn't say anything to each other. We just kind of walked off in the general direction of Herb's Café, where we hung out.

But as we were walking along, Shake said something that I didn't think I heard right—something that sort of summed up how he was, and still is.

"Well, it's a wrap on the squash," he said.

I muttered a huh, or something.

And Shake said, "I've been trying to think of what good there could be in my mom dying, and the only thing I can think of is that I won't have to look at any more fuckin' squash on the dinner table."

Shake Tiller has always had what some people might call a strange sense of humor.

People themselves have always been the funniest things of all to him. He's a good imitator and he could always listen to somebody talk for just a little while and then sound like them.

To this day, Shake can still imitate Big Ed Bookman so good it makes me and Barbara Jane collapse. Big Ed Bookman is Barb's daddy.

Big Ed Bookman is in the "oil bidness," as Shake would say. Big Ed talks a lot about a "tax break for the oil bidness." He talks about "buyin' pipe," and all of his production out in Scogie County. Things like that.

Big Ed is a big man in Fort Worth, which some people say is not so hard a thing to be. Fort Worth is not exactly Dallas or Houston. It's near Dallas, about thirty-five miles away on a toll road. But that's geography.

In looks and money and getting things done, Fort Worth is about as far away from Dallas as I am from Shakespeare.

I'm afraid my old home town is in that part of Texas which doesn't have the charm of the flat plains or the piny woods or the coastline or the mountains.

The land looks like it could be almost anywhere in twelve or fourteen different states. The wind that sometimes blows across it is the same wind that blows across Oklahoma—untouched.

We've played ball down there in ever kind of weather you can imagine. In October it can get as hot as summer. And there are days during the summer when you can see the heat in the air. It looks like germs.

It can also get colder than a nun's ass. I don't know

if many people outside of Texas know what a norther is, but a norther is when the sky turns the color of a battleship and you can feel the icicles stabbing you in the chest.

We've played a lot of ball in northers.

Fort Worth has some pretty parts. There are neighborhoods with little creeks running through them and lots of sycamore and oak trees. There's a river winding around called the Trinity, and this could add something to it if it wasn't always the color of meatloaf.

My old alma mater of TCU—that's Texas Christian University, of course—doesn't have quite as much ivy covering its great halls of learning as your normal McDonald's. It is just a bunch of cream-brick buildings and parking lots but the buildings are not so ugly compared to some grain elevators rising up on the outskirts of town.

The good things about the town are most of the people, who are honest, unpretentious and work hard. And the Mexican food and barbeque, not to forget the chicken fried steak and cream gravy. But I'm not sure this makes up for some kind of pride in ignorance that somebody like Big Ed Bookman seems to have.

There's an old city slogan that Fort Worth is "Where the West Begins," and I suppose at one time there were a bunch of cowboys hanging around instead of used-car dealers and Jaycees.

There used to be another slogan which went something like, "Dallas for Culture, Fort Worth for Fun." But none of us ever knew what fun they were talking about, unless it was trying to get on one of the thirteen roads leading out.

Maybe they meant the fun we had to dream up for ourselves, which was always plentiful.

We used to ask Barbara Jane why somebody as rich as Big Ed Bookman would stay in Fort Worth. She always answered the same thing. "Would a czar leave Russia if they weren't pissed off at him?" she'd say.

It still bewilders me somewhat. Big Ed Bookman can live anywhere he wants to, but he stays in a town where you still have to stop your car for freight trains and look at signs which need repainting or have one neon light missing.

Big Ed always said Fort Worth wasn't such a small town if you looked at it a certain way. If you took all the Jews out of Dallas, all the niggers out of Houston and all the spicks out of San Antonio, Fort Worth was a pretty good-sized place, he'd say.

Big Ed is big in everything in Fort Worth, of course. Big in "bidness." Big in golf. Big at River Crest, his country club. Big in TCU football, having bought the AstroTurf for the stadium when TCU fired a couple of assistant coaches he didn't like. Big in what passes for society in Fort Worth.

Big Ed Bookman is always flying down to Houston, where he keeps his "oil bidness" office, or he's flying out to Colorado to one of his ranches, or he's flying up to Washington, D.C., or he's flying to Acapulco.

For as long as I can remember, Big Ed has always been on the board of a lot of banks. And he's talked about the governors, senators and Presidents he's helped elect.

Doesn't seem like anybody—to this day—can do anything in Fort Worth unless they ask old Big Ed Bookman about it.

Big Ed is married to Big Barb, and in her own way Big Barb is as big as Big Ed around Fort Worth.

Big Barb has always been in charge of who got to be a Fort Worth debutante, as if there ever was such a thing. She's in charge of all kinds of charities and theaters. She's in charge of redecorating the country club. She's always in charge of everybody's party and vacation and clothes and schools and voting.

She's also some kind of history nut. I mean in the sense that she's always tracing the Bookmans back to Henry the Fuckin' Eighth or Sam the Fuckin' Houston.

I've got to say that they're still handsome people. Big Ed is tall and most of his hair he's still got. It's gray but thick. He always has a tan and he wears a whole pile of cashmere and double knits and tricky loafers.

Big Barb is pretty scenic her own self. She's still slender and fairly elegant of eyes and teeth. She can lay some hairdos on you, and some heavyweight jewelry. She goes around smiling most of the time and looking at herself in hubcaps, or whatever she can find that will cause a reflection.

She's a semi-brunette.

But I started out to say how Shake can imitate Big Ed, who has a deep, important voice.

Shake's favorite line to imitate is Big Ed in a restaurant.

"Uh, little lady," Big Ed will say, "I'll have one of your sixteen-ounce T-bones medium rare."

This is Shake doing his Big Ed routine:

"The thing that bothers the world today is a bunch of goddamn kids who don't have any respect for what made this the greatest goddamn country in the world.

"This country is great because of what the white man did with it. There wasn't a goddamn thing but savages around one time, and they didn't know anything about schools or golf courses or any other goddamn thing.

"But the white man came in and kicked the shit out of the blacks and the browns and the yellows and made the world a decent place that smelled better and had johns that flushed.

"It was the white man who invented the electric light and the airplane and the television and the air conditioning and every other goddamn thing worth having.

"If the white man had left it up to the black man or the brown man, we wouldn't have anything but a bunch of goddamn disease and lice and probably a hell of a lot of Communism.

"Kids today ought to look at the white man and stop lookin' at niggers and spicks. That's where they find out about dope and screwing off.

"If you don't mind me saying so, it's people like me—Big Ed Bookman—that made this country what it is. I employ about ten thousand people, one way or another, and I pay 'em good, too, as long as they work their ass off.

"Hard work never hurt anybody. I've worked hard ever since my daddy found oil in Scogie County. I could have just let our family fortune go to hell and played golf all the time, but I didn't. I only played part of the time, and there's not a goddamn thing wrong with recreation. It's American.

"Let me give you an equation that affects today's kids. One nigger plus one spick equals Communism and dope. It's all tied in together.

"Uh, little lady, I'll have one of your sixteen-ounce T-bones, medium rare."

I had to stop to answer the phone. It was Barbara Jane calling up to say that the place where they were at, something called the Macadamia Nut, had a comedian who was about as funny as a late night talk show and a singer who was at least as good as T. J. Lambert. She said they were leaving.

I said for them to go on, and call me again. I was still writing.

"I'm talking about your folks," I said.

Barbara Jane said, "Oh, shit. Did you put in there that Big Barb's ancestors invented the spinning wheel and the hunting dog?"

"And the hundred-dollar bill," I said.

'Say, luv, this place is a wrap," she said. "We think we'll go take a look at a new club called the Ho Chi Minh Trail. It's right there on Rodeo where everything else is. You can't miss it."

"Is it near the caviar joint?" I asked.

"Right," said Barb. "A block down from Nicholas and Alexandra's Caviarteria, and across the street from that sandwich shop where the out-of-work actors hang out. Poopoo and Ricky's Suede Cadillac. You'll see it."

"I'll find it," I said. "Sure sounds like a swell name for a club. You can expect a vertical assault from old Twenty-three within an hour or so."

"O.K.," Barb said. "You write that old book now, boy. You write that old book real good and we'll get you some quail and some brown gravy and some biscuits. That ain't no bad way to start off the day, is it?"

"Got to go now," I said. "Bye."

"Billy Clyde Puckett, you get down off that roof!" Barb said.

"See you in a while," I said.

"You come in this house right now before I take a switch to you," Barb said.

"Bye," I said.

"Love, luv," she said, and hung up.

By now you may have figured out that Barbara Jane Bookman has a bit of a satirical nature. She has always been able to make me laugh, just like Shake Tiller.

In terms of growing up, I'd have to say that Barb was most likely the first smart-ass I ever knew. Before Shake, even.

I could give you a fairly good example by telling about the time the three of us got expelled from Fuller Junior High.

It happened because the three of us were in old lady Murcer's music class one day in the high seventh, and old lady Murcer had to leave the room for a while and she let Barbara Jane, her pet, preside over the class.

Barb's job was to stand up at old lady Murcer's desk and lead us in a few songs until old lady Murcer got back.

Everything went along fine for a couple of songs, but then Shake Tiller held up his hand.

"Yes, Marvin, what is it?" said Barb, snootily.

Shake said, "Miz Bookman, I was wondering if we could sing something besides this daffodil shit?"

Barb laughed like hell, along with everybody else.

Then she said fine, we could sing whatever we wished, provided Shake and me got up in front of the class with her and helped lead the room.

We got up there and proceeded to lead the class in what we thought was the funniest song we'd ever heard.

What we sang was, "Down, Down, Down with R. E. Turner." R. E. Turner was the principal, naturally.

The song went:

> *Down, down, down with R. E. Turner.*
> *He's a dirty horse manure,*
> *Horseshit!*
> *They forgot to pull the chain,*
> *Consequently, he'll remain—*
> *Til they disinfect the*
> *Fort Worth city sewers.*

I don't recall how many times we sang it, or how far down the corridor anybody could hear it. But R. E. Turner heard it and when we finished it the last time, he appeared in the doorway of our room.

Seems like the three of us sat in R. E. Turner's office for about an hour before Big Ed got there.

Mr. Turner just sat there boiling and looking at some papers on his desk. We tried to sit quietly and not look at each other because we knew we'd giggle if we did.

At one point, Mr. Turner told Barbara Jane, "Young lady, I hope you realize that this may cost you the state spelling championship."

Shake blurted out, "Aw, gee. Not that. Anything but that."

And Barbara Jane bit her lip to keep from breaking up.

Mr. Turner told me, "It's not really your fault, Puckett. You've always been easily led."

When Big Ed came in, he insisted that we be allowed to stay in Mr. Turner's office and listen to their conversation.

"I don't have anything to say that I can't say in front of anybody in this great world. That's what it's like to be totally honest," said Big Ed.

Mr. Turner nodded.

Big Ed said, "Now, R. E., let's you and me try to remember our younger days when we got into scrapes of one kind or another. Thank God there was somebody around to help us out. That's my mission here. I'm here to stand by my daughter and these two young men that Mrs. Bookman and I know to be fine, clean, honest young men."

Mr. Turner said he appreciated Big Ed's concern.

"Now, R. E., I know that your immediate impulse is to expel these youngsters and teach them a lesson. But let's think about that for a minute."

Big Ed leaned forward and said, "You know what that would accomplish? You'd lose a possible state spelling champion, and I know for sure you'd lose the city junior high track and field championship next week."

Mr. Turner said those things weren't so important.

Mr. Turner said what we had done was so bad that we ought to be kicked out for the rest of the semester and made to take the high seventh over again.

Big Ed cleared his throat.

"Now, R. E.," he said. "I think you ought to give some consideration to the fact that if we kick these fine youngsters out for the rest of the semester, they'll fall behind the other kids, and the next thing we know, they'll drop out of school altogether and get involved in dope and start hanging around with undesirables like some of these unfortunates you've been busing in here."

Mr. Turner didn't say anything.

"Now, R. E., you just give some consideration to your own youth," said Big Ed.

Mr. Turner said he had never done anything like we did.

Big Ed then said, "Well, R. E., why don't you give some goddamn consideration to who the hell I am?"

Mr. Turner said we'd be out for three days. That was the best he could do, and Big Ed marched out like a winner.

Big Ed decided to drive all of us over to his house on Bookman Lane, which was Barbara Jane's old home before Big Ed built the new one on River Crest's tenth fairway, which he made the club sell him, even though it left

River Crest with a seventeen-hole golf course.

The drive was fairly quiet until Big Ed said, "Well, Barbara Jane, could you tell me just what you think of these two punks here who got you into all this?"

Barbara Jane said, "Mostly Dad, I think they're pretty rotten singers."

Big Ed fumed the rest of the way.

When we got there, he made us sit down in the den, where we could look at his golf trophies and his stuffed animal heads and his framed letters from various political studs, who thanked him for being for America.

Big Ed said Big Barb would be home in a minute and then we would all talk about our futures. Big Ed then left us alone in the den. I think he went to phone up Wall Street and sell Libya.

Barbara Jane said her mother was probably at a meeting of the Daughters of the Intimate Friends of the Dumb-Asses who stayed at the Alamo, or something.

Shake called his daddy at the store they owned, Tiller Electric, and told him what had happened and where he was.

I remember that listening to Shake on the phone I got the impression that his daddy didn't think any of it was a very big deal.

I remember hearing Shake saying, "Yeah, really, Dad. For singing dirty. Yeah, an old song about Mr. Turner. With a bad word or two in it. Yeah. Yeah. No, sir, it was mainly because Barbara Jane was doing it with us and she's a girl and all. Yes, sir. I'll tell her. Him, too. Yes, sir. O.K. Bye."

I would have called Uncle Kenneth but I knew there

weren't any phones on the fifteenth green at Rockwood Muny. Anyhow, he'd have only been interested in whether we would get back in school in time for the dashes and the broad jump.

Big Barb finally came in wearing big round yellow sunglasses, pants, rings on every finger, her hair pulled straight back like a Flamenco dancer, a short drink in her hand and a long cigarette.

"Well," she said. "This is certainly a new experience for the Bookman family. I'm so ashamed of you three that I'm actually numb."

Shake said, "It was my fault, Miz Bookman."

"Was not," Barbara Jane said.

Big Ed said that if it hadn't been for him we'd all be out for the semester.

Shake said he sure did thank Mr. Bookman for saving us, and he mainly wanted to apologize for getting Barbara Jane in trouble.

I said me too.

Shake said, "My daddy says he feels real bad about Barbara Jane being involved."

"Your father's a very nice man," said Big Barb. "I've shopped in his little store many times. I think that fixture in the hallway came from there."

Shake said it could have.

Barbara Jane said it probably did.

I said I didn't know.

"Is his little store still in the same place, over there by the bridge where the Mexicans have started moving in?" Big Barb asked.

Barbara Jane said, "Oh, terrific, Mom."

"Yes, Ma'am," said Shake. "Over there on Nelson Avenue is where it's still at."

I said that's right. Over on Nelson Avenue.

Big Barb said, "Barbara, I only meant that the town's changing faster than we can keep up with it."

"Sure," Barbara Jane said.

Shake cleared his throat.

So did I.

Nobody said anything for a minute or two, and then Big Barb said, "As a matter of fact, I think those two carriage lamps on the front door came from Tiller Electric."

Might have, said Shake.

Probably did, I said.

Barbara Jane sighed and put her elbows on her knees and put her chin in the cups of her hands and closed her eyes.

Big Ed said, "Uh, honey, these boys and your daughter have promised me that their behavior in the future will be A-O.K. I think these three days out of school will teach them a pretty good lesson."

"Of course, it will be talked about at River Crest," Big Barb said.

"I wouldn't worry much about that," said Big Ed.

"I'm sure you won't," Big Barb said. "You'll be in Houston."

Big Ed said, "River Crest don't talk about a goddamn thing that I don't tell 'em to talk about, so that's that."

Big Barb looked away and smoked.

Shake and me glanced at each other and Barbara Jane blinked.

Big Ed said, "This isn't exactly the end of the goddamn world. It isn't anything that intelligent white people can't handle."

Barbara Jane said, "I wonder how unintelligent black people handle it."

"What's that supposed to mean?" said Big Ed.

"I was just thinking out loud," Barbara Jane said.

"That wasn't very funny, Barbara," said Big Barb.

Me and Shake looked at each other.

"Let's wrap this up," Big Ed said. "Jake Ealey's gonna stop by in a minute and we've got to talk about what we're gonna do with that goddamn Alaska property."

We stood up.

"Be sure and tell your father hello," said Big Barb.

"He's a goddamn nice fellow," Big Ed said.

Shake said thank you. He would.

Big Barb looked at me and said, "How's your, uh, your Uncle Kermit these days?"

"Kenneth," I said.

"Yes, of course," she said. "Is he getting along fine?"

I guess so, I said. He still plays at scratch.

Big Ed said, "Kenneth Puckett was one hell of a golfer around here a few years ago."

Must have been, I said.

"There was a time when some of us at the club thought seriously about putting him on the goddamn pro tour," said Big Ed. "Probably should have. He'd have probably made us a ton."

"And him, too," Shake said.

"Damn right he would have," Big Ed said. "Well, listen, you hot shots. Mind your damned old singing now.

And keep my daughter out of trouble, all right?"

Shake and me smiled and said we would.

We were walking out the front door when Big Ed said, "What the hell's Kenneth doing these days?"

Shake said, "Near as me and Billy C. can figure out, he's got some kind of position in the Fort Worth underworld."

Big Ed and Big Barb managed a nervous laugh.

Then Big Barb said, "You boys don't be strangers now. You know you're welcome here any time."

"See you, Barb," said Shake.

"Later," I said.

We jogged off through the big yard but before we crossed the circular driveway, right at the iron gates, Shake stopped and looked back.

"Hey, Mrs. Bookman," he hollered. "Next time you're over at the store, don't mind all those Mexicans. All they ever do is go to sleep in the dirt. You can just step over 'em."

We heard Barbara Jane howling as we turned and trotted off. Even then, she had that great laugh.

Jim Tom Pinch has said that there ought to be something in the book about the life that me and Shake lead when we're not playing ball. Something about what we do during the off-season. And as he put it, "Something about your aptitudes and attitudes, other than football."

I think this is a lot of boring crap, Jim Tom, but I'll try to cover it quickly, if aptitude means what I think it does.

Actually, when I stop to think about this, it makes me kind of hot. Not you, Jim Tom, but the fact that there are those people who don't think a ball player is anything but a go-rilla.

I'd like to make it clear that me and Shake lead a very quiet and decent life in the off-season. We pretty much stay in New York through the winter and spring. And by that time, of course, it's getting near the start of another training camp.

Maybe a day or two a week we'll go off somewhere and make a speech at a luncheon or banquet. We get anywhere from three hundred to five hundred a pop, depending on how much the Sioux Falls Quarterback Club—or some such thing—can afford.

A lot of studs hold down steady jobs in the off-season because they have to in order to feed their families. We're lucky, I think. We make good money and don't have to do that. Work, I mean.

Now and then you have to spend the night somewhere on the banquet circuit. But this doesn't have to be total agony if some of the guys who've invited you out there will lay a kindhearted secretary on you, or maybe even some of their private stock.

I've been known to have me some good times in some surprising places. Akron wore my ass out once, and so did Omaha. And Shake Tiller always speaks fondly of Terre Haute and Oklahoma City.

When it warms up around New York, we try to play some golf.

I suppose that I ought to confess that the only thing

I'd ever be interested in doing besides playing ball would
be to run my own restaurant or bar.

That might be all right sometime, after I'm crippled.

I know the kind of place I'd want. It would have to
be located in the Fifties on the near East Side so the
clientele wouldn't have to worry about getting shot or
stabbed. It would serve a big drink and stay open late
and there wouldn't be any Frenchmen waiting tables.

I'd encourage a lot of wool to hang around for set
decoration. There'd be comfortable chairs and round
tables, and none of them very close together so the cus-
tomers wouldn't have to bore each other with their talk
about business or clothes or kids.

Nobody would wear a tie. Elroy Blunt would be on
the juke box. And you'd be able to get decent things to
eat like chili, real barbecue and black-eyed peas.

I'd probably call it something like the Triple Option
and hang some pictures on the wall of Shake Tiller.

But that's a few years off.

As for Shake Tiller, his interests run a little wider than
mine.

For one thing, he likes to jack around in the stock
market with our money. He likes the action. "There's a
new ball game every day," he says.

He does O.K., by the way, which he says is not surprising because most everybody in real-life business is a
dunce.

He likes to say, "I never knew a chairman of the board
of anything that I'd let run an elevator for me."

Shake says one of his great ambitions is to meet a smart

guy who's the boss of something.

I've heard him say, "Every time I'm introduced to somebody who's supposed to know all about television or politics or Wall Street, he's a goddamn drop case."

He's said, "So far as I can figure out, the only three ways to get to the top in business is to get born rich, marry it, or be so fuckin' dumb they can't do anything but promote you to get you out of the way."

We do a couple of other things during the off-season that have helped Shake form this opinion. We have lunch a lot with dumb-asses who are "friends" of the Giants, and we spend a few random nights in places like "Twenty-one" talking to other dumb-asses.

I guess we like to drink and laugh at the drop cases or we wouldn't do it.

In fact, Shake once said he'd be perfectly happy if the whole world was semi-dark and indoors. That's a pretty funny line that's been quoted by a lot of other people around Clarke's and Manuche's.

Maybe if Shake wasn't a ball player he'd be a stud in public relations because he's handsome, a dude dresser, and has the gift of bullshit. I think he'd be good in television, if he wanted to do it, and from the money he's made for us in investments, I know damn well he could run a curl pattern on Wall Street.

Our apartment is pretty much known as a landmark around town.

It's the penthouse on the eighteenth floor of a semi-new building at Sixty-fifth and First. We've got a big living room and a bar, two big bedrooms, a kitchen with

a bar, and a terrace. Shake has done it up pretty neat
with thick carpet all over and comfortable furniture.
And we've got a couple of fireplaces.

We've got stereo coming out of everywhere and color
TV's built in here and there. We've got some paintings
on the walls that Shake likes because you can make them
out to be whatever you want them to be. There are a
few blown-up photographs of us around, scoring touchdowns and getting our dicks knocked off.

There's a great big photograph of Puddin Patterson's
little cousins, Albert and Bowie, sitting on our bench on
a cold day at Yankee Stadium, sitting between me and
Shake.

Oh, yeah, and we've got a Siamese cat named Martha
Nell who's a rotten, surly bitch that hates us and tries to
eat up all of our cashmere sweaters.

Mainly, our apartment is known as a landmark because we have a considerable number of parties there,
some planned and some not. We always have one after
a home game. Most of the guys on the team come up to
see if we've discovered any new stewardesses in the
building, or if Barbara Jane has any new model friends
who might be half-horny.

When we first got up to New York we instituted the
regular Monday afternoon all-skate during the fall. This
was a thing where we got a few friends and a few light
hooks to come in, get drunk, take naked, and have what
we called an Eastern Regional Eat-Off.

Some of our TV friends that we met learned how to
drop by for lunch, take part in the skate, and still make

the old five forty-seven to Greenwich.

T. J. Lambert still holds the record for having performed the most formidable deed at a Monday all-skate.

One time there were these three spade hooks in attendance. They were hard-hitters and really good-natured. They let T. J. get them defrocked and boost them up on the mantel over the fireplace in the living room.

I can still see them sitting up there with their legs spread, singing like the Supremes, while T. J. took turns eating all three.

T. J. still refers to our apartment as "Sperm City."

Well, I got to go off to the bright lights of Beverly Hills now. Probably ought to just stay here in our palatial suite and drink milk shakes since the dog-ass Jets are coming up for us Sunday.

But like Shake is prone to say at times, "Can't a man ever unwind? Is it all just work and worry?" That's his way of excusing a few young Scotches and a couple of drags on those anti-God cigarettes that a man gets handed to him now and then.

Might be some of that tonight, in fact.

So this is Billy Clyde Puckett's last mercy message of the evening. The port side is starting to list. Clear the rafts. Hymn singers and female impersonators over the side first.

Hope I don't need my I.D. card to get a drink in the Ho Chi Minh Trail.

Which suddenly reminds me of what Shake Tiller used

to say when we were kids and somebody would ask our age before selling us a cold Pearl.

Shake would have the collar turned up on his khaki shirt and he'd have his shades on and a cigarette in his teeth, and he'd say:

"Nobody ever asked us how old we were in the Mekong Delta."

PART TWO

The Wool Market

When I think of all the men you must have killed
With those looks that you go lookin' at 'em with,
When I think of all the good homes that you've broke
With those promises you've whispered and you've spoke
Then I wonder why the Lord has gone and willed
That a Hard-hittin' Woman ain't no myth.

—from "Hard-hittin' Woman,"
a song by Elroy Blunt

An appropriate tune to be furnishing background music right now would be "Wore Out Mother," one of Elroy Blunt's first big ones.

The point is, I'm just a little bit tired after last night. It might have to be a wrap so far as my night life is concerned until after we've dough-popped the dog-ass Jets.

That place we were at, the Ho Chi Minh Trail, was what you might call semi-O.K. if what a man has on his mind is drinking and smoking and fooling around with goddess women.

Cissy Walford ran about eighth and even Barbara Jane would have been caught in a photo finish. That's how me and Shake gauged it at the peak hour in terms of sheer physical legs, lungs, asses, ankles and faces.

Now if you think that's not stronger than T. J. Lambert's underwear, then you can bust me.

Only the Old Skipper in the great beauty pageant in the sky could have known who most of those young things were. Or how they came up so glorious. It was just a whole pile of have bosoms, will travel; of long, tough legs; of extra-long, serious hair; and of soulful eyes.

Barbara Jane said they were what you call your southern California witches.

There isn't much to them, really, except physical stupendousness. They just sort of slouch around and toss their serious hair and do these slow dances by themselves, or with fags, with not too many clothes on. And if they speak at all, it is only something like, "Oh, hi. Didn't we meet at Screen Gems?"

We asked around who some of them were. We asked whether they were movie stars or semi-starlets or models, but you can't get any straight answers from people who live out here.

For instance, one of the persons we asked was the Western TV star, Boke Kellum, who sat with us, much to Cissy Walford's delight.

And all Boke Kellum said was, "They're all a bunch of silly pussies with *hideous* make-up."

Our general view was that the Ho Chi Minh Trail was a fairly nifty place, take away a few fags.

When you walk in, you go down some steps into a trench up to your waist and you begin to hear the muffled sounds of explosions and gunfire. And it seemed like we also heard some kind of serious voice reciting the Declaration of Independence off in the distance.

A fag spook in black pajamas comes up to you and asks if you're a member or anybody important. Then he leads you to a bunker where people are laying around on sandbags. The trench winds all around the place, to other bunkers, and other people. Everybody has to look up to the dance floor where the southern California witches are.

There are mosquito nets draped all around and everything is camouflaged in brown and yellow and green. It is sort of dark and there's a small spotlight that stays pointed at a portrait on the wall of Ho Chi Minh.

You don't hear the music so much in the bunkers because of the muffled gunfire and explosions and the Declaration of Independence. But up on the dance floor, you can hear it because it comes down out of the ceiling, out of guns mounted on the wing of an American jet fighter plane that seems to be halfway poked through the ceiling.

We thought the whole place smelled somewhat like grass.

This might have been because Boke Kellum didn't see anything wrong with lighting up a few times and passing the little darlings around. The waitresses didn't seem to mind taking a hit or two, which tended to have some effect on the service.

When I got to the bunker where my pals were, I couldn't tell for the dark who all was there at first. The first thing I saw was Boke Kellum sitting next to Cissy Walford. He stuck out his hand and said, "A real pleasure to meet a fellow athlete. I played a little football myself at Indiana State."

Like shit, I thought.

He had a real tough handshake like he was testing the stud hoss's grip, or trying to cover up the dicks he's swallowed.

Shake was propped up on a sandbag with his arm around Barbara Jane.

"It's our kind of place, Billy C.," he said, nodding

up toward the dance floor where the southern California witches were.

I looked up behind me and didn't see anything but a cluster of fantastic thighs and calves.

"I see what you mean," I said.

Barbara Jane said, "You'd better look a little closer."

I looked again. Well, sure enough, looking up there, if you looked close enough, you could plainly see that those lovely witches didn't have any undergarments on. So staring down at all of us was lots and lots of slow-moving, southern California witch wool.

"It do get distractin', don't it?" Barbara Jane grinned.

I was beginning to wonder if I might have to burn a flag or something to get myself a young Scotch when I sensed something warm and damp in my ear and something sort of nice pressing against my arm.

"Aren't you Billy Clyde Puckett?" the waitress asked.

"Same one," I said.

"Your friends said you were coming," she said.

"They were right," I said.

She said, "Would you like something to drink, or would you rather just sit here and cuddle?"

I said I might like both.

But I would start with a young Scotch and water.

"Groovy," she said. After which she pushed a whole blouse full of lungs against my arm and licked my ear again and left.

I looked over at Shake and Barbara Jane.

"Anybody got any idea what that dumplin' resembles in a better light?" I asked.

Shake said, "Pure Dirty Leg."

And Barbara Jane said, "Lower."

I said, "Ain't no Runnin' Sore, is it?"

"No," Barbara Jane said. "But you wouldn't race off and buy a whole pack of Binaca."

I said, "Stove or Stovette?"

Shake said, "In-betweener. A semi-Stovette, Dirty Leg, Kid at Home. You wouldn't put her on your arm and go just anywhere."

Barbara Jane giggled. "That's not to say you wouldn't eat her," she said.

A long time ago, way back in college at TCU, me and Shake and Barbara Jane to a certain extent had worked up this rating system for girls, or wool.

Mostly, it was Shake's terminology and we had never forgotten it.

Anything below ten was a Running Sore. That was something that only a Bubba Littleton or a T. J. Lambert would fool around with, but of course either one of them would diddle an alligator if somebody drained the pond.

From the bottom up, our rating system went like this:

A Ten was a Healing Scab. Had a bad complexion, maybe, but was hung and could turn into some kind of barracuda in the rack.

A Nine was a Head Cold. Good-looking but sort of proper and didn't know anything at all about what a man liked.

An Eight was a Young Dose of the Clap, but pretty in a dimestore kind of way, and not bad for an hour.

A Seven was just rich.

A Six was a Stove or a Stovette. A Stove was over thirty and preferably married. A Stovette was just under thirty, divorced, talked filthy, and tried to make up for all the studs she never got to eat because she got married so young.

A Five was a Dirty Leg. She wore lots of cheap wigs, waited tables or hopped cars, was truly hung, might chew gum, posed for pictures, and got most of her fun in groups.

A Four was a Homecoming Queen or a Sophomore Favorite and a hard-hitting dumb-ass. Fours married insurance salesmen and got fat and later in life stayed sick a lot.

A Three was a Semi, which a Texan pronounces sem-eye. You had to beware of Semis because you might marry them in a weak minute. Threes had it all put together in looks and style and sophistication. They could drink a lot and dance good and hang around and make conversation.

A Two was a Her. With a capital. If a Semi was tough, a Her was tougher. You might marry the same Her twice. Or three times. Barbara Jane was a Her, or a Two.

And there just never had been a One. Ever.

The day we made up the absolute grand majestic final list, we were sitting around Herb's Café drinking Pearl. Barbara Jane knew quite a bit about what a One ought to be, since Barb herself was in the running.

A One had to be extremely gorgeous in all ways from the minute she woke up in the morning until she fixed a man his cold meatloaf sandwich after love practice at four A.M.

A One never got mad at anything a man might accidentally do, no matter how thoughtless or careless it might be.

A One didn't care about having a lot of money.

A One had to be good-natured and laugh a lot and enjoy all kinds of people, no matter how boring they were. At least bores were funny, we said.

Words like *fuck* and *shit* and *piss* and *tit* and *fart* and *spick* didn't bother a One. In fact, she used them, but not recklessly. Just natural.

A One was a lady at all times.

A One could cook anything a man wanted fixed, quickly, and good, such as biscuits and cream gravy, fried chicken, enchilladas, meatloaf, navy beans, tunafish salad with pecans in it, barbecued ribs and strawberry shortcake.

If a One danced, she could cool out everybody else on the floor but she never asked to dance.

She ought to tan easily and not have any sort of blemish on her whole stud body.

Hair color and eyes were optional but streaked-butterscotch hair and deep brown eyes weren't too bad, since that was what Barbara Jane had, along with a semisleepy look and the ability to sweat daintily.

A One had to know, Shake said.

"Know what?" Barbara Jane asked.

"Whatever we want her to know at the time," Shake said. "She just knows and understands."

A One was well-read and smart and witty but not as well-read and smart and witty as some guys she hung around with.

It would help if a One had a great kind of laugh, sort of husky and boisterous at times, and highly appreciative of what a man said.

A One was stylish in the way she dressed. Not fancy but semi-inventive. What she wore didn't detract from her physical beauty but made it better, and it frequently outbutted whatever was fashionable among women.

A One didn't particularly care about ever getting married.

She was a happy drunk and never aggressive.

She was a talkative, funny high, but she probably preferred booze to dope.

Finally, we decided, a One really and truly, and without any hangups, enjoyed every kind of normal sexual adventure under the proper circumstances.

"Then she *can* come," Barbara Jane joked.

Shake said, "About every other time when she's getting fucked, but just as regular as a faucet if you eat her."

Barbara Jane finished off a Pearl, took a long drag on a Winston, looked at me and Shake across the table and said, "I'm a One."

I had a giggle fit for a while, and it was catching, and we all giggled through the ordering of another round of Pearl in Herb's.

And then Shake said, "Sorry."

"What do you mean sorry?" said Barbara Jane.

"Real close but you ain't a One," he said.

Barbara Jane looked at me.

"Missed by that much," I said.

We were grinning.

"I damn sure am," she said.

Shake said, "Nope."

I said, "You hit the tape at the same time. Probably both run a nine one. But you ain't a One because there's no such thing as a One that we know of."

Barbara Jane said, "Well, if I'm not a One, then who in the hell is?"

"Nobody," said Shake.

Barbara Jane looked off for a while. And then she said, "I know who you all think is a One. You think that bitch Emily Kirkland is because she's been to Europe and has her own Porsche. I don't personally think she's so good-looking."

We just laughed.

"She's got a thick waist, did you know that?" Barbara Jane said.

We didn't say anything. Just drank our Pearl.

"If you two think Emily Kirkland is a One, then you two are just a couple of rat bastard pricks," Barb said.

Shake laughed like hell and so did I.

Then Shake said, "Emily Kirkland is lighter than popcorn."

I said, "Barb, you're the only Two we ever knew. What's wrong with that?"

Barbara Jane said, "What's wrong with it is that I'm a goddamn One. That's what's wrong with it."

Shake said, "I'll tell you what we'll do. We'll give you

a one-week tryout as a possible One but if you flunk just one test, then you're gonna have to be content as a Two forever."

"And if I pass?" said Barb.

"Well, the test don't really ever come to an end," said Shake. "A One can stop being a One almost any time. Like if she would change in any way and start putting a lot of bad-mouth on a man for some reason. So if you're gonna get a One tryout, you're gonna have to stay hook-'em-up the rest of your life. Or not be a One, of course."

Barbara Jane said, "Since I'm a *natural* One anyhow, I don't imagine it'll be too difficult."

Shake grinned and said, "I just thought of something. If you're truly a One, then I don't suppose you'd mind doing me and Billy C. a favor right now, would you? All you'd have to do is get under the table for a few minutes."

Barbara Jane said, "Gee, it would sure be fun, guys. Right here in Herb's. But as a One, of course, I have to be well-read and smart and witty. So I gotta go to class."

She slid out of her chair, stood up, and swallowed the last of her can of Pearl.

"See you around the campus, as they say. Is that what they say?" she said.

Going toward the side door of Herb's, she stopped to say hello to old Herb, who was behind the bar.

"Listen, Herb," she said. "There's a couple of fur traders sitting over there who just blew in from the Yukon. Set 'em up with some of the good liquor. I'll be back after I do my next song and dance."

Then she slinked out, like one of those old dolls in one of those old movies.

Shake and me and old Herb, from across the small bar-type room where we were at, all shared a mutual grin for Barbara Jane Bookman.

We sat silent for a minute and Shake said, "You think I'm not about half in love with that sumbitch?"

"Always were," I said.

We kept on sitting there, sort of looking out the window at the parking lot, and across the street at the Esso station.

Shake said, "She's the strongest sumbitch I ever knew."

"Stronger than rent," I said.

Shake said, "I guess I really do love her, don't I?"

I said, "Old buddy, any time you decide that you don't, I know an old boy who'd like to try out for the part."

And Shake said, "Hell, Billy C., if you didn't love old Barb too, then you and me wouldn't have anything at all in common. We wouldn't even be fur-trading partners in the Yukon."

The name of that waitress dumpling at the Ho Chi Minh Trail was Carlene.

I found that out after she brought me three or four young Scotches and let me check out her lungs to make sure they were real. When my eyes had got used to the dark in there, I found out that Puddin Patterson and Rosalie were in the bunker with us, except they were asleep. I would have known they were there at first if they had been awake because they would have said something and I could have seen their teeth in the dark.

Things get into a man's mind when he sits in a place like that and looks up at a whole pile of southern Cali-

fornia witch wool and also has a Dirty Leg licking on his
ear and pressing her lungs against him.

Cissy Walford didn't seem to mind it too much since
she was busy talking to Boke Kellum about the fascinating
world of show business.

I hesitate to talk much about what eventually happened
last night. I'm afraid we had us one of those occasions
that me and Shake normally reserve for our New York
apartment after a home game.

We all came back to me and Shake's palatial suite
here at the Beverly Stars Hotel and eventually worked
ourselves into a group portrait.

I guess Rosalie Patterson might have been the rookie
star of the night after Puddin went to sleep. Boke Kellum
didn't do anything but watch, which figured.

Barbara Jane was only involved to a physical extent
where Shake was concerned, but she was sure an inspiration to everybody with her NFL body. And she kept
Cissy from getting too mad about the fact that Carlene
was a bit of a hog. Carlene, by the way, was everything
we hoped she would be, a semi-wild sumbitch.

She sure knew how to spread the wealth around, even
as far as Rosalie. They did a duet on the vibrators.

I've got to say that Rosalie was an awful good sport
when it came to playing some of Shake's favorite games,
such as Unhitch the Box Car, Flaming Cartwheel, Denmark Love Book and Down Range Target Practice.

I'm sure glad Puddin was asleep.

Barbara Jane remembered something funny in the
middle of one of our better heaps.

She said she thought she'd seen this kind of thing before in a magazine called *Climax,* back in the fifth grade.
"Let's get Miss Lewis on the phone," Barb said.

Miss Lewis was one of our fifth-grade teachers, and
she had once caught all of us looking at *Climax* and
snickering. Instead of writing our book reports on Babe
Ruth or somebody.

Barb told Miss Lewis that day, "I don't see how people
can eat things like that without catchup and fries." And
me and Shake laughed so hard and fell down so many
times we broke a desk.

I guess Barb was born funny and semi-grown up.

We didn't get expelled or anything that time back in
elementary school. Miss Lewis was ashamed to show the
picture to the principal. She wanted to keep it, I think.
Miss Lewis wasn't so bad for a teacher, and the mini-
skirts she wore suggested that she might have had a little
bit of hell in her.

Anyhow, we had us a semi-skate last night, is what
we did. We got some of the crescendos on tape, but I
don't think they'll be any good for the book, Jim Tom.

It's just a lot of laughing and semi-ecstasy words that
nobody can spell.

Man, you can always tell when it's getting close to
game time. That's when everybody from Big Ed Bookman to Hitler's nephews start asking for extra tickets
that don't exist.

Here it is Thursday, and between our meeting of the
offense this morning and our practice at UCLA this

afternoon, I guess I got five calls for tickets.

There'll probably be some more while I'm writing this. Downstairs in the lobby and in the bars, it is getting awfully crowded with Giant fans who have flown out for the big day.

Shake and Barbara Jane are down there with Big Ed and Big Barb, who have just arrived. Cissy Walford isn't back yet from going to a studio to watch Boke Kellum kill another fag in an episode of his TV series, which is called *McGill of Santa Fe*.

All we have to do tonight is something fairly quiet, thank the Lord. We have to stop by a cocktail party that CBS is having here in the hotel and then go to early dinner with Big Ed and Big Barb.

Big Ed and Big Barb don't normally arrive this early for our games. They usually hop in Big Ed's Firestream Two, his six-seater jet, and flog it in on Saturday night and then flog it back to Fort Worth on Sunday night in time for some drinks and boring talk at River Crest.

But since this is our first Super Bowl, Big Ed thought it was a special enough occasion that he and Big Barb had to be on hand early so he could tell us how to whip the dog-ass Jets.

There isn't anything that Big Ed doesn't know all about, especially football.

I think that if he had a loose sixty million that he wasn't "puttin' in the ground," as he says, he would buy the Giants from DDD and F just so he could sit on the bench and fire Shoat Cooper.

Which wouldn't be so bad an idea, to fire Shoat.

Big Ed thinks the only reason we're undefeated this season is because of the inside tips he's given us.

Big Ed's idea of strategy is to devise your game plan so that you run and throw at the other side's niggers.

Me and Shake have bust our butts laughing at some of Big Ed's serious ideas about football.

This is how Shake imitates Big Ed discussing football:

"Now if the other side has a fast goddamn nigger, you've got to get to him early in the game. Hit that black bastard a good lick on his big toe and he won't run so fast.

"Never give the ball to a nigger on third and three when you're behind and need the yardage. Goddamn it, they'll dog it on you ever time. It's too bad they've been raised that way, in Africa and Brazil and Philadelphia and Detroit and everywhere, but that's the way it is. One of these days when they've educated themselves better and shown some goddamn initiative at inventing things like—oh, I don't know, the offshore rig or the diamond drillin' bit, or something useful—then goddamn it, you can give a nigger the ball on third and three. But not now.

"I just wouldn't trust a nigger to make a big play for me any more than I'd trust a spick to fix a flat tire.

"Uh, little lady, I'll have one of your sixteen-ounce T-bones, medium rare."

Shake and me have pointed out to Big Ed that there are some fairly stud spooks on the Giants, such as Puddin Patterson and Sam Perkins and Euger Franklin in the offensive line, and Henry Knight and Perry Lou Jackson and Varnell Swist and Jimmy Keith Joy and Story Time Mitchell on defense, not to forget Randy Juan Llanez, our all-purpose stud who returns kicks, fills in at cornerback and behind Shake Tiller at split end, and is all kinds of mixed-up spook and spick blood.

Big Ed has said, however, "There are some goddamn exceptions to everything and as far as I'm concerned those boys are damn near as white as us because they've paid the price."

Speaking of our ball club, regardless of what colors we are or what Big Ed the Brain Trust thinks, this seems like a good time for me to go through our line-up and tell you a little something about each stud that you might find interesting.

I enjoy talking about these studs, anyhow, because I'm proud of what we've accomplished, both as a team and as what you might call your human beings.

At tight end, of course, we've got old Thacker Hubbard who just walked into camp one day. He'd been drafted and cut by Detroit and nobody wanted him. Granted, he's slow. But he'll catch it if Hose Manning doesn't make him reach too far, and he can block.

Thacker keeps to himself and does his job. He's from Idaho and likes sheep. He's about six three and two thirty-five.

Seems like Thacker said something funny back during the season but I can't remember what it was.

Sam Perkins is an offensive tackle on the right side of the line. Sam is just one of those spooks who never complains and gives you a whole lot of effort. He's about six feet and two fifty and he's been around long enough to know every kind of secret way there is to hold on a pass block.

Sam played college ball at Oregon State but he comes from Los Angeles. That's where he lives in the off-season, somewhere around here, like Compton. He's got a real good off-season business designing women's clothes, they tell me.

Some people say Sam might like boys better than girls, and that's why he's never been married, but I hesitate to believe something like this about a friend.

Anyway, I don't see how the Lord would make somebody an interior lineman, and black, *and* a fag.

Puddin Patterson is our right guard on offense, as you already know, and of course Puddin is simply one of the all-time immortals. He must be the fastest big man that ever was, and he's such a good buddy that if I ask Puddin to kill somebody for me, he wouldn't say anything except, "Where you want this cat's body shipped?"

Because I like country music so much, Puddin calls me his "closet red neck," but he knows I love his big ass, and Rosalie, and his two little cousins, too.

Through our connections, me and Shake helped Puddin get a beer distributorship in Lafayette, Louisiana, where he's from, and we also put his mamma in the pie-making business, in which she is about to get semi-rich.

One of the things I think me and Shake will do one of these days when Puddin retires from pro ball is give his old school, Grambling, a ten-thousand-dollar scholarship in his name.

Puddin says that won't make up for the fact that we're white.

He says, "You cats know how much better ball you'd play if you didn't feel so much guilt?"

We tell Puddin to go play the saxophone, or whatever it is spades do.

At center we've got a peculiar old boy named Noba-kov Korelovich from Notre Dame. He's got a monk's haircut, no front teeth, real white skin and a cross eye. Everybody calls him the Pope and he kind of grins.

The Pope goes about six four and two sixty and one of the fascinating things he can do—for money—is drink a can of beer in four seconds. He just sucks it out in a giant inhale.

The Pope broke in as a rookie last year, and I'm sure he would have made All-Pro if he hadn't beaten up a sports writer from Chicago when we were out there play-ing the Bears.

It was on Saturday night before the game and some of us were in Adolph's having dinner and some drinks when the sports writer saw us and came over to our booth and started kidding the Pope about Notre Dame losing to Tulane.

The sports writer found out that only two things make the Pope mad. One is the guy he's blocking on, and the other is a joke about Notre Dame football.

The Pope vaulted out of the booth with a big steak bone in his mouth and grabbed the sports writer and lifted him up in the air by his neck. He held him up in the air near the piano bar and slapped him a few times, growling through the meat in his mouth.

Then he took the poor old sports writer out on the sidewalk, right there on Rush Street, turned him upside down and shook him. He took the guy's money and threw it down the street, and took the guy's glasses and ate them.

He just chewed all the glass out of the rims and swallowed it, growling some more, and went back in Adolph's and washed it down with some beer.

We got him calmed down and the Pope just sat there the rest of the night and said, "Fuckin' literary fuckers."

The sports writer didn't press any charges. In fact, he wrote what I thought was a funny story in the paper the next day about how to interview Nobakov Korelovich.

What I mainly remember was the guy's opening paragraph.

He wrote:

"Outlined against a blue-gray October sky, the Four Horsemen rode again last night. You remember them. Pestilence, Famine, War and Korelovich."

Our other offensive guard is Euger Franklin. Euger is from Nebraska and he's about as close as anything we've got to what some people might call a troublemaker.

There's no worry about Euger in a football game. He's a strong-shouldered old boy with a hell of a physique and he's quick as a turpentined cat. He weighs about two forty and stands about six one.

Shoat Cooper refers to Euger as his "malcontent."

Since I've been around Euger, which is roughly three seasons, he hasn't been overly friendly with the white studs on the team. He never hangs around with any of us, even when there are other spooks in the crowd. Even Puddin Patterson, who sort of keeps Euger cool.

Euger is about the only spade on the team that you wouldn't get too funny with, in terms of race or anything. It's strange, too, because actually he's a lot lighter than the rest.

Euger, in fact, could damn near pass as a Mexican or an A-rab.

Euger was a No. 1 draft choice of the Giants, and also an All-American and a Lineman of the Year at Nebraska.

He's married to a good-looking chick named Eunice, who's not a bad blues singer and who's been in the movies. He makes good money with the Giants. He's probably the highest-paid lineman we've got, next to Puddin. Or maybe higher, considering the bonus he got.

But Euger Franklin's been right there with every kind of spook movement that's gone on in the league. Like the white-shoe movement, which was when all the spooks decided they would only wear white game shoes. Things like that.

Shake Tiller somehow gets away with kidding him. A little bit.

Like today at practice.

We were working on a tricky reverse where Euger has to fake a pass block, then circle out and around and go downfield and try to get the safety.

We ran it four or five times and messed up the hand-offs, and Euger, meanwhile, was going downfield and coming back.

He just walked off and sat down, pissed.

Shoat Cooper strolled over to him and said something and Euger said something back, waving his arms, and standing up and kicking his helmet.

Puddin hollered at him, "Hey, boy. You get that mean and we'll whip them cats on Sunday."

Euger took a few steps back toward our unit, cupped his hands, and shouted at Hose Manning. He shouted:

"Say, baby. Why don't you let those cats back there *fair-catch* those handoffs, you dig?"

Shake Tiller grinned and so did Hose Manning.

And Shake called to him:

"Come on, Euger. Get your white ass over here. A little extra running can't hurt anybody as mean as you."

Euger said, "I don't get paid to take laps, baby."

Everybody whooped and hooted.

"Get over here, Euger," said Hose Manning. "Let's work, gang. Here we go."

And Hose whistled loudly and clapped his hands.

Euger Franklin started walking to the huddle, slowly, talking to himself.

"Tell you what, Euger," said Shake. "When that big black tribunal takes over, your trouble-makin' ass is gonna be the first one they execute."

Euger fastened his chin strap and spit.

We ran the play a few more times and Euger dug out harder than anybody.

Our other offensive tackle is just a big old country boy named Dean McCoobry from the University of Texas. He's a rookie who hasn't said anything that I know of since training camp when we made him try to sing "The Eyes of Texas" every night after dinner until he got the words right.

The first time he sang it was just about the funniest thing I've ever heard.

Dean's idea of the tune was semi-close but the words came out about like this:

> *The eyes*
> *Of Texas were upon*
> *it.*
> *All*
> *the lifelong thing.*
> *The eyes*
> *Of Texas were because, if*
> *They thrilled me*
> *all their days.*
> *Do*
> *Not think you can despise it,*
> *From now*
> *Til every afternoon.*
> *The eyes*
> *Of Texas went behind them*
> *Til Garland goes back yet.*

Of course, nobody ever said an offensive tackle had to be able to sing or know the lyrics to his school song. He knows our plays, which is good enough. And he can blow me through a hole for five and six yards at a pop.

Dean's six five and about two fifty-five, he's got buck teeth, wears glasses off the field, and has a bit of a puzzled look on his semi-baby face. We call him Baby Dean, and he collects match folders.

Our split end is Marvin (Shake) Tiller, of whom you may have heard me speak. Shake Tiller. Pimp. Sex maniac. Dope fiend. Wanted for manslaughter in Joplin, Missouri.

We have a flanker who can't do much except outrun everybody, but that's really all he's supposed to do.

He's Al (Abort) Goodwin, the ex-Olympic hurdler.

I'll tell you. If you ever need anybody to run three and a half miles over brush and timber, you'd better get Al (Abort) Goodwin.

On a straight line, I don't think there's any doubt that Al Goodwin could outrun anybody in football. The thing he gives us is the deep threat. Real deep.

Al runs so fast down the sideline that he very often gets sixty or seventy yards gone on a single pattern, but of course Hose Manning just can't throw it that far. Still, the defense has to assign one man to Al, basically on the chance that Hose will try to hit him once a game, he'll underthrow, and the defensive back can intercept.

It must have been two seasons ago that Al Goodwin caught his touchdown pass against Philadelphia. I remember Hose had the wind.

Al (Abort) Goodwin is a real nice fellow who lives in Boulder, Colorado, teaches history at the university, is married, and has four kids. He's never seen a day of the year when he didn't run some laps, or do some sprints, even in the snow.

He usually flies in on Sundays for our games, wherever

we are, and just suits up and goes out and runs his sideline sprints on every play. He doesn't really have to know the offense.

Al will probably be getting in here tomorrow, or the next day.

Long before now I should have mentioned our fullback, the guy who takes over some of my ball-carrying duties now and then and does a fine job of pass-blocking for Hose Manning.

Our fullback is Booger Sanders from Alabama, and he's one of the best sumbitches who ever breathed air.

In the eight years he's been up from Tuscaloosa, Booger's had a lot of bad luck with his career. He's had every physical thing happen to him from a broken back to the clap.

Two wives have just hauled off and left him.

Booger's kind of short and stumpy but he's run under more than one tackler in his day. This is the first season that things have gone smooth for him. No injuries. And he's come up with a nice girl friend who might not rob him.

She's a cashier in the first Howard Johnson's you come to on the Jersey Turnpike after you go through the Lincoln Tunnel. Booger likes to drive her home after work every night. I think she lives in Hartford.

Booger's prematurely bald and he's starting to get a belly on him, but he can still scoot, and there just isn't an ounce of give-up in him.

Now we come to a fellow I just can't say enough about.

This is our cerebral leader, Mr. Quarterback himself,

otherwise known as Hose Manning.

Shoat Cooper calls Hose Manning "the best milker on the farm," meaning he's the best quarterback in pro ball. I agree.

It's a known fact that a football team can't go very far without a good milker, and in my five years with the Giants we didn't really start going anywhere until we got Hose from the Vikings.

That was two years ago.

We got Hose from Minnesota after a turn of very sinister events that spring. We got Hose because the Vikings thought he would never be able to play ball again after he was in a terrible car wreck back in his home town of Purcell, Oklahoma.

The story behind the trade is semi-fascinating and I think I'll reveal it. It would make a damn movie is all it would do.

Hose had gone home to Purcell, like he always does in the off-season. He'd gone home to look after his chain of filling stations. Purcell is a little town near Norman, which is where the University of Oklahoma is. Purcell is also where they have the annual Old Fiddlers' Convention and Contest.

The Old Fiddlers' Convention and Contest is an event where old fiddle players from everywhere gather for a few days and fiddle their asses off.

Down there that same spring to scout Oklahoma's spring training one week was Tom Stinnywade, the Vikings' chief scout. One day Stinnywade had nothing else to do but drive over to Purcell to hear some of the old fiddlers who were having their contest at the same time as Oklahoma's spring practice.

By a strange coincidence Stinnywade happened to be passing along the highway just outside of Purcell at the exact time that Hose Manning's Cadillac got hit from the blind side by one of those old yellow-dog school buses. You've seen those old yellow-dog buses. The kind with the straight back seats. The kind junior college teams go to games in, and throw Kentucky Fried Chicken bones out the windows of.

When Hose's car got hit, it turned over two or three times, they say, and rattled all the dishes in Grayford's Truck Stop Diner on the other side of the street.

Tom Stinnywade actually saw the crash, hopped out of his own car, ran over and saw Hose laying on the ground, unconscious.

What Stinnywade did next is the key to the whole thing.

Instead of seeing how bad Hose was hurt, Stinnywade ran into Grayford's Truck Stop Diner and called the front office in Minneapolis and got hold of Herb Fannerbahn, the Vikings' general manager.

"Trade Manning," Stinnywade said. Or something like that.

Now the plot thickens.

Herb Fannerbahn phoned up Burt Danby in New York and asked him if the Giants had found a quarterback yet. Burt obviously said no. Fannerbahn asked if Burt would like to have Hose Manning. For the Giants' first four draft choices?

Burt Danby is sometimes not so stupid and he put Herb Fannerbahn on hold and said he'd get back to him within an hour.

Burt then phoned up Shoat Cooper, who was down on his ranch near Lubbock, Texas. The Vikings want to give us Manning, Burt said, but there must be something wrong. Could Shoat find out what it was?

It just so happened that Shoat Cooper had a friend in Purcell that he could call. It was a waitress in Grayford's Truck Stop Diner named Louise the Tease.

Shoat had done some scouting in his day and like most scouts he knew every beer joint and truck stop and waitress in America.

Shoat called up Louise the Tease and asked her if she had heard anything about Hose Manning lately?

"All I know is what I can see out the window right now," said Louise the Tease, "which is Hose Manning layin' in a ditch."

Shoat asked Louise the Tease to do him a big favor, like run across the street and see if Hose was alive, and, if so, did he have all his arms and legs and hands, and, possibly, could he call an audible?

"I'll go see," said Louise the Tease. "But personally I wouldn't give you two cents for him. He taken something from between my thighs once and now he don't never come around."

Louise the Tease called Shoat back in less than five minutes and said Hose seemed to be all right. She said he even managed to smile and suggest something she could do that would make his crotch feel better.

Shoat phoned this news to Burt Danby, who immediately phoned up Herb Fannerbahn and made the trade.

And that's how we got our milker.

I don't know whatever happened to Tom Stinnywade. Last I heard he was an assistant coach in a vocational high school on Chicago's south side. And Herb Fannerbahn is a tour guide now at Hoover Dam, I think.

Hose Manning fit right in with us, of course. He not only gave us the arm we needed but he's a fine punter and field goal kicker. A real all-around stud who nearly won the Heisman Trophy when he played for OU.

Hose is a tough leader. And he's not bad-looking for a guy with an Oklahoma face. He's got deep creases in his face and what's left over from a childhood case of semi-acne. He's got black, stringy hair, and he's about the only quarterback left who wears high-top shoes. He's over six feet and weighs about two hundred. He's got a quick release and he throws what we call a light ball. The nose is up and it's easy to catch.

The only thing Hose lost in that wreck was one kidney. But like he says, "If I'd lost it earlier in life, think how much less I'd had to piss."

As for our defensive unit, I don't know so many personal things about very many of those studs, other than T. J. Lambert.

In pro ball the offense and defense are like two separate clubs. We never work together. The defense is always down on the other end of the field figuring out its own problems.

Shoat Cooper's number one assistant is an old fellow named Morgan Bujakowski and he handles the defense. Shoat calls Bujakowski "Ol' Army" because he played at both West Point and Texas A&M during World War II.

Most of the players call him the star-spangled Polack because he's still got a crew cut, keeps his shoulders reared back and wears an old Aggie cavalry hat to practice.

The star-spangled Polack likes to kick players in the butt and tell us that we don't know what real football is. He says face-guards have taken fear out of the game.

What I'll do, I think, is just run through the defensive line-up for you, sort of quick.

T. J. Lambert of course is on one end, and you've already gotten acquainted with that great American poet. On the opposite end we've got F. Tolan Gates, who's from Stanford. He's a good fellow whose family is about half-rich.

At one defensive tackle we've got Henry Knight from Arkansas AM&N, which the star-spangled Polack once said stood for Agricultural, Mechanical and Nigger. The other tackle is Rucker McFarland from North Carolina State, who met his wife on a float in the Peach Bowl parade.

That's our down four.

Our three linebackers are Perry Lou Jackson, Salter Bingham and Harris Jones. Perry Lou's from Texas Southern. You might have heard of Perry Lou's older brother, Bad Hair Jackson. He got famous a couple of years ago for killing four prison guards at Huntsville.

Salter Bingham played at UCLA and his sister was a well-known actress named Stephanie something. Harris Jones comes from Michigan State, where some people might recall that he was better known as a basketball player.

In the secondary I'd guess that we've got more speed than a bunch of hookers at a convention.

Jimmy Keith Joy and Story Time Mitchell give us the two toughest corners in pro ball, I think. Jimmy Keith Joy is from Kansas State and Story Time Mitchell is a rookie from Purdue whose whole life got changed by football. In the spring of his junior year at Purdue, Story Time Mitchell got caught being a lookout on a grocery market holdup. The school decided, however, that it wouldn't be a good thing for an All-American, which he was, to have to go to jail. And the team voted that he ought to get to stay on the squad, figuring it would help rehabilitate him, and that way he could also keep returning punts and intercepting passes.

This has just reminded me that when I made one of my best runs this season against St. Louis, Jim Tom Pinch called me up that night to tell me he'd seen it on TV and that during the run when I side-stepped two tacklers I had made "the greatest move since Story Time Mitchell went from armed robbery to probation."

Story Time Mitchell has played real good for the Giants and stayed pretty much out of trouble with the law, although his roommate on the road, Perry Lou Jackson, says, "It sure is a lot of trouble all the time to have to take a shower with your money in your hand."

This leaves only our free safety and our on-safety and they happen to be absolute streaks named Varnell Swist and Bobby Styles. Varnell Swist is from San Diego State and I don't think there's a better free safety in football. And Bobby Styles is from LSU, where he was a running back. In Baton Rouge, they say, the radio stations still play a recording of Bobby's great run which beat Ole Miss a couple of years ago.

The radio stations play Bobby's run every fifteen minutes all day long before a Saturday night game. Shoat Cooper likes to kid Bobby and tell him, "I don't see how you can be any kind of coon ass legend when you ain't got no *x*'s or *u*'s in your name."

Shoat means of course that everybody from LSU seems to have a name like Bou-ax and Loubedo.

Well, this just about takes care of everybody important on our team, except for Randy Juan Llanez, our utility stud. All I can say about Randy Juan is that he comes from somewhere in South America, played college ball at Florida State, and says he learned to run fast in riots after soccer games.

So there they are, folks, the New York Giants. Get 'em, Giants.

Cissy Walford came in a while ago and she's getting dressed for the CBS cocktail party, and for our dinner with Big Ed and Big Barb, so I am doing some more work.

She said everybody in the whole world was in the hotel lobby. This means there are six or seven people down there that she knows from around midtown New York.

She said Burt Danby was down there with Camille Virl, the movie queen, and he was really having fun introducing her around. She said Shake was signing a lot of autographs around the table he was at with Big Ed and Big Barb in the Eucalyptus Bar, just off the lobby.

She said some photographers were there and they were setting up a picture of Shake and Camille Virl when Boke Kellum rushed up and hugged Camille Virl in the middle of the photograph, and got himself in it.

She said several writers were hanging around, getting funny statements from Shake about the game.

And here she comes now, folks, right out of heaven, as I'm talking into the old tape recorder. I do believe this little pet is wearing fewer duds than she did at the *Sports Illustrated* party.

All I can see from here are these elegant thighs and that long yellow hair streaming down off an angel's face. Get over here, woman. As T. J. Lambert once said, "Psycho wants pussy."

Well, this is Friday morning, friends, and this is Billy Clyde Puckett, the disk jockey's disk jockey. I'm here to wake you up with tunes of pleasure and semi-sadness as sung by that merry philosopher Elroy Blunt.

Here's our first tune by Elroy. It's titled "Watch Old Billy Clyde Brush His Teeth and Throw Up."

Now I'm back from doing my household chores. Washing my face and hands and teeth and body parts and all. Everybody else is still racked in and I guess I'm up early because this is Friday and it will be our last serious workout of the week. I believe I'm getting my game-face on.

We won't do anything tomorrow, Saturday, except play catch and trot for about thirty minutes in shorts.

We probably won't even look at any more film after late this afternoon because Shoat Cooper has already said, "The hunt's over. It's time to piss on the fire and call in the dogs."

This of course has not been an ordinary week in terms of how we prepare for a football game.

If this were just a regular season game, the week would go sort of like this: nothing on Monday, see the film breakdown of last Sunday's game on Tuesday, run through our entire repertoire on Wednesday, set the draws and screens on Thursday, light-polish on Friday, rest the legs on Saturday, and then kick the pee out of somebody else on Sunday.

This being the Super Bowl, it's different.

We've had two weeks to get ready since we dough-popped the LA Rams for the National Conference championship back in good old Yankee Stadium.

We had a three-day rest and victory celebration after that because it was such a colossal thing that the Giants won their conference. They hadn't won anything in fifteen years except a few coin flips.

Then we started boning up on the dog-ass Jets, who had dusted off Oakland thirty-five to ten for the American Conference title. Dreamer Tatum broke two Oak-

land jaws in the game and personally caused six limp-
offs.

Ten days before the Super Bowl we left New York and
went to Rancho La Costa, which is near La Jolla and
San Diego. Shoat Cooper worked it out for us to go to
Rancho La Costa and do our hard preparations. It was
warm there, and, besides, Shoat knows a cocktail
waitress there who is sort of a Stove but she likes
coaches.

We got here to the Beverly Stars Hotel last Monday,
pretty much ready to play a ball game. We know what
to do. It's only a matter of polish, timing and execution.
And, anyhow, the last few days before a Super Bowl are
given over to talking and interviews and mental health.

What the dog-ass Jets did was stay back in New York
practically the whole time. This meant they got their
asses caught in several blizzards and ice storms and had
to practice in Madison Square Garden in the mornings.

Rudi Tambunga, the coach of the dog-ass Jets, was
quoted in the papers as saying that if he had it to do over
again he would take his team to Fiji.

They got out here Tuesday on their charter jet after
what I read was a fairly hectic flight. First, they had to
sit on the ground for seven hours at La Guardia because
of the blizzard. And then when they arrived, the smog
was so heavy that a small private plane nicked them in
the wing tip on their approach.

Nothing real bad happened on the landing, however,
except for some minor burns to the pilot. The collision,
they say, caused him to spill coffee on one of his hands

and drop a lighted cigarette in his lap.

The papers have been full of a lot of junk about the trip out here taking something out of the dog-ass Jets, but nobody can fool me. I know they're ready.

The dog-ass Jets are professionals and I have plenty of respect for them, both as athletes and as people.

Physically and technically, they have been completely rebuilt since the Mastrioni brothers, Angie and Tony, took over the team and hired Rudi Tambunga for a coach.

I know that everybody said they wouldn't make a comeback after Joe Namath retired a few years ago, but they've had some good drafts and made some stud trades.

One of the slickest moves the Mastrioni brothers made four years ago was getting the dog-ass Jets to lose their last five games so they could finish last in the whole NFL and be allowed to draft Dreamer Tatum.

In case nobody knows it, the last-place team gets the first draft pick. I heard a story that the dog-ass Jets celebrated their final loss to the Patriots in Shea Stadium by carrying their quarterback, Boyce Cayce, off the field because he had thrown four interceptions for touchdowns.

"This is a great bunch of guys," the papers quoted Rudi Tambunga. "I'm proud to be associated with a bunch that wants the first-round draft pick as much as the management does."

After the dog-ass Jets got Dreamer Tatum, they made a stud trade with Dallas and got Jessie Luker and Gruver

Allgood to pep up the offense.

Jessie Luker is a hot dog from Alcorn A&M who's got hands on him like snowshoes. Instead of his name on his jersey across the back, he's got "See You Later" stitched on there for guys to read when they're chasing him.

In the regular season he caught the most balls of anybody other than Shake Tiller.

Why Dallas gave up on Gruver Allgood has baffled a lot of people. He only gained a thousand thirty-five yards last season for the Cowboys and took them to the Super Bowl, where they lost down in Mexico City to the Chiefs, fifty-six to three.

Gruver was popular in Dallas despite his two arrests on sodomy. And that scandal he got into when he got caught stealing women's underwear off the clotheslines in backyards.

He's sure done a fine job for the dog-ass Jets, and he's stayed fairly clean in New York.

There's another old boy who makes the dog-ass Jets what they are and that's Boyce Cayce. I don't think he's any Hose Manning but you'd have to put Boyce in your top half of quarterbacks around the league.

The sports writers have been calling him "the grand old man" for several years although he's never played on a great team until now. Boyce started out with the Rams about twelve years ago, I guess, and since then he's been with the Redskins, Saints, Oilers, Raiders, Browns, Bears, Dolphins, Chiefs and Broncos.

The dog-ass Jets got him four years ago and he sort

of became a different person. Rudi Tambunga has handled Boyce real good. They say Boyce has cut down a lot on his fights in bars. He hasn't stolen a city bus in a long time. You don't hear so much about his drinking in public or his betting.

It's hard to pin down the personality of the dog-ass Jets. Some say they're about half-rowdy, off the field. They've always been cocky. As I've said, I don't know any of them too well because they mostly live in Queens and low-rent places like that and they hang out in bowling alleys, or somewhere.

I think you'd have to say that Rudi Tambunga is the dominant personality of the whole outfit.

He's a natty little man who always wears a gray felt hat with a wide brim, a black shirt and silver tie, and a striped suit.

Tambunga calls all of their plays during a game; all but the ones that Boyce Cayce rejects because he hasn't learned them.

Tambunga hangs around lower New York City and you can nearly always see him in a restaurant on Mulberry Street sitting with his back to the wall. The name of the place is Paloggia's and it is popular with Italians when it isn't being blown up.

Rudi Tambunga is very thick with the owners of the dog-ass Jets, the Mastrioni brothers, Angie and Tony.

Somebody once told me they all grew up together in Newark.

I do know that Rudi Tambunga introduced both Angie and Tony to their present wives, April Mastrioni and

Dawn Mastrioni. Not bad lookers for Vegas shills, in fact.

I saw them once at Jimmy Weston's on Fifty-fourth Street when all of them were having dinner and entertaining Dreamer Tatum before they signed him. Weston's is kind of a supper club for horse players.

The wives, April and Dawn, were sitting on either side of Dreamer and whispering in his ear. Angie and Tony and Rudi Tambunga were whispering to each other.

I was there with Shake and Barbara Jane, and when Barb saw the Mastrioni wives in their stacked-up amber hair and their stacked-up lungs and their dark glasses and their white fur coats around their shoulders, she said, "It's One and One-A."

We decided it would be polite to go say hello. This was our first introduction to Dreamer Tatum. He reached out between April and Dawn and shook hands and smiled. But nobody else looked up at us.

I think I said something like, "Hope you come up here. It's not a bad town."

Without even looking at us, Tony Mastrioni said, "It's the only town."

We would have stood around exchanging pleasantries a while longer except that either April or Dawn peered at us over the top of her dark glasses through a stream of cigarette smoke and said, "You could do us all a very sincere favor if you'd fuck off."

We laughed and went back to the bar up front and Barb said, "I kind of like her. I think I'll put her up for the Junior League."

It seems everybody is waking up now. Me and Shake have a meeting to go to, and then that luncheon at the Century Plaza, and then our last workout. Later I'll tell you about last night's dinner and the CBS party.

Semi-hilarious is all they were.

I mark the exact time at six oh two P.M. upon a Friday night in January in Beverly Hills, California. It is about forty-eight hours until the minute when the gun sounds to end the Super Bowl and the New York Giants will be champions of the world in professional football.

I have marked the time on my old East-West Shrine Game wrist watch, which is laying on the toilet seat while I am enjoying a lemon-lime bubble bath in the bathroom of me and Shake's palatial suite in the Beverly Stars Hotel.

Shake is enjoying a boysenberry-blackberry bubble bath in his own bathroom of his own bedroom of our palatial suite.

We have come back from our last stud workout and from that low-rent lunch at the Century Plaza where nothing happened except that Dreamer Tatum had to get up and make a short talk about me and I had to get up and make a short talk about him. Some phony fuckin' emcee thought that stunt up.

Dreamer said, "I respect Billy Puckett as the best running back in the National Conference (he wouldn't say the whole league), and I just hope to slow him down some on Sunday."

I got up and said, "Obert Tatum has proved he's the

best cornerback in the game. I say this with all due respect to my good buddies sitting down there who play for us—our own stud hosses at corner, which are Story Time Mitchell and Jimmy Keith Joy."

I also said, "I want to say, too, that as the captain of the Giants it is a real thrill for us to be here in the Super Bowl."

And I said, "So far as the game itself is concerned, I don't know what's liable to happen. Probably a big break one way or another will decide it. But I do know this. Our side is *ready*."

I was real flattered that when I said that, all of the New York Giants stood up and clapped.

It made me feel good and warm inside to see our men do that, although it also embarrassed me when I looked down in the midst of it and saw the dog-ass Jets giggling and whispering to each other.

Later on at workout at UCLA, I thought I had some real spring in my legs, and I thought Shake looked slick catching balls from Hose Manning.

I really do believe we're ready.

I have forgotten to say where Barbara Jane and Cissy are.

They are in the living room of our palatial suite, as it happens, entertaining a whole mess of folks, including Big Ed and Big Barb, and Burt Danby, and some television people, and Boke Kellum.

And there is an ugly rumor circulating that Elroy Blunt his own self is due in tonight.

Our plan is to stay around the hotel tonight and not

exert ourselves too much, just like we will tomorrow and tomorrow night.

I guess a lot of people will be dropping by our palatial suite during the evening. Me and Shake have told Barbara Jane to order plenty of everything to eat and drink for everybody.

All I know is, for the next hour, old Billy Clyde is gonna lay here in his lemon-lime bubble bath and write on his book and relax.

Maybe Cissy Walford will drop a young Scotch on me from time to time.

Now about last night.

We started out at the CBS cocktail party, which was semi-massive.

That was perhaps the high point because that's where T. J. Lambert did his number.

The party was held in the Señor Sombrero Café on the second floor of the hotel. It was a big L-shaped restaurant room, all glassed-in with a view of all of the smog from Sunset Boulevard down to little Santa Monica. It had a terrace outside the sliding glass walls, which hung out over one of the hotel swimming pools.

It used to be that players didn't go to parties like this because there was drinking and the coaches and the old commissioner, Pete Rozelle, frowned on it. Commissioner Cameron, however, took a more modern view when he came into office on the forty-eighth ballot. He said players were going to drink anyhow and he said they might as well drink in public because that way maybe they would drink less.

That holds true for some, I guess. But it doesn't hold true for somebody like T. J. Lambert.

The party which CBS gave was mainly for the National Conference people, which are their friends, and therefore there weren't any dog-ass Jets around, or any of their dog-ass fans.

What caused the trouble with T. J. Lambert, I think, was the fact that the CBS bars pretty quickly ran out of any decent Scotch and T. J. started drinking gin mixed with rum and brandy and tequila.

I remember Puddin Patterson telling him, "Say, cat, if you drink that kind of mess, you liable to catch a silver bullet before *this* night's over."

T. J. has a big old pink freckled face and small squinty eyes, and he said,

"Shit, I've drink everything from dishwater to polio vaccine in my day, Daddy. I don't never kill nobody. And I don't never puke."

T. J. Lambert is not the sort that anybody tells what to do, ever.

He had once been shot in the belly, point blank, by an irate husband. And all he did was drive himself to the hospital and recover. That was in the off-season once, back in Tennessee.

I personally saw T. J. beat up four cops one night in Dallas, the night before a game with the Cowboys. We had rented a car and driven out on the highway to a place called Dorine's Paradise, a country music place. We wanted to unwind a little, and take our minds off the game.

Coming back to the hotel, however, T. J. was driving and he started going across people's front yards and scraping the car off the sides of office buildings on the sidewalks.

Two squad cars finally hemmed us in on a neighborhood street. Fortunately the cops recognized us and put away their guns and offered to escort us back to our hotel and not say anything about it.

But just as we had it smoothed over, T. J. Lambert farted two or three times real loud, and hollered:

"They's a number of things in the world that's overrated and one of 'em is how tough a goddamn cop is."

Then he said, "I believe I'll make me a sandwich out of these sixty-dollar-a-week motherfuckers."

And he did. He sure did.

The Giants and the Cowboys got together and kept our arrest quiet. We got to play in the game. I think the Giants had to give up a high draft choice to the Cowboys when it was over.

But the best testimony I can give as to how mean and tough old T. J. is has to do with a hunting trip some of us went on last year. Several of us went out on Big Ed Bookman's farm near Fort Worth one day to shoot birds. We killed birds all day and then we built a fire and started drinking.

Everybody got fairly drunk and started throwing everybody else's hat up in the air and shooting at it. A hat would go sailing up in the air and it would sound like Saigon on election eve. This went on for a few minutes until it was Hose Manning, I think, that threw T. J.

Lambert's Stetson up in the air.

And there wasn't a single shot fired.

That's how tough that sumbitch really is.

Well, with all this in mind, you can understand why it got a little awkward at the CBS cocktail party in the Señor Sombrero Café when T. J. Lambert picked up the movie star, Camille Virl, and held her upside down by her ankles over the swimming pool off the terrace rail.

T. J. just stood there snickering while Camille Virl screamed and cried, and while a whole crowd of people begged T. J. to bring her back up and not harm her.

It was Barbara Jane Bookman, I'd say, who rescued Camille Virl. T. J.'s wife, Donna Lou, might have been able to do something if she had been there, but I think Donna Lou, who is a pretty good Stovette, had slipped off with Burt Danby for a spell.

Barbara Jane went over to T. J. and said, "T. J., I always did think a woman looked better from this view, don't you?"

T. J. said, "There's her old wool right there. See it?"

Barbara Jane said, "What are you going to do with her?"

"I don't know," said T. J.

Barbara Jane said, "Why don't you drop her in the pool?"

T. J. swayed a little and said, "Won't she get her wool wet?"

Barbara Jane said, "Why don't you lift her back up here with us?"

"Naw," said T. J. "She'll scratch and bite me."

Barbara Jane said, "What did she do to make you mad, T. J.?"

T. J. belched and said, "Aw, I don't know. I was talkin' to her and she was comin' on kind of strong like a damned old prick teaser so I said why didn't we go somewhere and I'd shit on her chest."

"I see," said Barbara Jane, nodding.

"She told me I was about half-foul and ought to be in a prison, so I picked her up and dangled her, which is where she is now."

"Yeah," said Barbara Jane. "I don't blame you. But now you've scared her, so I think you ought to drop her in the pool or bring her back up."

T. J. said, "I think I'm gonna puke."

Barbara Jane got Camille Virl's attention and asked if she could swim and she said yes, goddamn it.

"Drop her," said Barb.

"I'm gone puke," said T. J., frowning.

"Let her go," said Barb.

T. J. dropped Camille Virl into the swimming pool, about twelve feet down.

A lot of cocktail party drunks applauded and some others gasped. Camille Virl could swim, and pretty good, which was a stroke of luck. Because she had no sooner hit the water than T. J. Lambert's vomit did and she barely managed to get out of the way.

Cissy Walford said, "That was such a pretty dress."

Boke Kellum ran down to the pool with some towels.

Shake and me and Barbara Jane died laughing. And

we convinced Big Ed and Big Barb that it was really
sort of funny, after all. Camille Virl was nothing but a
phony movie star who was only trying to get publicity,
and she deserved what happened. In fact, she would
profit from it, we argued.

T. J. Lambert said he felt a lot better, now that he
had puked, and he said he was just sorry he never had
puked before in his life, since it sort of revived a man
and allowed him to start drinking again.

"Let's go somewhere and get a good piece of beef,"
said Big Ed. "I'm buyin'."

"I'd like a sixteen-ounce T-bone, medium rare," said
Barbara Jane.

I just took time out here in my lemon-lime bubble
bath to smoke a cigarette and think. That doesn't hurt
football studs, by the way. To smoke, I mean. Not to
think. Most of us smoke a little, and you run it off.

I was just thinking about Barbara Jane and all of
us.

And I was thinking about a conversation that Shake
and me had one evening at our New York apartment
during the regular season.

We were just laying around drinking coffee and reading papers and listening to an Elroy Blunt album. It was
one of his new albums, the one called *Flip Top Heart,*
which features that song. We were just laying there, anyhow, trying to decide whether to wander over to P. J.
Clarke's and eat some bacon cheeseburgers and argue
with the owner, Danny Lavezzo, about the Giants and

other intellectual things.

Barbara Jane wasn't in town at her own apartment over on Fifth Avenue and Sixty-seventh Street, which is where it's at. She was down in Palm Beach making a commercial for DDD and F.

We had just talked to her, in fact, on the phone. And she had said that Palm Beach was the same old place— a lot of semi-rich Stoves running around with busted-out fags, and old ladies whose husbands had died, leaving them thoroughbred farms.

Shake and me had always had conversations every so often about what the world amounted to. We didn't generally get too serious.

Shake always questioned things more than I did, maybe because he read so many books. I always just believed a man ought to do the best he could, whether it involved playing ball or something else. I thought a man ought to laugh a lot. And then I thought a man turned up one day and just wasn't breathing any more. And that was that.

We were talking about Barbara Jane that night in our apartment and I said, "Old buddy, do you realize that Barb has never mentioned getting married?"

"I guess she hasn't," Shake said.

"What do you think about that?" I said.

"Good," he said.

"Is it?" I said. "I don't know."

"It's good," he said.

I was stretched out on a sofa with the coffee cup balanced on my chest, looking up at our trophy shelf with the game balls on it and at some pictures.

I laid there for a minute and said, "Yeah, but I wonder where we're all going?"

"Clarke's, I hope," Shake said, who was in a chair behind an issue of *Sports Illustrated*.

I smiled and said, "In what you call your life, I mean."

"Oh, *that*." Shake laughed.

And he didn't add anything to it.

After a while I said, "It's hard for me to think of myself ever not playin' ball."

"Not me," Shake said.

"Really?" I said.

"Yeah," he said.

"Since when?" I asked.

"I don't know. Lately, maybe," he said.

I said, "What's that mean?"

"Nothin' actually," he said.

I raised up and leaned over and turned down Elroy Blunt, even though he was singing "Tell Me, Mister Tooth Brush."

"You like it better than me, old buddy," I said. "And you got a chance to play a lot longer."

Shake said, "You realize how long you and me have been at it?"

"Fifteen years, I guess, starting with the Pee Wees," I said.

"Hasn't it ever privately bothered you that we're gettin' close to thirty and we aren't anything but football players?" he said.

It hadn't.

And I said it hadn't.

"Well, you just asked me about what you call your life," he said. "That means you must have thought about it."

I said, "Well, all I meant was, I wondered if we were ever gonna be married, like you and Barbara Jane, and me and somebody, and whether we would ever be living someplace like Greenwich and mowing the lawn or anything."

"Speaking for myself," Shake said, "I can tell you that I'm not ever gonna be in Greenwich."

I laughed.

"I sure hope I'm not, either," I said.

He said, "I might be in Marrakech, however, or on a ranch in Buenos Aires, or hiking in the rain forest on Kauai."

"You can't get the scores in any of those places," I said. "You're gonna have to be here in the fall."

Shake grinned and said, "Well, I'll always know that TCU didn't beat anybody but Baylor and that Big Ed fired the coach."

Shake got up and went to the kitchen to get some more coffee.

He said, "When you think about it, we've done about all there is to do, except win a Super Bowl."

We never won State for dear old Paschal High, I pointed out.

Shake, coming back to his chair, said, "Yeah, but they fucked us out of that. Hell, you scored *twice* from the one and they didn't give it to us."

I said, "It was raining pretty hard."

"Yeah, but remember how hot we were when we saw the films later?" said Shake.

I said, "Have you ever felt as bad in your life as we did that night after the game?"

"Just killed is all," Shake said.

"I must have kicked in every door in that locker room," I said. "Hell, I knew I scored."

Shake laughed to himself and said, "Did you ever see your Uncle Kenneth any drunker?"

I laughed, too.

"I don't know what he lost, but I'm sure it was everything in the envelope," I said. "He still carries an envelope, you know. He's still got the old bank and office right there in his coat pocket."

Shake looked off for a minute. Then he said, "Spring Branch. Rotten fucking Spring Branch. And we had those sumbitches down by fourteen at one time."

"Only time I ever saw Barb cry," I said.

"Hell, we all cried," Shake said. "You can take your wars and your starvation and your fires and your floods, but there's no heartbreak in life like losing the big game in high school."

I sat up and folded my hands behind my head.

"Well, it makes you a man," I said.

Shake said, "That's right, boy. Give 'em a few heart-breakers along the way. Straighten 'em up."

"Take away their parents," I grinned.

"You bet," Shake said. "Make a lot of 'em poor."

"Turn some of 'em black," I said.

"Mix in some cripples," he said.

"Mostly the black ones," I said.

"That's what the world needs more of," said Shake. "Poor black cripples."

"Who can't get hard-ons," I said.

"Kill some of their mothers, too," my old buddy added.

"Oh, Christ," I said.

And we kind of shook back and forth in laughter, and then sighed, and then didn't say anything for a while.

Shake lit up a cigarette and slouched down in his chair and sipped on his coffee and said, "Billy C., you know what I been thinkin' I might do? If we were to win the Super Bowl this year or next, which I think we got a chance to do?"

"Run for office?" I said, being funny.

"Nope," he said. "I think I might hang old eighty-eight up and let 'em take it on to Canton, Ohio."

"Yeah, me too," I said. "Next case."

"I'm serious," he said, and he was.

"You're serious, aren't you?" I said.

"I believe I am," he said.

"Well, that don't make me feel so great," I said.

"I don't know, really," he said.

"You got a lot of records you can break," I said.

"Records don't mean shit," Shake said.

I lit up a cigarette my own self.

"What the hell would you do if you didn't play any more ball when you're still able?" I wondered.

"Not play ball," he said.

"And then what?" I said.

"Not bust my ass and run my ass off and stay sore all the time from takin' licks," he said. "And not talk to a whole pack of dumb shits all the time. And not have to go to camp. And not look at a bunch of film. And not go to luncheons and dinners. And just not think about it any more."

I shook my head.

"That doesn't make any sense to me," I said.

"Well, that's right," Shake said. "You see, you're gonna play until you drop because you really love it, and then you're gonna be the coach of the Giants some day, and you're gonna be goddamn good at it. But that's not what I want to do, and I'm almost thirty."

I guess I knew that Shake never wanted to be a coach.

And I guess I thought that what he'd do when he quit playing ball would be to take care of our investments and make us even richer, and maybe become a vice-president of the club, or something, and marry Barbara Jane, and we would all just keep on hanging around New York.

I guess that's what I had always thought.

I remember that I sat there for a while and tried to imagine what it would be like to play on a team without Marvin (Shake) Tiller on it. Because I never had.

It didn't sound like fun.

"What about Barb?" I said. "What does she say about it?"

"I don't know," he said. "But it doesn't really matter."

Shake said, "Barb is Barb and she doesn't care what we do as long as it's what we truly want to do."

I said, "O.K., so you hang up old eighty-eight and then you go to Marrakech, or some fuckin' place. Is that all right with Barb, to leave New York?"

Shake said, "Well, old Barb wouldn't be going where I go, wherever that is."

I must say that this struck old Billy Clyde by surprise and also made him feel sick for a second.

"I just don't believe that," I said. "Or any of the rest of it."

Shake then said that this was the way his head was shaping up at the time being, and that it certainly was true how he felt.

He said that he and Barbara Jane always had agreed that they would probably never get married legally because that would fuck up their friendship as well as their love.

He said that, anyhow, he and Barbara Jane had probably been married, in spirit at least, ever since the fourth grade, and that sure was a long time.

He said that this didn't mean he didn't love Barbara Jane more than almost anything he had ever known but he was just frankly tired of the responsibility of loving anything or doing anything, if I could understand that.

I remember I said, "Owl shit." Or something.

Shake went on and said that, of course, it was perfectly all right for Barbara Jane to accompany him to Istanbul or Marrakech or Tahiti as long as he didn't have any responsibility. As long, he said, as she didn't mind letting him sit in semi-open bars with bamboo curtains and ceiling fans and without a shave and looking for a young Rita Hayworth from the old movies to walk in.

He said that being a pro football stud was probably

keeping him from ever doing some of the things which
had always intrigued him. Like sitting at a sidewalk café
in San Sebastian or being a spy in Geneva or a fur trader
in the Yukon or getting drunk and painting a picture
on a small island near Java and waiting for a tidal wave.

He said he might want to own and run a bar in Puerto
Vallarta or Trinidad or Positano. Or he might want to
own and run a fishing boat somewhere around Japan. Or
he said he might just want to go sit around a lighthouse
in the South China Sea and listen to waves crash against
the rocks and think up poetry.

I told him that all of that was very interesting, but
that he could go do all of it in the off-season, with Barbara Jane as well. And maybe I would go, too.

"Not the same," Shake said. "I want to disappear for
a while, from everything I've ever known. I think that
would be fascinating."

"If I couldn't get the scores," I said, "it wouldn't do
anything but make me hot."

"In your case, that's right," he said.

I said, "Listen, old buddy. There never has been a
more fired-up ball player than you, or a better leader.
Don't that tell you something? Don't you know what
you really love?"

"What are you gonna tell me I love?" he said.

I said, "You love—aside from Barb, I mean—you
love catchin' balls and stickin' your hat in somebody's
gizzle."

Shake said, "Yeah, well, what I'm trying to say, Billy
C., is that I'm burnt out. I've been gettin' up for games

for fifteen years and playin' my ass off, and I'm gettin' close to that time, I can feel it, when I'm gonna flame out."

Then he said, "I would like to win a Super Bowl though."

"There you are," I said. "Let's go to Clarke's and get on the outside of some bacon cheeseburgers."

Shake said, "You know, the thing that would ruin Barb would be for her to be married legal."

I asked how come.

"Well," he said, "it's because, basically, deep down, and she can't help it, she's a fuckin' woman."

I said I thought that was a pretty lucky break, as a matter of fact.

"Think about this," he said. "None of us have ever had an argument or a fight or hurt the others' feelings, ever, have we?"

I said that's right.

"So, all right, let's say me and Barb got married and lived somewhere and she was happy," he said. "Happy with the place, whether it was Tangier or wherever. And I was happy there, running my bar with the ceiling fans and the bamboo curtains and all the spies coming in and out. Do you know what would happen one day, just as sure as hell?"

I didn't have any notion.

"I would forget something," he said.

He said, "I would forget one day to pick up bread for dinner or maybe I would forget to hang up my clothes. Or I might even forget to fuck her. Well, Barb, now being a legal wife, which would make her an *owner* of sorts, would say something about it."

Possibly, I agreed.

"She might say something smart-ass, or she might just utter a small complaint. But sooner or later, she would say something. Do you know what would happen then?"

I sure didn't.

Shake said, "Well, what would happen is, she would blow all those years I'd ever known her and loved her. She would piss me off about something that didn't make a shit and it would leave a scar and it would all be ruined."

I thought that over for an interlude and listened to the soft background of Elroy Blunt singing "Tear Me a New One."

"Seems a little harsh," I said.

Shake said, "Naw, that would do it. She'd bitch one time, sooner or later, and the whole thing would be ruined. Women can't help it. It catches up with 'em. At one time or another, they got to bitch about something that don't make a shit."

"Seems like Barb ought to get the privilege of one bitch in a lifetime," I said.

"Why?" he asked.

"I don't know," I said, honestly.

"Has she ever bitched?" he said.

"Not that I know of," I said.

"Well," he said, "you let her become a legal wife, an owner, and then you would see some dissatisfaction expressed."

"Even Barb?" I said.

"That's the thing, Billy C.," he said. "No matter how great she is—and she's the best—she can't help the fact that she's a woman. It'll finally catch up with her, and I just don't want to be there when it happens."

I asked my old buddy how he knew all this.

"Books and movies and knowing people," he said.

I busted up laughing.

Then I asked him what about men who bitched.

"Men don't bitch like women and even if they do, you don't take it seriously, and you can tell 'em to go shit in their wallets and they don't get their feelings hurt and they don't hold grudges," he said.

Women were certainly a different problem, I said.

Shake went on, "Women take things personally when they shouldn't. For example, if you forget the loaf of bread, they have a tendency to think that you forgot it because you don't love 'em as much as you did yesterday. And that's not why you forgot the loaf of bread. You forgot the loaf of fuckin' bread because you were drunk, or it wasn't important enough to remember."

I said, "It might have been important to the woman. She might have needed it to cook you something good."

Shake said, "Then she could fix navy bean soup instead. Or enchilladas."

"Oh, that's right." I giggled. "I forgot."

Shake said, "It's too bad about women, and especially Barb, but that's the way it is."

I said I guessed so.

He said, "You were wondering where we're all going

and that troubles me a lot more than it does you, like I said. The thing is, you see, where we're going now doesn't lead anywhere."

"We're living," I said, "and laughing."

He said, "Yeah, but it would all be ruined by Barb not getting her loaf of fuckin' bread some day. See, I've known the all-time girl and I've loved her and she's loved me. I've had the all-time pal, which is you. And I've played a game as good as anybody ever played it. Now I think I want to do something else."

"Find some spies," I said.

"Just do something different. It bothers me that all I've ever done is be a split end and fuck around," he said.

"It doesn't matter that you've been loved and happy and famous and rich?" I said.

"Anybody can do all that," he said.

"All you got to do is want to," I said. "I forgot again."

"Right," said Shake.

"In other words," I said, "you want to go see if you can round up some misery somewhere."

Shake said, "Well, I'm not exactly looking for any misery. I've always been dead set against hunger or being thirsty, as you know. I think what I'd like to find is something different to look at and something different to listen to, but I don't know what."

"What's your position on being lonely?" I asked.

Shake said, "Nobody's lonely who's got any sense. And if it's female companionship you're speaking of, well, you know old Shake 'Em Up, Shake Loose ain't gonna be without a pretty face with a set of dandy lungs, although the colors may differ as he travels about."

I said, "Old buddy, what you're telling me is that love doesn't matter."

"Naw," he said. "Love is great. Love is flowers and oceans and mountains and laughing and a Her or a Semi to share 'em with. But maybe I'm tired of all that. It's not so important any more."

Not as important as what else, I wondered.

"I don't know," he said. "A new kind of talk, maybe."

I said, "Well, why don't you go the fuck up to Harvard? They'll talk to you."

He said that wasn't quite it, and he said that he supposed I couldn't really understand what he was trying to say since I had to be somewhere so I could get the scores.

"All I know," I said, "is that if a girl like Barb loved me the way she loves you, I would have found everything I was ever looking for. And I would bust my ass more than I do on Sundays for the New York Giants trying to make her happy. Old Billy Clyde is the one who ought to be looking for something instead of you."

Shake said, "Aw, yours will turn up. She'll walk right into a New York bar one night, a vision of loveliness and lungs and good nature."

"For fifty or a hundred," I smiled.

Shake said I was probably right about all of it and that he was probably crazy, but maybe he would be less crazy with a couple of bacon cheeseburgers down his neck at Clarke's.

"You don't want to hang around with spies, anyway,"

I said. "Most of 'em don't even speak English, I hear."

"That's right," he said. "And they're mostly men, too, aren't they?"

I laughed a yeah.

"Piss on spies," said Shake. "Let's go eat and talk about football, or something that makes sense."

"Just do me a favor, old buddy," I said.

"Yeah," he said.

I said, "Don't disappear on us until we've had a chance to draft a good split end."

Well, friends, I am finally out of my lemon-lime bubble bath and I'm sitting here on a stool by the dressing table, but I am going to have to take a shower now, because of something that took place in the past thirty minutes.

There I was, all comfortable in my tub with my tape recorder and a cigarette, when the bathroom door cracked open and this voice came floating through.

It was singing.

What the voice sang was:

His achin' muscles soaked in that old tub where he was sittin',
A day's drive was done and that was good.
But his drivin' never ended, just like a woman's knittin',
And his life was just as lonely as that engine 'neath the hood.
Oh how he'd drive, drive, drive that big old truck

It was Elroy Blunt, naturally.

He poked his head in the door wearing a large floppy-brimmed suede hat.

"Clyde!" he whooped. "They told me you was in the tub so I made that up from the living room to here. Good to see you, son."

I told Elroy he was still a genius and I was delighted to see him. And I was.

"They's good times ahead, Clyde," he said. "Nuthin' but good times."

How's it going? I asked.

"Just as smooth as the inside of a little old girlie's thigh," he said. "How 'bout your own self?"

Good, I said.

"You look good, son," he said. "Takin' them old fag baths and all. Marvin Tiller looks good, out there in the livin' room wearin' his pirate shirt and his velvet pants. Barbara Jane looks her same old delectable self, just as if the Old Skipper sent her to us from upstairs. And I want to congratulate you on that there Cissy what's-her-name. Hmmmmmmmmm, son. *Strong.*"

She's comforting, I said.

"Clyde, that Cissy what's-her-name's got to be stronger than a family of Mexkins," he said.

She's understanding, I said.

"Lookie here, Clyde," said Elroy. "Now you know I'm always thinkin' of your fantasies. Ain't that right? Well, I done brought you a present."

I wasn't sure whether that was good or bad.

But it was O.K.

What Elroy Blunt brought into the bathroom was what he described as a debutante from Savannah. Name of Sandi.

"This here's Sandi," he said.

I said it was a pleasure.

Sandi was solid built and she had orange hair piled up, and her eyes were painted dark purple, and she looked somewhat bored.

Elroy said, "If you will note, Clyde, young Sandi here is a lady with a whole dress full of titties."

She certainly was, I said.

Elroy said, "Now, Clyde, if a man was to rate this particular set of delectable lungs on a scale of Small, Medium, Large, Gigantic and Just Right, where would you say they stood?"

Pretty close to *all right,* I said, and they were.

"Strong, ain't they?" Elroy grinned, squeezing on one of Sandi's enormous lungs and kissing her on the cheek.

Sandi didn't seem to change her expression much. Her lashes flapped, that's all.

"Now, Clyde, one of the things they teach a Junior Leaguer in Savannah, I found out, is to start their tongue on a man's big toes and work their way all the way up to the backside of his teeth. With intermittent stops, of course," he said.

Of course, I said.

Elroy looked at Sandi and said:

"Say somethin' to my old podner here that'll get him excited."

Whereupon young Sandi knelt down by my tub and stuck her arm in my lemon-lime bubble bath.

"Let's see what I can find down here," she said.

Elroy said then, "Well, I think I'll leave you two love-birds alone for a while. Clyde, son. By God it's good to see you. And there ain't nuthin' ahead but good times. Don't worry about your guests in the livin' room. The star's here. He'll entertain 'em."

Well, friends. All of this was just a while ago. Young Sandi has now finished practicing her hobby. She's dressed again, and already gargled, and gone into the living room, where I'm sure she received a warm reception from Cissy Walford.

Now I got to take me a shower and join my guests.

There I was, all clean and smelling good, and then Elroy brought me that Junior Leaguer for a present.

With him around a man never knows what's liable to happen.

Anyhow, I got to get after it. We'll chat later.

Yawl come see us again in Savannah now, you heah?

I DON'T KNOW HOW ALL OF THE OTHER GREAT BOOK writers do it but I like a little quiet and semi-solitude myself.

It's after one A.M. right now, which means that it has turned Saturday, the day before the game.

I am laying here on the bed where Cissy Walford has gone to sleep in a mound of movie magazines. Everybody left our palatial suite pretty early, about midnight.

That was just what me and Shake wanted to have. An early night.

All we did was sit around, mostly, and talk about how we were going to dough-pop the dog-ass Jets.

Elroy Blunt got out his guitar and sang about seven thousand tunes, which was fun, and relaxing.

Big Ed and Big Barb don't go much for country music and they kept requesting things like "Moon Over Karakaua," and "Palm Frond Mamba," and "You're the Twist in My Cocktail."

Once, Big Ed and Big Barb tried to do their version of the Fort Worth Slide when Elroy sang "You Can't Peel the Bark on a Redwood."

It wasn't so good.

Right in the middle of the evening Shoat Cooper showed up, as he is known to do. He was having his usual case of pregame second thoughts and worry.

He wanted me and Shake to go out in the hall with him and have a "gut check."

Shoat said he had been down in Hose Manning's room chewin' on his cud, as he put it, and there was something troubling him about the game.

"I believe our defense is ready to stick 'em," he said. "I ain't worried about the defense. Their navels is gonna be screwed to the ground and they'll scratch and bite and spit at 'em."

Shoat said he figured our defense could hold the dog-ass Jets to seventeen or maybe twenty-one points. Twenty-four at the most.

"What this means," he said, "is that our offense is gonna have to stay off the toilet seat."

Me and Shake shook our heads in agreement.

"What troubles me," he said, "is that I dreamed the other night that they ain't gonna stay in their tendency defense. I think them sumbitches have so much respect for our runnin' game they're apt to give us a new look."

Shake said, "They can't overload anywhere. We got too many ways to fuck 'em."

Shoat said, "They can do one thing we ain't thought about."

Me and Shake looked at each other, and back at Shoat.

"They can Man you with Dreamer," Shoat said, looking at Shake Tiller. "And send the whole rest of their piss ants after stud hoss here."

"Dreamer can't play Man on Shake," I said. "Shake'll dust his ass off."

Shoat said, "Why's that?"

"He just will," I said. "Nobody's ever been able to play Man on Shake. And the best have tried."

"Dreamer ain't tried," said Shoat.

"So what?" I said.

"It's just something that come to me in my sleep," said Shoat. "It'd be a gamble for 'em. But I think it's what I might try, if I had me a Dreamer Tatum."

We all stood there in the hall and looked down at our feet.

"What else this means," said Shoat, "is that you're gonna take some licks in there, stud hoss. You got to hang onto that football out there Sunday. We can't give them piss ants anything."

I hardly ever fumble, by the way, and I reminded Shoat Cooper of that.

I looked at Shake as if to ask him about all this.

Shake said, "Coach, if I had one wish in life it would be for Dreamer Tatum to cover me Man. The whole fuckin' game."

Shoat Cooper thought about that. Then he said:

"Well, it would be an interestin' thing to look at in the screening room some day, or maybe at a coaching clinic. But I don't know as though it would help us win this football game."

Shake said, "If he tries to cover me Man, he'll get at least three interference calls, and I can beat his black ass all day on deep."

"He cheats," I said to Shoat.

"He wouldn't cheat if his job wasn't to stop no sweeps or pitches," said Shoat. "If his job was only to intimidate old Eighty-eight here and climb inside his shirt, he wouldn't cheat for the run."

We stood there some more, and I made up my mind.

"If they use Dreamer that way they're more dog-ass dumb than I ever thought," I said.

"It's just somethin' that bothered me in my sleep," said Shoat. "I just wanted to know what you studs thought about it."

Shake said, "What'd Hose think?"

Shoat pawed at the hall carpet and said:

"Aw, old Hose, he just smiled. He said he kind of hoped Dreamer would be Man on you because at least if he was, then Hose wouldn't have to worry about gettin' blind-popped from a corner blitz."

We grinned, me and Shake.

"Everything's cool, coach," said Shake. "If they play that way, old Billy C. here might not get his hundred and thirty-five rushing but we'll get everything else."

"You hosses feelin' good?" Shoat asked.

"Ready as we'll ever be," I said.

"Feelin' *fierce,* coach," said Shake, hugging old Shoat on the back. "Ready to rape, ravage and plunder."

Shoat said, "You hosses get a lot of rest in these last few hours. I want them legs to have spring in 'em. It's gonna be nigger on nigger out there Sunday."

"We're ready," I said again.

And we said goodnight to old Shoat, who probably went and drew circles and *x*'s for five or six more hours.

Shake and me stayed in the hall after Shoat walked off.

I said, "Is there any possibility whatsoever that Shoat could be right?"

Shake said, "None."

"No team gives up its basics and takes chances in a big game," I said.

"Right," said Shake.

"It's all down to who executes. And besides that, they're favored," I said. "Or were."

"They think they can play normal and cover us *up* with busy," said Shake.

"And they can," I said.

Shake had started back into our palatial suite, but he stopped and grinned and said:

"Goddamn, Billy C. Nobody ever said it wasn't gonna be semi-tough."

On Thursday night when we had dinner with Big Ed and Big Barb we had a fairly pleasant night, as it turned out. Which was an upset.

You don't just go looking up Big Ed and Big Barb for dinner. Mainly you don't because you know that Big Ed will take you through the whole history of the "oil bidness" again. And he'll go right from that to what's wrong with pro football, specifically the coaching.

Generally, Big Ed will also get mad at one or two waiters or waitresses, so much so that people at other tables will stare at you. And so much so that the food and service will be pretty miserable for everybody.

But, anyhow, it wasn't bad. We went to that steak place on Rodeo where a place called the Daisy used to be. The name of it was Beef Jesus.

Big Ed was on his good behavior, as I say. Except for a few remarks about Hollywood having more Jews than it used to have—in a fairly loud voice.

"Sorry you kids missed Hollywood back in the days when you could tell the women from the men," he said.

Another time, he said, "By god, I loaned some Jews out here some money one time and came out to check up on it and had me a hell of a time. That was before you, Mrs. Bookman."

Big Barb only smiled the whole time and kept glancing around Beef Jesus to see what the other women were wearing.

Big Ed did have a bit of a problem with the menu and the waiter, who looked and was dressed like straight Jesus and carried a big cardboard cross on his back as part of his costume.

"Hi, there," said the waiter. "I'm Jesus Harold. I've *come back* to serve you."

Big Ed spoke half to Jesus Harold and half to his menu.

"I don't know where you came back from, young man, but it looks like you didn't grab anything but your underwear when you left," he said.

And Big Ed looked around the table to see if any of us thought that was funny.

The waiter said, "The menu doesn't actually mean much. The specials, I think, will intrigue you a lot more. The menu is mostly for, well, you know, people from *Iowa,* or somewhere."

Jesus Harold adjusted his cross and stood with one hand on his hip.

Cissy Walford wanted to know what the specials were.

"To start," said Jesus Harold, "I've got avocado and aku, *cold,* of course, with Macadamia nut dressing. Very nice. I've got spinach and mushroom pie. Unbelievable. I've got asparagus soup, *cold,* of course, with some heavenly little chunks of abalone in it. I've got celery spears stuffed with turkey pâté. Incredible. And I've got civiche *without* pitted olives. It's terribly marvelous."

Big Ed looked up at Jesus Harold and said:

"Now tell us what you've got to eat."

I was on Big Ed's side for once.

Jesus Harold said, "On the *menu,* I'm sure the light in here is good enough for you to find a shrimp cocktail, a salad with roquefort, and a New York cut."

Jesus Harold looked away while he was writing on his pad.

"A little dish of vanilla for dessert?" he said. "All around?"

Big Ed said for Jesus Harold to hold on there for a minute. He said he wasn't interested in any of the specials. And he didn't think any of the rest of us were. What we really wanted was some good beef. Nothing to start. Just bring us some more drinks and six good pieces of beef with maybe some asparagus and sliced tomatoes.

"I don't suppose you've got a sixteen-ounce T-bone out there, do you?" said Big Ed.

Jesus Harold said, "If we do, I will *personally* rope it and drag it out here."

We all smiled at Jesus Harold, who wrote down our order. Or Big Ed's.

"Thank you very much," said Jesus Harold. "I'll tell Jesus Barry to bring you another round of drinks."

"Those are all medium rare," said Big Ed.

"Of course they are," said Jesus Harold. "Life *itself* is medium rare."

Our waiter left, straightening the cross on his back and clomping his sandals across the floor.

The steaks weren't bad. Big Ed and Big Barb asked Cissy Walford several questions about her parents. They decided they knew some rich people her parents knew. Big Barb asked Barbara Jane if she had done several things to her apartment since they had last seen it.

Big Ed discussed a number of things that were wrong with the current economy. He reviewed TCU's football season for us. They were three and eight. He also reviewed next season's prospects and said that one of TCU's problems was they had too many niggers on offense and a couple of Jesus Harolds in the secondary.

As Big Ed always does, he proposed a toast when dinner was over and Jesus Harold had sent Jesus Barry around with some stingers. It was the same old toast.

It was the toast where Big Ed says that you come into the world naked and bare, or something, and you go through the world with trouble and care. Then he says you go out of the world you know not where. But if you're a thoroughbred *here,* he says, getting louder, you're a thoroughbred *there.*

Me and Shake and Barb have learned to listen to the

toast with blank expressions. We raised our glasses again when Big Ed finished.

And Big Ed said, "Goddamned if I don't love a thoroughbred in life. And we've got a whole table of 'em right here."

Big Ed then spoke for a while on how he had molded most of our lives and helped us become thoroughbreds. Except for Cissy Walford, of course.

He said her daddy, being a wealthy man, had probably done the same thing for her. He said he and her daddy had a lot in common. "Respect for the American dollar," he said. "What's good for America is good for the world," he said. "If the world stops believing that, we may have to kick 'em in their chink asses again," he said.

Big Ed went through some of his fond memories about me and Shake and Barb. Big Barb joined in occasionally. Cissy Walford yawned once or twice.

Big Ed said he couldn't be happier to have turned out such a handsome daughter who seemed to have all of her mother's good taste. He said he didn't understand some of her wit, but, hell, this was another generation.

Only a couple of things had disappointed him, he said.

He said he was sorry a few years ago that Barbara Jane had refused to become a Fort Worth debutante like her mother had planned it. Which would have been the exact same year her mother got herself elected president of the Assembly and the Junior League and the Republican Women for White Freedom—the triple crown, so to speak. The Assembly was a club that picked debutantes.

Big Ed said he would have thrown a hell of a debutante

party for Barb. He said he would have brought in Freddy
Martin's orchestra and Bert Parks and a lot of other show
biz celebrities that he knew.

He said he was sorry, too, that Barbara Jane had gone
to TCU instead of a place like Mrs. Bellard-Ronald's in
upstate New York. "I'm for TCU as far as our town's
concerned," he said. "What the hell we got down there,
other than a bomber plant and a bunch of goddamned
apartment builders on the city council? But you can go
too far with your loyalty. Barbara Jane should have gone
off to a lady's school."

"Clarice Stuart in Ironwood, Virginia, would have
been *perfect*," Big Barb said.

Barb said, "Terrific."

Big Ed said his other major disappointment was when
his very own daughter and some other girls got caught
spending the night in the athletic dorm at TCU.

"I never expected such a thing from a Bookman," said
Big Ed.

We began laughing.

"I've never *felt* so destroyed," Big Barb said.

Shake said, "It all worked out. It was a joke, anyhow."

And Big Ed said, "You goddamn right it worked out.
After I *worked* it out. I thought for a while I'd have to
buy the Fort Worth *Light & Shopper,* and I'd just as soon
own a dry hole in Egypt."

"Bookman Heiress Shacks Up with Football Studs,"
said Barb, teasing. "Hell of a story. Aw, come on, Daddy.
Jim Tom Pinch wouldn't have ever printed the story. You
know that."

"It's funny now, huh?" said Big Ed.

"It's pretty funny, I think," I said. "That was some night. That was the night after the varsity picnic at Lake Worth. The spring before our junior season."

Shake said, "The night we scuttled Bobby Roy Simpson's forty-footer."

Barb said, "You mean the night Bubba Littleton did."

"Well, Bubba did the work but I think it was our idea." Shake grinned.

Big Ed said, "Wait a minute. Somebody sank somebody's boat that night?"

Shake said, "It didn't matter. Bobby Roy Simpson was a rich kid who liked to hang around with the football studs. He had several boats."

Big Ed said, "Well, I've got several boats myself but I'll be goddamned if I want anybody sinkin' 'em."

Barbara Jane laughed and looked at us.

"It didn't matter, Daddy. It really didn't," she said. "If you had known Bobby Roy Simpson, you would have sunk his boat with him *in* it."

Big Ed said it still didn't seem right, somehow. A man's boat and all. A private property deal.

Shake said, "I don't remember why we thought it would be all right to bring the girls back to Tom Brown Hall. It seemed like the thing to do, though."

I said, "Wasn't that the same night that Bubba Littleton tore the pay phone out of the wall?"

"Sure was," said Barbara Jane. "And threw the Coke machine down two flights of stairs. Double-header."

Shake said, "Well, you know why he was so hot?"

Me and Barb broke up. We knew.

Bubba Littleton was hot because Honey Jean Lester had caught him that afternoon flogging it underneath the dock as I have mentioned earlier.

"I don't see how any human being who's white could do things like that," Big Ed said.

"He was just mad at his date about something," I said.

"Well, Bubba Littleton wasn't a good enough football player at TCU to get away with things like that," Big Ed said. "Destroying property is what chinks and Commies want."

"He was a pretty mean tackle," Shake said. "He'd hit somebody."

I said, "He was about half-mean all the way around."

Shake said, "How about those poor Aggies?"

I wished Shake hadn't said that just when I had my young stinger up to my face. I nearly spit in it from laughing.

On a Friday night in Fort Worth one time before a game we had against Texas A&M, Bubba Littleton went downtown to a pep rally the Aggie cadet corps was having because he wanted to get him some Aggies as captives, for a joke.

I never knew any other TCU man who would go around an Aggie rally by himself. But Bubba of course could go anywhere he wanted to. He used to go look up truck drivers and try to get them to fight him to see who bought the beer.

Anyhow, Bubba went downtown and got him four Aggie cadets and brought them back to his dorm room.

The first thing he did was shave off all of their hair, what little they had, being Aggie cadets. Then he made them get naked and shave all the hair off of each other's bodies and vital parts.

They were just scrawny little old Aggies whose daddies had made them go there in the first place, to Texas A&M, I mean, which is kind of like going to Sing Sing. So they couldn't do anything except what Bubba Littleton wanted them to do, not unless they wanted to get an arm broke.

The next thing Bubba did was take some purple paint— purple is TCU's color—and make the Aggies stand at attention while he painted something on each one's chest. What he painted so that you could read it when they stood in a certain order was: AGGIES . . . IS . . . SEMI-
. . . RURAL.

Bubba finally let the poor souls go after they sang the TCU fight song to his satisfaction, and after they had a beat-off contest.

We carried on a little more with Big Ed and Big Barb about our growing-up days.

Big Ed said that one of the things which pleased him the most is that me and Shake and Barbara Jane had never needed any of his money.

Like all rich guys, Big Ed said he didn't have a whole lot of money but that he had managed to keep *some* from the government. And he said it was always there if any of us ever needed it for something important.

Big Ed said that what he planned to do with what little money he had, when he died, if none of us needed it for something important, was leave it to various things around Fort Worth, in his memory.

He said he hoped TCU would take some of his money and upperdeck the entire stadium and call it Big Ed Bookman Coliseum.

He said the family's first oil pump was still out in Scogie County but that he hoped the city would one day want to bring it to town and put it on the lawn of the Convention Center. He said it would be interesting history.

"Who are you going to leave your heart to?" Barbara Jane asked in a wry way.

Big Ed looked at Barb as if she was a Communist.

"Big Ed's heart goes with Big Ed," he said. "That's just goddamn foolishness, giving up things like that."

Big Ed said, "Wouldn't I be in a fine fix to come back on Earth some day without a goddamn heart?"

Barbara Jane howled.

"I don't want to talk about that kind of thing," said Big Ed. "I know everybody has different ideas these days. I just don't give one goddamn how many transplant cases are walking around healthy. They're supposed to be dead, like God wanted 'em to be."

Shake said, "Damn right. If God wanted a man to have two hearts, he'd have given him two hearts. If God had wanted a man to drink more, he'd have given him two mouths."

Big Ed said, "Go ahead and be funny about it. But I'll tell you this, Eighty-eight. You go out and get yourself a nigger's heart and then we'll see how many footballs you catch on Sunday."

"Can you *believe* it?" said Barbara Jane, looking at us.

Big Ed said we'd do well to listen to him. He said he guessed he would have to educate us, once and for all. Why in the hell did we think Barbara Jane was such a beautiful and great girl? Why was that?

He said, well, he would explain it to us. By God, it was because she was a thoroughbred, he said. She came from good stock. Bookman stock. And don't think that didn't mean plenty, he said.

Big Ed said that God wasn't so dumb that he didn't know there had to be a few people around in history to see that the world ran right.

He said that God tried to turn it all over to mankind once and it just didn't work. A whole goddamn bunch of chinks and niggers got born, along with a whole lot of spicks and Mongol hordes. That pissed God off, he said. So God took over again and God's been trying to straighten it out ever since, without ruining his image.

He said God would sneak a tidal wave in every now and then, or an earthquake, or a volcanic eruption, and then a few wars, to get rid of several million undesirables outside of America.

It's a slow process, Big Ed said, because it got so far out of hand, and God has to be careful and do it slowly, and not make everybody so hot they won't like God any more.

Now then, he said, sipping on his stinger.

While all of this has been going on, God has allowed some carefully selected people he could trust to get born and take rich and be able to run things.

These are people, he said, like all of the great rulers and businessmen of history. Well, he said, they're people like the Murchisons and Hunts were, or like some corporation presidents he had known, and some generals, and himself.

The Bookmans, he said, went back a long way. God sent the first Bookman over on the Mayflower to help get America started off right. The reason, he said, was because God knew that America would be able to get the rest of the world to shape up. Eventually. Like today.

The Bookmans, he said, distinguished themselves in all of the wars, including his own self in World War II, which none of us could much remember, he guessed. The big war, where we kicked the shit out of those that had it coming, and did it right.

He said that God obviously didn't want him to get killed in that war, basically because he had some big money to earn and some jobs to provide later on, and that's why God had given him the intelligence and the aristocracy to go into the army as a colonel at the age of twenty.

He said God knew what he was doing when he worked it out that Big Ed got to stay in Washington, D.C., throughout the big war and help out with many of the important decisions that were made about who to kill next.

Now then, Big Ed said again.

One of the wonderful things that came out of him being preserved and not killed, as God had shown the good sense to do, was that he got to meet Big Barb in college when they were at the University of Texas, after the big war. Big Barb had come from a fine family herself, he said. The Huckabees from Waco, he said.

And out of this union had come Barbara Jane, he said, with her hair of streaked butterscotch, her deep brown eyes, her olive complexion, her splendid cheekbones, her full lips, her perfect teeth, her big bright smile and her keen mind and, according to her mother, her flawless carriage and good taste and her incredible body.

"It took a lot of Bookmans to produce that," said Big Ed in conclusion.

"And one hell of a lot of earthquakes," said Barbara Jane.

I SEE BY THE OLD EAST-WEST SHRINE GAME WRIST watch that it's about time for Billy Clyde to grab his eight or nine hours.

The time is beginning to pass very slowly, I think. It's always this way before a big game.

When I wake up it will be Saturday morning, and that's still another twenty-four hours before we can put on our hats and get after the dog-ass Jets in the biggest football game there is, the old Super Bowl.

My plans for Saturday are to lay around a lot and rest my legs and not eat anything but steak and eggs and fruit, and maybe some wool.

I may not even have more than a couple of drinks.

Elroy Blunt of course is going ahead and having his party in the mansion he has rented for the weekend in Bel Air. That's where a lot of studs live out here who have fucked people out of some serious money.

I guess we'll attend the party but just for a short while. Elroy said he would have some steaks for those of us who have a game to play and don't want to log up on eight or ten dozen barbecued ribs and beans and potato salad.

Elroy said he was laying in a Mississippi River of Scotch, a Lake Michigan of vodka and an English Chan-

nel of beer. He said if anybody wanted anything to drink
other than that, which he would not be able to understand or even tolerate, they could smoke dope instead.

He said he had two footballs stuffed with the best grass
any A-rabs could smuggle in.

Elroy said he had invited several of his country rhythm
picker friends, a couple of rock groups for dancing on the
lawns, a few semi-starlets, and several debutantes for
those who didn't have dates or wives, or even for those
who did.

He said there shouldn't be more than a hundred people
in all.

He said he had taken the precaution to arrange for
fourteen Cadillac limousines with TV's and telephones
and bars in them to arrive at ten A.M. Sunday and ensure
that everybody got to the Los Angeles Coliseum in time
for the game.

He said there would be two or three doctors on hand
with B$_1$ shots and Dex and penicillin to handle various
things like hang-overs, fatigue and the clap.

"You don't know about some of these debutantes," he
said. "If they look a bit worn, you ought to take some
penicillin just to eliminate the mental grief."

Me and Shake told Elroy he sure was thoughtful of his
guests. We asked what the whole thing was going to cost
him.

"Nowhere near as much as it ought to, considering the
bigness of the occasion," he said. "I can probably get
away for three or four thousand whip-out."

Elroy said that would include tips for the debutantes.

*　*　*

There was a minute or two in the living room of our palatial suite tonight—or last night, I should say, seeing as how it's almost two A.M.—when Barbara Jane and I talked about my literary effort. And about ourselves.

She said she had now listened to everything I'd spoke up to a day ago and she said she thought it was still semi-honest and half-funny.

But she said she thought it was a little embarrassing for her own self.

"I think you make me sound like a goddamn priceless emerald or something," she said.

"I'm going to tell Jim Tom to tone me down with some editing. In terms of the characterization of Barbara Jane Bookman, you are writing what they say in the magazine business is an all-out, no-holds-barred, hard-hitting puff."

I told her that if Jim Tom Pinch changed anything drastic about her, I'd see to it that he wound up his career writing bowling scores. Got that, Jim Tom?

Barb put her hands on my shoulders and kissed me, gentle like. Then she wrapped her arms around my waist and put her head on my chest.

I held her there for a while, with my chin resting on top of her streaked butterscotch hair, which was parted in the middle and hung down quite a ways, soft, straight and pretty.

We squeezed on each other like good friends and kind of stood there.

She said, "I wonder what I've missed, not ever knowing anybody very well except Old Twenty-three and Old Eighty-eight?"

"Hardly anything," I said.

"I've never even *cared* about anybody else, not really," she said. "Damn it, nobody else ever laughed enough."

I said, "If you ever had cared about anybody else, you couldn't have been a Two."

"One," Barb said.

"Two," I repeated.

"One," she said softly, looking up and kissing me again, and then putting her head back where it was.

I smiled and I think she did too.

There was another pause. And then Barb said, "A serious question, O.K.?"

She said that to my shirt.

"Anything, anytime, anywhere," I said.

"What's the story on the game?" Barb said. "Do we win or do we lose?"

I said, "Straight deal?"

"Straight deal," she said.

"No owl shit?" I said.

"No owl shit," she said, looking up. "Just unbutton your shirt and let your heart fall out, boy."

I kind of cleared my throat and took a breath and said, "Well, I think we've got a better team. I think we've got more character."

"Is that an answer?" Barb said.

"Big Ed says we've got better niggers." I smiled.

We untangled and Barb held my hands and looked into my eyes as if there was a scoreboard in there somewhere.

She looked at me for several seconds and I looked at her, which is always a delight.

Finally, she squeezed my hands tight and said, "We'll win."

Barb went on off across the room, then, presumably to see if she could rescue anybody that Big Ed and Big Barb were boring to death.

And now I, Billy Clyde Puckett, am going off to stack me up some Z's.

See you around the campus, as they say.

Is that what they say?

PART THREE

Game-Face

Will they play a Super Bowl in Heaven?
Will the fans be drinkin' beer?
Will any long-haired, lovely girls
Be there to cheer?

    —from "The Ballad of Billy Clyde,"
      a song by Elroy Blunt

I MAY HAVE TO DOUGH-POP CISSY Walford before I
ever get around to the dog-ass Jets.

What she has done is semi-unforgivable and a rotten
thing to do to somebody that she is supposed to be about
half-crazy about, which is me.

I am hotter than a pot of butter beans right now, as
you might can guess. Shit, I'm hot.

What Cissy did was go squirt off her mouth to Boke
Kellum, our friendly neighborhood fag Western hero,
about this book I am writing.

And what Boke Kellum did was go squirt off his
mouth to the newspapers about it, and here it all is,
right here in my hand in the Saturday morning Los
Angeles *Times*.

The dog-ass headline says:

PUCKETT TURNS AUTHOR FOR SUPER BOWL.

The story says:

All-Pro Running Back Billy Clyde Puckett, who
may hold the key to the New York Giants' chances
in tomorrow's Super Bowl, will be taking notes on
the sidelines throughout the game.

The *Times* has learned that Puckett is keeping a
diary of Super Bowl Week and will turn it into a

hard-cover book for a major publishing house next fall.

Puckett's book will be most revealing, according to reliable sources.

It is understood that Puckett is delving into many personalities involved in the Super Bowl attraction, and will present some of the darker sides of the game of pro football itself.

Much of the book, the *Times* has learned, will be devoted by Puckett to describing exactly how the Giants prepared for the contest.

It is also believed that Puckett will describe how he developed his rip-roaring running style, a style which has made him the leading rusher in the NFL.

Parts of the book will also touch on some of Puckett's close friends, such as Boke Kellum, the handsome star of the hit TV series, *McGill of Santa Fe*.

There's some more but mainly it's quotes from some of the dog-ass Jets, like Dreamer Tatum, about me being so talented as to be able to prepare for a big game and write a book at the same time.

Boy, I am so hot right now that I could turn into some kind of T. J. Lambert.

If there was ever a bad time for something like this to come out, it is the day before the Super Bowl.

Cissy Walford has already cried a few times this morning and tried to make everything all right by grabbing me in the crotch but it hasn't helped.

I've told her that if I lay my eyes on Boke Kellum again I was gonna leave him every way but alone.

Man, I'm still hot. And all of this hit me more than an hour ago when I got up. I don't usually get hot like this for anything other than a football game. But I am hot.

Shake says that I shouldn't be so hot because a lot of other stud athletes have written books and everybody just figures that it's what a stud athlete does for money these days.

Barbara Jane said she didn't think it was anything to be bothered about.

"It's not as if we've just lost to Spring Branch." She smiled.

Barb said the best way to look at it was that the dog-ass Jets wouldn't know what to do, going up against a real live intellectual book writer.

I said what bothered me most was having to go to a squad meeting pretty soon and take a lot of shit from my pals.

But it's something I've got to do. And right away, in fact.

See you in a little while, gang. If there's anything left of me after T. J. Lambert gets through.

If not, I'd like my ashes pitched out of a taxi at the northeast corner of Fifty-fifth and Third.

That's where P. J. Clarke's is, of course.

It's probably asking too much of the owner, Danny Lavezzo, to hang my photo on the wall, back there in the back room where all the celebs hang out; back there with the checkered tablecloths and the Irish waiters.

There wouldn't be much status in having it hanging
in the middle room, behind the front bar—the room
where everybody stands in line, hoping and praying for
a table in the back. There's nothing in the middle room
but too much light, and some drunks standing around a
garbage pail.

I guess I don't know of anybody who ever got his
picture up on the wall in Clarke's, without dying. Not
even a Greek ship owner or a columnist. If Frank Gif-
ford or Charley Conerly or Kyle Rote couldn't do it
from the old Giant glory days, I don't know how I could
expect it.

Maybe my only chance is if T. J. Lambert turns me
into a tragic legend.

"Oh, what could have been," they'll say in Clarke's.
And hang my picture.

*Feelin' you is feelin' like a wound that's opened
    wide,*
Feelin' you means troubles by my side.
Feelin' you ain't easy,
Don't know how much I can take.
Feelin' someone gone is feelin' nuthin' but an ache.

*When you took my credit cards and headed north
    across the bay,*
When you piled up all my clothes there in the hall,
*When your anger made you laugh at all the bills I'd
    have to pay,*

I could hear you laughin' louder while I kicked and
 beat the wall.

You ain't nuthin' but a servin' wench, it's true.
Serve it up and grab a tip or two.
Eggs fried greasy, coffee dark,
Donuts hard as sycamore bark,
But you'll trap another fool like you know who.

I just hope you'll keep on movin' down the road.
Movin' faster than I'm drivin' this old load.
Much more heartache I ain't needin',
Though your looks have got me bleedin',
I'm just about to get your memory throwed.

But feelin' you is feelin' like a wound that's opened
 wide,
Feelin' you means troubles by my side.
Feelin' you ain't easy,
Don't know how much I can take.
Feelin' someone gone is feelin' nuthin' but an ache.

Nothing helps trouble and woe, I think, like listening to music. I've been listening to some Elroy Blunt tunes here on the portable stereo we brought with us to our palatial suite.

One of my favorites among his new songs is "Feelin' You," which is those words I've just recited, in a semi-tuneful way.

It's late in the afternoon upon this Saturday in Janu-

ary. I've been back from the squad meeting for quite a
while and had lunch up here in the suite.

Some of the Giant fans who have flown out for the
game are having a party down around the cabanas by
one of the swimming pools. That's where Barbara Jane
and Cissy are. Shake Tiller and Hose Manning have
gone over to the Beverly Wilshire to talk to some *Sports
Illustrated* writers and editors and reporters and photographers.

We'll be heading out to Elroy Blunt's mansion for his
party in a while. He drew up directions for our rented
car on how to get there.

This hasn't been too good a day for the stud hoss, unfortunately.

All of my teammates had read that story in the Los
Angeles *Times,* and of course they all clapped when I
walked into the squad meeting.

I caught a whole bunch of heat.

Varnell Swist said, "Say, baby, you ain't gonna write
anything about what a cat does on the road, are you?"

Puddin Patterson said, "Tell us about that rip-roarin'
runnin' style. Do you just jive it on in there for six by
your own self?"

Puddin said, "Er, uh, say, baby. Do you rip first, or
do you roar first?"

There was lots of giggling among my pals.

Euger Franklin said, "If me and Puddin ain't blockin'
nobody's ass, he just lay down, baby."

Varnell Swist said, "What you gonna say about the
road, baby? Some wives is gonna read that mother you

writin', you dig what I'm sayin'?"

Puddin Patterson said to the squad, "Lookie here, cats. Lookie here at the cat who holds the key to the whole jivin' tomorrow. Ain't he a dandy? He just gonna go out there tomorrow by his own self and win his self a Super Bowl."

I was trying to grin while I blushed.

Puddin said, "Cat gonna put that rip-roarin' jive on them other cats and they just gonna say, 'Oooo, he hit har-rud.' Cat just goes shuckin' and jivin' out there with nobody but his own self. Lookie here at this mean cat."

Jimmy Keith Joy said, "Say, baby. That *dark* side of pro football you gonna jive about. You ain't talkin' about brothers, are you?"

Euger Franklin said, "Show us that key you holdin' to the game, baby."

"It's them moves," said Puddin Patterson. "Say. Say, lookie here. The key is in them big old strong legs that lets this cat go rippin' and roarin'."

"Make my hat hum he hit so har-rud," said Euger Franklin.

Puddin said, "Everybody get down and cat say hup. Cat say hup-hup. Cat say hup-hup-hup. And old Billy Clyde go jivin' for six. Crowd say oooo-weee, he run so har-rud because he's a-rippin' and roarin'."

O.K., I said. Go ahead on.

Puddin said, "Everybody get down and cat say hup again. Cat say hup-hup. And Billy Clyde go hummin' for six. And crowd say oooo-weee, he run so har-rud and he writin' a book while he rip-roarin'."

T. J. Lambert hadn't spoke until he finished the sack of chili cheeseburgers he brought to the squad meeting.

He finally stood up and licked his fingers and bent over, with his butt toward me, and he cut one that must have been the color of a Christmas package.

"That's all I got for tootie fruities what write books," he groaned.

In the serious part of the squad meeting, Shoat Cooper explained to us what the drill would be for Sunday, in terms of what time everything would occur.

Shoat said we would start getting our ankles taped at eight o'clock tomorrow morning. Those that needed special braces and pads taped on, he said, ought to get to the taping room thirty minutes earlier.

He said he hoped everybody on the team could have breakfast together at nine in the Señor Sombrero Café on the second floor.

He said we would leave for the Los Angeles Coliseum about ten-thirty. It would be about eleven-fifteen when we got there, he said, and that would give us plenty of time. "To get frisky for them piss ants," he said.

The kickoff wasn't until one-fifteen, he pointed out. It had been set back fifteen minutes by CBS, he said, in order for the network to finish up a news special it was doing on some kind of earthquake that wiped out several thousand chinks somewhere yesterday.

It was news to me and Shake and we shared some kind of look which had to do with Big Ed Bookman. News about the earthquake, I mean. Not about the kickoff.

Shoat said that both the offense *and* the defense would be introduced, on both teams, for television before the game. He said we should line up under the goal post that would be appointed to us and carry our hats under our arms when we trotted out to our own forty-five yard line and faced the dog-ass Jets and stood there for the "Star-Spangled Banner."

That would be the last thing we would do before the kickoff, Shoat said. Therefore, he said, this would come after we had warmed up and then gone back into the dressing room and crapped and peed and drank some more Dexi-coffee. Them what needed it, like the interior linemen.

"A little spiked coffee never hurt nobody's incentive," Shoat said. "Especially them lard butts who have to play down in that trench where the men are."

Shoat said we might have a long time to lay around the dressing room after we warmed up because the National Football League had a fairly lavish pregame show planned.

Shoat said he understood that both the pregame show and the halftime show would have a patriotic flavor.

"That can't be anything but good for football," he said.

According to Shoat, here's what was going to happen before the game:

Several hundred trained birds—all painted red, white and blue—would be released from cages somewhere and they would fly over the coliseum in the formation of an American flag.

As the red, white and blue birds flew over, Boke Kellum, the Western TV star, would recite the Declaration of Independence.

Next would be somebody dressed up like Mickey Mouse and somebody else dressed up like Donald Duck joining the actress Camille Virl in singing "God Bless America."

And right in the middle of the singing, here would come this Air Force cargo plane to let loose fifty sky divers who would come dropping into the coliseum.

Each sky diver would be dressed up in the regional costume of a state, and he would land in the coliseum in the order in which his state became a United State.

When all this got cleaned up, Shoat said, United States Senator Pete Rozelle, the ex-commissioner of the NFL who invented the Super Bowl, would be driven around the stadium in the car that won last year's Indianapolis 500. At the wheel would be Lt. Commander Flip Slammer, the fifteenth astronaut to walk on the moon.

Riding along behind the Indy car, Shoat said, would be two men on horses. One would be Commissioner Bob Cameron on Lurking Funk, the thoroughbred which won last year's Kentucky Derby. And on the other horse, Podna (the horse Boke Kellum pretends to ride in his TV series), would be the current president of CBS, a guy named Woody Snider.

Finally, Shoat said, the teams would be introduced and two thousand crippled and maimed soldiers on crutches and in wheel chairs and on stretchers would render the "Star-Spangled Banner."

Shoat told us the halftime was likely to run forty-five minutes. It would be a long one, at any rate, "which might be a good thing if we got some scabs to heal up," he said.

The length of the halftime, Shoat said, would depend on whether CBS would decide to interrupt the Super Bowl telecast with a special news report on the earthquake, which might still be killing chinks with its fires and floods and tidal waves.

"I never knowed a dead chink, more or less, to be more important than a football game," Shoat said. "But maybe if a whole gunnysack of 'em get wiped out, it's news."

Shoat said it was too bad we would all have to miss it but the Super Bowl halftime show was going to be even more spectacular than the pregame show.

He said there would be a water ballet in the world's largest inflatable swimming pool, a Spanish fiesta, a Hawaiian luau, a parade stressing the history of the armored tank, a sing-off between the glee clubs of all the military academies, and an actual World War I dogfight in the sky with the Red Baron's plane getting blown to pieces.

The final event of the halftime, he said, would be an induction into the pro football hall of fame of about twenty stud hosses out of the past, including our own Tucker Frederickson, the vice-president of DDD and F. United States Senator Pete Rozelle would preside, Shoat said, along with Camille Virl, the actress, and Jack Whitaker, the CBS announcer. When the induction ceremony was over, Shoat said, then Rozelle and Whitaker and Camille Virl would lead the inductees in singing a parody on the "Battle Hymn of the Republic," which was written by somebody in the league office. The title of it, he said, was "The Game Goes Marching On," and he understood it might make some people cry.

Shoat said CBS hoped the whole stadium would join in the singing, since all 92,000 people would have been given a printed copy of the lyrics.

The last thing in the halftime would be some more birds. While the stadium was singing this song, Shoat said, several thousand more painted-up birds would be released and they would fly in such a way overhead that the likeness of Vince Lombardi, the great old coach, would appear.

This was about all that was discussed at the meeting.

Shoat said for all of us to start getting our game-face on.

"When we take that field," he said, "I want you pine knots to be in a mood to stand them piss ants ever way but up."

I got a collect long-distance call from Fort Worth a while ago and of course it was from my Uncle Kenneth.

He just called up to thank me for the fifty-yard line seat I sent him along with a first-class round-trip plane ticket.

Uncle Kenneth said that as much as he wanted to be out here, he didn't rightly see how he could go off and leave an acquaintance he had made with an old boy who thought he knew all about how to play gin.

I said I understood. That when a good business opportunity presented itself, a man had to act on it.

Uncle Kenneth said he would certainly be watching
the game on color TV, however. He said he had four
large bet on it—at pick—and how did I feel?

Perfect, I said.

I told him he could cash that plane ticket in for some
whip-out, if he wanted to.

Uncle Kenneth said he had done that, already. But he
said he was going to keep the game ticket as a souvenir,
if I didn't mind.

"How's old Shake 'Em Up, Shake Loose?" he said.
"He fit and all?"

Sure was, I said.

"And old Barber Jane?" he said. "Still prettier'n a
crocheted afghan, I guess."

You bet, I said.

"Well, Billy, you have a good ball game now," Uncle
Kenneth said. "Remember what I've always said to you.
A lot of first downs'll take you to that land of six."

That's right, I said.

"First downs, Billy," he said.

O.K., I said.

"Comin' second ain't nuthin'," he said.

You got that right, I said.

"The YMCAs are full of all 'em that come second,"
he said.

Sure are, I said. Take care now.

"First downs, Billy," said Uncle Kenneth, hanging up.

*   *   *

All I wanted to do just now was clean up and be ready to go to Elroy Blunt's party. That's sure all I wanted to do but of course I didn't get to do that because I had me some visitors.

Burt Danby, the head of DDD and F (and therefore the head of the Giants) stuck his self in the door of our palatial suite and held up his hand.

"Got five?" he said. "I can come back."

I said he might as well come on in and get a seat before the Communist army got here.

"I just wanted you to meet a *super* guy," said Burt, who was wearing his go-to-southern-California outfit. His pink sports coat and pink scarf with white pants and white shoes that were tight and soft like little old white and soft gloves.

It was just my own self at home, I said. Shake Tiller was still over at *Sports Illustrated*'s penthouse in the Beverly Wilshire, and the girls were down at the swimming pool.

"Saw the girls, saw the girls," said Burt. "They're in splendid hands down at the cabanas. *Hell* of a party going on down there. Christ, it looks like Manuche's at Monday noon after we've won a biggie. My God, it's like Shor's in the old days down there. Jesus, it looks like Weston's when Sinatra used to drop by. Fantastic! It looks like Elaine's when the King of Morocco's in town. The place is crawling with top guys. *Crawling*."

I said there wasn't any party going on up here unless somebody cared to watch me take a shower. I had on my shorts.

Burt Danby came on in and behind him he brought in this tall, sunburned fellow who had a drink in his hand and was dolled up in such a way that nobody could ever have guessed that he came from Madison Avenue and had to be one of those Eastern, lockjaw motherfuckers who wouldn't know shit from tunafish.

Burt's friend had on some light-gray pants and a navy blue coat and some shiny buckled loafers and the last of the Brooks Brothers white button-downs and a green-and-gold striped tie. He also had on a big button, pinned to his coat, which said: ALCOHOLICS UNANIMOUS.

It only took me an instant to figure out that I had seen the guy before. He was that empty suit from the *Sports Illustrated* party that Shake Tiller had made sport of.

Burt Danby said, "Stud hoss, say hello to a *hell* of a guy. Put it in the vise with Strooby McMackin, the *president* of Kentuckian Cigarettes."

I said hidy.

"President," Burt Danby said. "As in *who* runs the store. As in how do I love thee, *let* me count the ads."

I said hidy again.

Strooby McMackin had a voice no louder than your average lift-off at Cape Kennedy. He said, "I met the stud the other night. Unfortunately—heh, heh—I was shit-faced and don't remember much. Hello again."

Burt Danby said Strooby McMackin was a *hell* of a good guy and a *super* client of DDD and F, even if he was sort of a sentimental Jet rooter.

"Oh, I like all football," said Strooby McMackin. "I

guess I became a Jet fan a few years ago before I took over this company. You have to be Jesus Christ to get a Giant ticket."

Burt Danby said, "You've got 'em now, fellow. For next year. As many as you need."

Burt laughed heartily and patted Strooby McMackin on the arm.

"Get you a pop?" Burt said to his friend. "Another tightener? Just down the hall. Won't take a second. How about another train-misser? Want a little see-through?"

Strooby McMackin said no, he was fine.

He said, "Puckett, I saw those young ladies you were with at the SI party. They're down around the cabanas with your whole New York Giant gang. Mike was down there a while ago, and Jerry and Felix and Stanley. All the die-hards I see around midtown."

Good, I said.

"The whole goddamn gang," he said, "Danny's there, Susan, Norm, Jimmy, Teddy, Eloise, Jack, Crease. Goddamn place looks like the back room at Clarke's."

Burt Danby said, "Strooby walked up and said, 'Can Frankie get me a table here?' *Christ,* that was funny, Stroob."

I tried to smile.

Strooby McMackin said, "Anyhow, I apologized to your girl friends for all the language the other night. *Dynamite* girls, by the way."

Sure are, I said.

Burt Danby said, "By gosh, we'll convert Strooby yet. You *ought* to be in the Giant camp, Stroob. You *really* should."

Burt looked at me and said, "He'd better go with a winner, hadn't he?"

I said, "It's gonna be semi-tough, but we're lookin' forward to it."

Burt Danby said, "Hey, Stud. Listen. Strooby here has a couple of the niftiest damn teen-age boys you'll ever meet. Really a nifty couple of kids. Chip and Clipper. Thirteen and fourteen. *Terrific* sailors and *plenty good* at paddle tennis."

That was good, I said.

"Oh, hell, they're sports fans, all right," said Strooby McMackin. "They read *Sports Illustrated* from cover to cover every month, and of course they don't miss a Colgate game. I was Colgate 'Fifty-one."

No kidding, I said.

Burt Danby said, "Stud, I know you want to relax, and we're leaving. But take just a minute here and write something to Chip and Clipper on this menu from the Señor Sombrero Café. Just anything. 'Hi, Chip and Clipper, all the best, from the All-Pro himself, Billy Clyde Puckett.' Anything at all."

Strooby McMackin said, "Hell, they'll put that right up on their wall with the poster of Robert Redford."

Then he said, "Puckett, I really do feel badly about being so shit-faced the other night. I was totaled, believe me. And Burt knows that I can usually outdrink any-body at the Creek or Twenty-One or the Frog, or any-where."

I wrote something fast on the menu to Clip and Chip-per, or maybe it was the other way around.

"Super," said Burt Danby, slapping me on the bare

back. It stung, as a matter of fuckin' fact.

I couldn't resist asking the president of Kentuckian Cigarettes, since he hadn't mentioned it, if he recognized that girl with Shake Tiller the other night, the one down at the cabanas. Barbara Jane Bookman.

"Yeah," he said. "That was, uh, who was that?"

I took considerable delight in telling him that she was the girl in all of his Kentuckian ads right now, on all of the signboards and on the backs of magazines.

"The hell she is," he said. "Well, that just goes to show you how much a president knows."

"*Plenty* good-looking girl," said Burt Danby. "And the ad's a real winner, Stroob. Our creative guys just did a *super* job."

I said she worked a lot at what she does and that she might be the most familiar girl in advertising. I said she had been the Ford Fatigue Girl and the Chrysler Catastrophe Girl and the Mercury Malaria Girl.

Strooby McMackin said, "Well, I'll have to keep an eye out for her. Say, Burt. If this girl's working for me and she's a Giant fan, I guess I'll have to cheer a little for your guys tomorrow."

Burt Danby looked at me and said, "Is he a *top* guy? You're too much, Stroob. You *really* are."

They said they had to go.

"Have a good game, Puckett," said Strooby Mc-Mackin. "And may the best team win."

"As long as it's us." I smiled.

Burt Danby whooped. "Is that something, Stroob? Is that *positive* enough?"

As they left Burt Danby turned back toward me and gritted his teeth and made a gesture with his doubled-up fist like he was hitting somebody in the stomach.

"Let's get 'em *good*," he said.

I said O.K. I'd get 'em if he would.

I think I've just heard Shake and Barbara Jane and Cissy come in. So I guess this is all the news for now from Walter Cronkite.

I'll try to get up early enough tomorrow morning to share a few experiences from Elroy's party with you before I go to get taped and eat breakfast with the team.

Might help me calm down some to get up early and do that.

Don't know as though I'll be able to sleep much anyhow.

As Shoat Cooper says about big games, "I believe I see in the papers where we got us a damned old formal dance comin' up."

We sure do, if there is any truth in all captivity.

And old Billy Clyde is gonna be asked to dance ever dance.

Hit them biscuits with another touch of gravy,
Burn that sausage just a match or two more done.
Pour my black old coffee longer,
While that smell in gettin' stronger,
A semi-meal ain't nuthin' much to want.

Loan me ten, I got a feelin' it'll save me,
With an ornery soul who don't shoot pool for fun,
If that coat'll fit you're wearin',
The Lord'll bless your sharin'—
A semi-friend ani't nuthin' much to want.

And let me halfway fall in love,
For part of a lonely night,
With a semi-pretty woman in my arms.
Yes, I could halfway fall in deep—
Into a snugglin', lovin' heap,
With a semi-pretty woman in my arms.

The stereo in our palatial suite is turned down fairly low so that nobody can get waked up by Elroy's singing, or my own humming. That's while I sit here in the early dawn on Super Bowl day and try to believe what I'm looking at, which I hope will cure my headache.

Reading from left to right on the coffee table in the living room here, we've got—let me see—a cold bottle of Coors, a pot of hot coffee, a tall glass of milk, a tall glass of tomato juice, a pitcher of ice water and a small bottle of Anacin.

I have gone up and down the row a couple of times and it's beginning to help a little bit. Not much. But I'm not dead, at least.

I ought to be, however. Dead, I mean. I ought to be dead for drinking up a young Pacific Ocean full of Scotch. And I ought to be dead from being shot, for having drank it the night before the Super Bowl.

When this book comes out about seven or eight months from now, Jim Tom old buddy, nobody is going to believe what they read about the things which happened the night before the biggest sports event of the year.

It was stronger than a used-up high school date is all it was.

As parties go, I suppose Elroy's would have to rate right up there with Hurricane Carla.

When the four of us got there it was just about dark and the party obviously had already started. We had to park about two blocks away but we could hear some music and hollering without any strain.

Elroy had rented one of those semi-castles in Bel Air, up there near the golf course. It was one of those old stone mansions that look like somebody in the family went crazy and got sealed off in one wing.

It had a big old hedge all the way around it, and a big old yard, and a big old swimming pool, and a lot of big old eucalyptus trees, and it was all lighted up.

The first thing we noticed when we walked into the yard was about two hundred people we had never seen before. It probably would have looked like a costume party to most people from Fort Worth.

The guys were dressed like everybody from Jesus Harold to John Wayne. And the girls who weren't dressed like Indian princesses or bathing beauties or rodeo trick riders were dressed like light hooks. Which was with short, tight skirts, high heels, squeezed together lungs and sullen faces.

Pretty visible through it all, however, was an awful lot of southern California witch wool—stewardi, semi-starlets, or whatever they were—who were running around acting like Elroy's hostesses.

The reason they were visible is because they weren't wearing anything but man-sized white T-shirts with some blue and red printing on them. The T-shirts said: GIANTS 28, JETS 17.

What I mean by nothing on underneath the T-shirts, is nothing but skin and wool. Which a man could easily tell when one of them bent over or sat down, or when a man simply stared at the various feasts of lungs which jiggled and poked around in the semi-thin T-shirts.

At first, we just kind of explored. We were looking to see where everything was.

Food and drinks were almost everywhere, indoors and outdoors. A big old buffet of barbecued ribs—Texas style, which means smoked and not chinked—was stretched all across a part of the back lawn. A slightly smaller one was in the living room.

The living room looked like some kind of fuckin'
cathedral with a big old pointed ceiling and paintings
hanging everywhere of a bunch of guys who looked like
they used to be Popes but weren't. Or some kind of
Frenchmen.

There was a bar with a bartender in every room, including the semi-huge bathroom off of what I think was
a master bedroom upstairs in one wing.

It must have been the master bedroom because it was
about fifty feet long with a fireplace across one wall, a
lot of bookshelves, and a big old desk with several
Academy Award statues on it. There was also a big
painting of a pretty lady. And a bed the size of Fuller
Junior High.

The bathroom off of it looked like Greece, or what I
guess Greece looks like. It had a big old step-down
marble tub, a waterfall, two or three basins, a stereo, a
color TV, a leather chair, some statues of studs and
goddesses, thick carpet, a balcony, and a fishing stream.

A few times while we were milling about, some of
those T-shirted little dandies with the no-panties and
the dinner lungs came up to us and chatted.

One that came around was about twenty-two, I'd say,
and had long black hair and big blue eyes. She also had
a big, blue homemade cigarette in her hand about the
size of a pregnant Winston.

She said we could all find one for ourselves if we
would lift up the tops of the silver trays next to the ribs
on the buffet tables.

She said the name for this kind of anti-God cigarette

was a "Waimea Rush," but in New York they probably called it a "Village Lunch." Or used to, she said.

She was pretty enough to make our traveling squad, I thought. Not the team's. Ours. Me and Shake's.

She said her name was Linda and she mostly skied at Aspen and mostly surfed at Waimea Bay and mostly danced at the Ho Chi Minh Trail. She said she flew for Pacific Basin Airlines and she lived at the Sunset Boulevard Towers—five four two, eight six three one—and that she mostly liked to smoke dope and talk nasty and fuck athletes.

"What do you do for fun?" Barbara Jane asked her.

There was another one who came up to us and had blond hair going off in different directions and a pair of funny glasses on her nose and was eating a rib.

She said her name was Felicia and that she had gone a year to UCLA, a year to the University of Texas, a year to Radcliffe and two years to a lettuce farm in Salinas.

She said Zebba Den Karab had a better idea about things than Jesus Christ or even Hitler, who was grossly misunderstood, she said.

She said she didn't like Europe any more because it was trying too hard to "catch up." She said Rippy, Iowa, had it all over Europe.

She said the best thing about the South Seas was to go there and get tremendously sunburned and have somebody beat on your back with long, wet leaves.

She wanted to know if Barbara Jane or Cissy wanted to eat her. She said she had chocolate candy, marshmallows, peanut butter and buttered popcorn in her "fun kit."

She wasn't bad-looking for an intellectual.

Shake Tiller asked her, "Where'd Zebba Den Karab wind up after he lost his kickin' foot and the Cowboys traded him?"

Felicia just stared at all of us and shook her head and wandered off into the night with the rib in her mouth.

There was another one that was real healthy-looking. She was a bit meatier than the rest, and taller. Being taller, her T-shirt didn't hang down quite far enough to cover up her wool more than halfway.

She had strong thighs and strong arms but she was semi-inviting for the man who sometimes gets in the mood for a gold medal swimmer.

She said her name was Nancy and she was studying to be a nurse.

Nancy said the party seemed pretty dull to her. Nobody wanted to do anything, she said, but eat and drink and smoke dope, which was corny. Or stand around and pose and make silly talk. There was nobody "alive," she said. *"Nothing* is happening."

I couldn't help but ask Nancy what was wrong with dope and booze and music and sex.

"Easy for you to say," she said. "What about the rest of us?"

What about them, I said.

"Like me," she said.

What about her, I asked, in all seriousness.

"Look, I've been here maybe three or four hours,

right?" she said. "And there are, maybe, fifty or a hundred guys around, fair? Fifty or a hundred?"

O.K., I said.

"Well, I must have asked at least half of them to come have some fun with me, and not one has taken me up on it," said Nancy.

Me and Shake asked about the same time what Nancy had wanted those chaps to do.

"Just something that would please *me,* that's all," she said.

Shake said he didn't see how that ought to be a problem at all. I didn't, either.

I do remember at this point that Barbara Jane was smiling at us and saying, "Boy, you guys are dumb."

Nancy went on, "Nobody knows where it's at. Nobody."

Shake said, "I can see part of it."

Nancy scoffed and said that figured. We were just like all the others. Selfish. Crude. Insensitive. Unimaginative.

She looked at us and said, "Don't you know what's *fun* for a woman? Look, I'll tell you. Have you been up to the master bedroom?"

We said yeah.

"Have you seen the bathroom off of it?" she said.

We said yeah.

"The thing that would *most* turn me on," she said, "would be to get naked and stretch out in that marble tub and have six guys come in and do the number."

Could she be a little more explicit, Shake said.

"Christ," she said. "The world is really a goner. I'll

spell it out, O.K.? Look, I want to get in that marble tub and simply stretch out and let six guys piss on me. What else?"

Barbara Jane busted up and clapped her hands like a gospel singer and did a kind of little old spook-rhythm dance step.

"All right," Barb said.

Me and Shake looked at Nancy. I guess I was thinking what a shame it was to see that gold-medal body wasted.

Shake finally said, "I think we can turn this party around for you if we can find a friend of ours here named T. J. Lambert."

I just had to run off to the phone there for a minute. It was that Pulitzer prize-winning journalist Jim Tom Pinch who said he wanted to know how I felt and what was going through my mind on the morning of the big game.

"I was only trying to remember what color the dog-ass Jets wear," I said. "Don't they wear green?"

Jim Tom said he thought so.

"I believe that's Baylor's color, too, isn't it?" I said.

Jim Tom said it was last week.

"Well," I said, "how in the hell can anybody expect Old Twenty-three to get worked up over a team that wears the same goddamn color as Baylor?"

Jim Tom Pinch said I sure sounded like I got a lot of rest last night.

"Hey, Stud," he said. "Can't you get somebody around there to draw you a warm tub of Visine?"

I asked Jim Tom how it was going in Fort Worth with Crazy Iris and the Port Lavaca Sandcrabs and the lovely and charming Earlene Padgett.

"I'm more concerned about the book," Jim Tom said. "Have you got lots of stuff on tape?"

I said I was the most prolific mother he'd come across since Big-un Darley.

"How's the detail?" he asked. "Got lots of insights?"

I said that I had paid a particular mind to detail. That I had made absolutely certain that whenever I had a young Scotch and water it was either J&B or White Label.

"Paschal win big in last night's semi-final against the Corbett Comets. Astronaut Jones got thirty-two wearing dark glasses with a bandana tied around his head," Jim Tom said.

I asked who Paschal played tonight.

"Paschal plays Astronaut Jones. Jones plays the Port Lavaca Sandcrabs, who beat the Itasca Wampus Cats like they were fags," Jim Tom said.

Paschal got a chance, I wondered.

"About as much chance as they'd have against Africa," Jim Tom said. "Port Lavaca took the precaution of bringing along some seven-foot Mau Maus."

No chance, I said. Right?

"Did a one-legged man ever win an ass-kickin' contest?" Jim Tom said.

My collaborator said his home life was going along pretty smooth. Earlene had only broken a clock radio lately, throwing it at him, and broken a window pane in the bedroom, throwing a jar of cold cream at him.

"Sounds like you might have been seen in the company of Crazy Iris," I said. "I don't think you ought to go on those midday picnics down there in Forest Park where everybody in the world can drive by."

Jim Tom said that what happened was, he'd been with Crazy Iris and got home at four in the morning, drunk, and that Earlene had got up ahead of him and found his underwear stuck in the pocket of his sports coat.

I asked what his explanation had been.

"I said they weren't mine and I didn't understand the question," Jim Tom said.

"Well," I said, "that certainly would have satisfied me if I'd been your wife."

Jim Tom said, "Stud, don't let anybody ever tell you that marriage isn't the greatest thing there is. By God, it beats being blind and crippled any time."

I said I had to go hold my head. Besides that, I was writing on a book. And, oh, yeah, I had a game to play.

"Keep in mind that it's a whole lot better book if you studs win that game," said Jim Tom.

Glad he reminded me, I said.

"You think you'll just bring all the tapes down here or something after the game?" he asked.

"Not immediately after," I said. "But eventually."

"Then you're definitely coming down to Fort Worth?" he said.

"After I rest," I said. "I got some things to do and some places to go, but I'll get down there and we can go over everything and you can type it up and we'll get it to the publishers in time for it to come out next season."

Jim Tom said, "By the way, did some goofy woman interview you out there?"

I said yeah.

"She called me and interviewed me, too," Jim Tom said. "Sounded like some kind of semi-intellectual or something."

"She *thought*," I said.

"What's that for?" Jim Tom said.

"I don't know," I said. "Some fuckin' women's magazine. I gave her a lot of shit."

Jim Tom said, "Did she ask if you ever had any bestial tendencies off the field?"

I said, "Aw, she wanted to know what went through my mind when I took a handoff and what sign I was born under and what I thought about the *condition* of the athlete's mind. That kind of shit."

Jim Tom said, "I think she might be well known around New York. In those literary circles and so forth."

"She was a cunt," I said. "I met her in the Polo Lounge over at the Beverly Hills and she had a cup of tea and said hello to a whole bunch of hebes with tans."

"Was her name Cynthia Harnett?" Jim Tom asked.

"Maybe," I said.

"Hard-hitter," Jim Tom said.

"Just a Stove with a lot of lip," I said.

"Big timer," he said. "Books and everything. Hope you came off O.K."

I said, "Well, she did seem a little disappointed that I wasn't more impressed with her. She seemed to throw out a lot of first names of guys that I wouldn't have known their *last* names. She kept saying she didn't know anything about sports. I think she said something about sports being the intellectual enema of Western Man."

Jim Tom said, "So you fucked her, right?"

I laughed.

"No, I just breathed heavy and looked off a lot and acted weary and concerned about the ball game," I said. "She felt my arm once, though, so I guess that was an indicator."

Jim Tom said he had to go rewrite some of Big-un Darley's headlines and I said I still had to hold my head. He said good luck in the game and I said we needed thirty-five points more than luck.

To get back to the party, we finally found Elroy under a tree with his guitar in the middle of a runaway monologue.

"And I say to you again, friends, that it's entirely possible for a man to experience an orgasm with his eyes open despite the overwhelming evidence to the contrary," Elroy was saying.

"Now you take these two volunteer couples that have just joined us," he said. "I've asked these kind people to be here tonight at their own expense to prove my point.

"I'd like for you to meet Mr. and Mrs. Harless Wilburn from Boise, Idaho, on my left, and Mr. and Mrs. Pervis MacAdoo from Hiroshima, New Mexico, on my right," Elroy said.

"No applause, please, until they've finished the demonstration," he said. "Too many things in this world go easily rewarded. But that's another story. Maybe not. Maybe it's part of this one. We'll see."

Elroy played a chord on his guitar and said, "Now, then, Mr. and Mrs. Wilburn and Mr. and Mrs. Mac-Adoo, before you demonstrate the all-important warming-up process, I'd like to explain to the audience a little something about how important food is to being able to have an orgasm with your eyes open."

"A proper diet might be the most important thing of all." Shake grinned.

Elroy said, "Would you care to rephrase that?"

"Not at the time being," said Shake.

"May I continue?" said Elroy.

"Only if you want to," Shake said.

"I thought you'd see it my way," said Elroy. "I certainly thought somebody would. I knew it probably wouldn't be the Texas Rangers or the FBI, but I thought somebody would."

Shake said, "Your well-taken point before you were interrupted, sir, was food."

Elroy said, "Yes, food. And about goddamn time, too. Where in the hell are all the pork chops and where's the biscuits?"

Barbara Jane held up her hand.

"Who's that?" said Elroy. "Is that Mrs. MacAdoo with her hand up? You're a pretty thing, Mrs. MacAdoo. Ever fool around?"

Barb said, "Sir, I was wondering if you wanted us to demonstrate the warming-up process with or without props?"

Elroy took an inhale of a pregnant blue Winston and strummed a chord on his guitar.

"That all depends on what the props are," he said. "Props differ around the country. In some cities I lecture in, barbed wire is considered a prop. In other cities, barbed wire is only considered to be wire, with barbed on it."

Barbara Jane said, "Yes, I think we've all had the same basic experience. It's the same thing you find with thirteen-year-old nymphomaniacs."

"Not quite," said Elroy. "With thirteen-year-old nymphomaniacs, you find many, many more men who can't stand up straight. That's one of the myths of thirteen-year-old nymphomaniacs."

Barbara Jane said, "Would you care to elaborate, sir?"

Elroy said, "Not in the least. I'd be most happy to elaborate because I think this subject is grossly overlooked in most of our classrooms today. It's a subject that America has been silently brooding over far too long, and it's groups like this one, which are forming all over the country, that will help to educate the broader pockets of misunderstanding that you find in the Midwest, the North, the East and parts of Louisiana. Thirteen-year-old nymphomaniacs ought to be eat more."

He said, "Now then. What exactly was my original subject?"

"Food." Shake laughed.

"Little girls," said Barbara Jane.

"Swallow 'em both," said Elroy.

I'm afraid that as we all sat there on the grass some

of those homemade cigarettes made the rounds.

We partook of some, I'll have to confess. Mainly, I believe, because we felt they would enhance the flavor of the barbecued ribs. It turned out that Elroy didn't have any steaks. Not by the time we got there, anyhow. Somebody said the debutantes ate them all, or stole them for their kids and dogs.

Incidentally, I only smoke that trash every now and then. Dope, I mean. Not kids and dogs.

I would like for the youth of America to understand that old Billy Clyde prefers a young Scotch any old time to what you call your joints, although I think joints are fairly harmless and won't make you any kind of major league A-dict like the State of Texas says.

Of course at Elroy's party I had both. What happened was, I started out on a young Scotch and decided I hadn't ought to drink so much before a game. Seeing as how it was a party, however, I wanted to enjoy myself to take my mind off the game. So I went to joints. But that only made me hungry and I didn't want to log up on too many ribs, so I went back to Scotch to keep from eating. And by that time, I was fuckin' high schooled. So I just drank myself into a street rummy, which is how I am now with my hang-over.

If a stranger walks through the living room in a minute, I'll try to borrow a quarter and go downstairs and lay down on the curb. Shit, I feel awful.

But back to the party.

I guess we sat around with Elroy under the tree with those other folks for another hour or so before it got so rowdy, and these curious things happened that nobody might believe.

I think it was after quite a while, and all of us had started to get tired of listening to Elroy, that this photographer came up.

Elroy said he wanted a photographer there to take some pictures for his den, and maybe something for an album jacket.

Anyhow we were all still sitting there on the lawn and jabbering and giggling when we noticed that one of the supposedly straight girls at the party—meaning a non-debutante or somebody without one of Elroy's T-shirts on—had gone over to pose for the photographer.

She was one of the Indian princesses who was wearing a headband and a lot of suede stuff with fringe on it. Good-looking sumbitch. Black hair. Kind of tiny. Smart-ass looking. Semi-mean.

Anyhow, the next thing we knew the Indian princess had slipped out of all but her hip-grabbing suede pants and her headband. Which meant that she was displaying her lungs for the photographer and smiling.

Apparently she was drunk or stoned. What she would do, anyway, was hold her suede top in front of her lungs and then she would drop it down and reveal her lungs to the crowd—and the photographer—like it was a big deal for anybody to see her lungs.

A lot of dumb-asses gathered around and applauded and shouted when the Indian princess dropped the top of her suede deal down, and tried to look sultry.

We watched for a few minutes and Barbara Jane, who

by now had jacked her own head around a little, said, "If I could stand up I'd give 'em a better show."

Me and Shake laughed.

Cissy Walford said, "Damn right. Me, too."

Elroy Blunt said, "Yeah, I'm always hearin' that big talk in my travels but nobody ever backs it up."

Barbara Jane said, "Yeah, well, if I could stand up, you'd see, boy."

I said it was a good thing she couldn't.

Elroy said, "What would you do for us, little lady? Would you do your panty hose commercials, or just what?"

"You'd see," said Barb, kind of giggling.

"Damn right," said Cissy. "Barbara and I could outlung that girl, anytime. Did I say that right, Billy? Outlung?"

That was about the best thing I'd ever heard Cissy say.

Elroy said, "Well, I been on six or eight continents, even some nobody knows about. I been to a shrub-judgin' and seen a queer there and I been to a football game in Dalhart. I been to Floyd's Tote-It Grocery in Sumpter and I've stepped across the Main Street of Selma with niggers on it. But I ain't ever seen no New York model show her dandy old lungs in public. And I ain't ever seen a society girlie from Long Island do it. That's somethin' I'd like to see."

He said, "Of course, I don't know about ever-body else."

Barbara Jane said, "If I could stand up, you'd see plenty."

Elroy said, "Maybe we got some volunteers around

here to help these two lovelies get up on their feet. How
'bout it? Anybody else want to look at some new titties?"

Nobody said anything. Just chuckled.

"Oh, well," said Elroy. "It's probably not important.
I guess a society girlie's lungs and a New York model's
lungs are pretty much like everybody's."

Barbara Jane had been lying down on the lawn with
her head propped up on her hand, which was supported
by her elbow. She started trying to sit up.

"I tell you what," said Elroy. "Why don't we just get
old Clyde and old Shake 'Em Up, Shake Loose here to
describe to us what the lungs of these servin' wenches
look like in the shower?"

"Nope," said Barb, struggling up to her feet with a
young Scotch in her hand.

"It's something we really ought to share with the
world at long last," she said. "Right, Cissy?"

Cissy Walford said, "Terribly absolutely. Goddamn
right."

Barbara Jane was wearing a flowered semi-Western
shirt that fit tight and had long sleeves and buttoned up
the front, and she was wearing snug, faded Levi's that
clung to her hips without a belt. Cissy was wearing an
apron, more or less, so far as I could tell, that was covered
with real jewels over a pair of pants that looked like
bikini bottoms, or fit like it. She also had her long
yellow hair tucked up underneath a head scarf and she
had on great big funny-shaped dark glasses and rawhide
boots that came up to her knees.

As Barbara Jane got up to her feet she said, "Ha!"

Cissy said, "How'd you do that?"

"Just another of my many tricks," said Barb.

Shake and me exchanged some kind of look which didn't mean much except wonderment about how far our women folk intended to carry on their joke.

Barbara Jane stuck her hand in her mouth and whistled two or three times, pretty loud, like men do, as if she was calling a New York taxi or a little niece who'd pissed her off.

She giggled to herself and whistled again, to get the attention of whoever was in range.

"Fifties and hundreds over here," Barb said, looking down at me and Shake to see if we appreciated her wit. Fifties and hundreds over here is what Burt Danby is known to say when he takes a client into an action bar in New York and is looking for hooks.

Some people began to meander over to where we were at. Those who didn't mind leaving other parts of the lawn where the rock combos were playing. And those who didn't mind leaving the Indian princess, who had started talking to a couple of Elroy's guests who wore suits and drank beer.

"Help me up," Cissy said.

I said, Why?

"Because I have to take off my clothes," she said, seriously.

That's right, I said. I forgot.

Cissy got up with my help and stood next to Barb with her hands folded behind her back and looking out across the yard at nothing in particular, I think.

Barbara Jane said, "I would like everyone's very close attention because it's show time."

Elroy played two or three chords on his guitar.

"What the show consists of," said Barb, "is mostly just Miss Earthquake and Miss Volcano, who happen to be smashed, trying to slip out of their duds."

Barb said, "I, of course, am Miss Earthquake. You probably all guessed that. At least you should have. I don't actually give a shit. Anyhow, this over here is Miss Volcano. Say hello, Miss Volcano."

Cissy Walford smiled and waved at everybody.

Barb said, "Now before we start, I want to know who stole my drink?"

Elroy strummed a chord on his guitar.

Shake handed Barb her young Scotch.

"You did that very nicely," Barb said, glancing down at Shake Tiller. "Remind me to put in a good word for you with Obert Tatum."

Barb took a sip of her drink.

"Now then," she said. "if somebody will hold my drink, I will attempt to unbutton my shirt. Thank you, Miss Volcano. That was a kind gesture on your part."

Barbara Jane started unbuttoning her shirt while Cissy held her drink.

Barb got her shirt unbuttoned and turned her back to everybody and slipped it off, and then turned back around holding her shirt up in front of her chest like the Indian princess did with her suede deal.

Then she pitched her shirt down to Shake.

Elroy Blunt strummed a chorus of "Flip Top Heart" and a number of people applauded. Barb's lungs, not Elroy's song.

Barbara Jane took her drink back from Cissy and reached down and captured a fresh cigarette from Shake, a straight Winston. She drew on it and sipped her drink, and then just stood there with her arms at her sides, holding the drink by the rim of the glass, and displaying her major league lungs. And looking casual.

If I hadn't known Barb and didn't understand the humor she was attaching to the whole thing, I would have thought she was being about half-brazen.

I suppose I should say that Barbara Jane's lungs are not exactly gigantic but are closer to what most men might think of as being semi-perfect.

They are certainly very large, but they are also firm and nicely shaped, and they have the good nips. Which is to say that Barb's nips are not big and dark but sort of rose-tinted and they perfectly set off her plenty large, nicely shaped lungs like a gold money clip can set off a roll of green whip-out.

I think most everybody who ever got to see them would agree with me that if there are any lungs to be found that you would classify as ideal, they would be Barbara Jane's.

After she had stood there smoking and drinking for a minute or two, she said:

"This isn't all the show, folks."

She said, "I would venture a guess that if there's anything all of us hate in this world—all of us humans, I mean—it's to come upon a pair of really *great* tits like these and not have a really *nifty* cunt to go along with them. Right?"

Elroy Blunt shouted something that sounded like whooo-ha.

And there was assorted applause from all around, of course.

Shake looked up at Barbara Jane and said, "You'll surely never find me around one without the other."

"Precisely," said Barb. Then she added:

"As luck would have it, it just so happens that I believe I've got one of those with me here tonight."

She started to wriggle out of her faded Levi's.

"It might not be the best you've ever seen," she said. "But, well. Some people say it smells better than a soft new Italian loafer. And some people say it tastes better than strawberry shortcake. That's what some people say."

Barb then started balancing on one foot, struggling with her Levi's, and giggling, with her cigarette between her teeth.

"What her wool actually is," said Shake to the crowd, "is semi-tough."

"Oh, it's a worker, all right," Barb laughed, kind of loud. "What the hell do you expect from Miss Earthquake? A can of Campbell's Chunky Beef?"

Barbara Jane balanced on one foot and got one leg out of her Levi's, and then she stood on the other foot and got the other leg out, holding her cigarette between her teeth, with her streaked butterscotch hair tossed all around, partly covering her face, flowing and dangling.

"Get on after it," she said to herself, finishing up.

And there she was in all of her smooth, curvy, tanned, elegant and total naked glory, seeing as how she had a habit of not wearing any underpanties, anyhow.

"Did it!" she said.

Everybody hollered and clapped and whistled.

Elroy stared at Barb and then leaned quietly over to Shake Tiller and stuck out his hand. "Son," he said. "Tell the truth. It ain't better than fried chicken, is it?"

Shake looked solemnly at Elroy, clasping his hand, and said:

"I got to be dead honest, Roy."

And Elroy said yeah, lay it on him.

Shake said slowly, "For a Lesbian who gave up the only real love she ever knew—Sister Francis at Our Lady of Victory—and for a person who can't make it any more with nothing but an electric toothbrush, she's the finest I've ever had."

Elroy whooo-haaad again, and looked back at Barbara Jane.

She was doing some fashion model poses, and the photographer was taking so many flashbulb pictures of her, you would have thought Barbara Jane was raising the flag on Iwo fuckin' Jima or something.

Guys in the crowd, which was getting bigger, started hollering some of the predictable things, like, "When's that old ground gonna crack open there, Miss Earthquake," and, "Make mine a double-dip banana nut," and "Show us your lava flow."

Barbara Jane stopped posing presently and proceeded

to turn Cissy Walford around and begin unfastening whatever it was that held up Cissy's jeweled apron. "Let's get with it, Miss Volcano," said Barb.

The apron came off and Cissy kind of blush-giggled and hid her lungs with her arms. She said to Barb, "Your body is just so incredible, I feel actually silly even *standing* here."

Barb then took Cissy's scarf off her head, letting Cissy's long yellow hair tumble down on her shoulders and her back where it belonged.

Barb then unsnapped something at Cissy's hips and began to yank down her pants, or whatever was supposed to be the rest of her outfit. Cissy was wearing white lace underpanties, bikini types, and Barbara started peeling those down.

Barb brought them down past Cissy's dark golden wool—it's about the color of a game ball, I'd say—and then started pulling them over Cissy's rawhide boots.

Barbara Jane stopped for a minute and burst out laughing and looked over at me and Shake.

"Jesus," she said. "I'm getting horny."

Pretty soon, Cissy was as bare as Barbara Jane, except for the rawhide boots, which stayed on. That seemed to be O.K. with everyone. And her big dark glasses, which was O.K., too, I presume.

So there was Miss Volcano in all of her own physical glory, which is pretty damn glorious, as I've said before.

While everybody was whistling and clapping and hollering again, and while the photographer was flashing away and sweating like a middle guard, Elroy jumped

out and got between our two women folk and put his
arms around their high waists. Way around and upward,
I noticed, so he could catch a feel of a delectable lung
resting on each of his forearms. One of Barb's and one of
Cissy's.

Elroy had one of those homemade cigarettes in his
mouth and his big old floppy-brimmed suede hat on.

"Goddamned if this ain't the jacket on my next album," Elroy said.

"I'm gonna write me some songs about the lungs and
wool of some little old society girlies, and how it's just
the nicest thing in the world, and how it's really what the
niggers have been after all along," he said.

Right about here, the scene sort of began to deteriorate
and lose some impact because a lot of other girls suddenly turned up naked.

They were Elroy's hostesses who had taken off their
T-shirts and pitched them up in the air in such abundance
it looked to me like a bunch of Annapolis cadets had
thrown their white caps in the sky because Navy had
fuckin' scored on Army.

One of the rock bands came over and whipped it up,
so a lot of people started dancing on the lawn, naked
and otherwise.

A couple of fags danced with Barbara Jane and Cissy,
and kept looking off into the night, or studying their own
moves, instead of looking at Barb and Cissy, where they
should have been looking. Fags are fags, I guess.

For quite a while it was a sight that can only be
described as quadruple unreal, with all of that naked

wool moving around in the night to some fairly good spook music.

I felt like a couple of other fags got the wrong idea about the whole thing because they slipped out of their duds, too. And somehow I didn't get the notion that too many people at the party gave a fuck about seeing naked fags who weren't built any better than a first-down chain.

Besides that, they looked in their faces like they were dying of something awful.

Shake and me and Elroy just sat there on the lawn and tried to watch all of it and pick out who we might want to invite to some future all-skate. Little old Linda the Stew was certainly a must, we decided, after she had danced by and stopped and had another brief chat with us.

"Groovy party," she said to Elroy as she stood there naked with her tough little old white body and her big blue eyes. She was puffing on a joint.

"Hey, I want to ask all of you something," she said. "What's your favorite audible?"

"In a game or in bed?" Shake said.

Linda the Stew said, "In bed of course. You know. Like when you're really jivin'. Heard any good audibles lately?"

We all thought about it for a minute or so.

Elroy said, "I think I heard, 'Fuck me, fuck me, fuck me,' not so long ago."

"Me, too," I nodded, seriously.

Linda the Stew said, "Oh, you hear that all the time. That's no good. 'I want all your come,' isn't bad. I heard that about a week ago from my roommate Kathy when we were doing a couple of pros from the LA Open."

I suppose we all thought about that for a while. I know I did.

Shake said, "How about, 'I know you won't believe this but I got a cramp in my leg'?"

Linda the Stew laughed appreciatively.

She said, "The really best ones are the really slimy ones, I think. Like, 'Oh, God, my God, put two fingers in each.' Or, 'Let me taste my own.' Those are neat."

"You've got some good audibles," I said.

Linda the Stew said, "Want to hear my all-time favorite?"

We didn't have to take a vote on it.

Linda the Stew said, "My all-time favorite is my own, and I just sort of said it not too long ago right after I'd caught a really neat load. I looked up at this guy and I said, 'I wonder who found out first that getting a mouth full of this was really fun?' "

Elroy got up right after that and went off with Linda the Stew toward the house, and Shake and me made it a definite point to memorize that five four two, eight six three one, for a future reference.

And we discussed a few more audibles.

We decided that some of the funnier ones were:

"Is Martha Nell Burch a real person or what?"

And—

"Where did you say you skied?"

And—

"Well, what'll we do after I do that?"

I think it was about right then, while Shake and me

were still sitting there on the lawn, and Barbara Jane and
Cissy were still up dancing naked with the fags, that we
heard this familiar noise which cut right through the
spook music.

It was T. J. Lambert who had slipped up on our blind
side and cut one that would have even made Donna Lou
stagger, even though she's used to it. He cut one that
surely must have been the color of a Hawaiian sunset.

And I've got to say that even though the young Scotch
and the anti-God cigarettes had me on third-and-long, I
was utterly shocked—shocked all to shit—at who T. J.
had with him.

T. J. had with him none other than Dreamer Tatum
and Boyce Cayce of the dog-ass Jets.

"Lookie here at a couple of tootie fruities I done
found me," said T. J. pointing at Dreamer and Boyce.

"I found 'em over at Tommy's puttin' some cheeseburgers in their bellies after they been to a movie," T. J.
said. "I told 'em I thought I knew where they could lick
theyselves some wool, so here we are. By God, there's
some here, too, ain't they?"

T. J. had already put away about forty-five beers, I
estimated.

Me and Shake stood up and shook hands with Dreamer
and Boyce and exchanged hidys.

Dreamer was wearing a leather and velvet suit and
high-heeled, candy-striped shoes, and a ruffled shirt with
a stand-up collar on it that came halfway up the back of
his head.

Dreamer has a big old thick head of spook hair, a
mustache, a thin beard that goes all the way around his

face. And he was wearing dark glasses.

Dreamer was also wearing a joint in his hand, and he was semi-stoned.

"I like your style, Billy," said Dreamer, soft and cool. "This here's some kind of mess, baby."

Then he looked around the yard and said to himself, "Tell this nigger somethin' *about* it."

I didn't think Boyce Cayce was drunk or stoned either one. In fact, he was drinking a Coke in a bottle, and he looked sort of unimpressed with the party as he stood there in his knit shirt and his pants which had cuffs on them. Well, that's what I thought at first, until I realized that Boyce Cayce's bottle of Coke also had a good deal of Jack Daniels in it.

Boyce Cayce was just so drunk he couldn't say much. He's from Georgia, anyhow.

There wasn't much we could chat about, except the fact that we sure hoped Commissioner Cameron wasn't at the party somewhere to see us all together.

Commissioner Cameron doesn't care so much about what we do as long as nobody can see it.

It's sort of against the rules for studs from opposing teams to get together the evening before a ball game. The theory behind the rule is that studs might get together and decide what the score of the game ought to be. And then somebody will call up a fellow like Uncle Kenneth, let's say, and bet four or five large on it, and then the game will happen to turn out like the studs talked about it beforehand.

At least Commissioner Cameron says this is what

people in public will think if they see some studs together in a public place before a game.

But what people think is not so accurate. I want to go
on record as saying that I have never known of a fixed
game, although I have heard rumors.

For instance Boyce Cayce is supposed to have set a
record of going half a season once without completing a
screen pass, but I think that's when he had a sore shoulder. With the Rams.

And I can remember hearing about all the heat Boyce
received when he was with the Oilers that time they made
the playoffs and got beat in sudden death by the Chiefs.

Boyce got criticized for electing to kick rather than receive after he won the coin flip. It's who scores first in
sudden death, of course. And then he got even more
blame for missing three straight open receivers when it
would have moved the Oilers into field goal range.

And even though a sports writer on the sideline
claimed he overheard Boyce say something incriminating
after the loss, that's just the writer's word against Boyce's,
as far as I'm concerned. The writer claimed he heard
Boyce say, "Hey, ho, who won the dough, eh, gang?"

You can just take all this for whatever you think gossip
is worth. Personally, I've never known a ball player to
lay down unless he was tired. I look at it this way, anyhow. If eight out of every ten NFL games are honest,
that's a hell of a lot better percentage than you can get
in that pro fucking basketball.

Who I worry about, mainly, in pro football are the
zebras. The officials. They do a good job, by and large,

but they could call holding on any play, and occasionally they sure choose some funny times. Once last season, for example, we had *defensive* holding strapped on us after Dallas missed a field goal. How can you defensive hold on a field goal?

They called it on T. J. Lambert and he turned so hot he almost got himself banned from the sport for life. He picked up the official who threw the flag, dangled him by his ankles, and said, "I'm gonna shake this fuckin' zebra til the fix money comes out his wop neck."

Well, anyhow. There we all were at Elroy's party, sort of embarrassed to be in each other's company.

Barbara Jane and Cissy noticed we had some strange company, so they quit dancing and came over and put their clothes on quickly and sat down on the grass.

Barb recognized Dreamer and Boyce immediately and straightened up somewhat. It was a little awkward, however, when I introduced them to Cissy Walford and she said, "Aren't you the dog-asses?"

Dreamer couldn't talk much for gazing around at several of Elroy's hostesses who were still dancing naked. Neither could Boyce Cayce.

T. J. cut one again that was absolute thunder, and in fact, it put him to sleep, sprawled out on the lawn, it was such a good one.

Boyce Cayce said, "He don't do that when he's rushin' the passer, does he?"

Shake and Dreamer, after a while, did a little playful sparring with each other about the game.

"You gonna play the wide field, Dreamer?" Shake asked him. "Even when old Eighty-eight's into the side line?"

Dreamer smiled and said, "I think I'll just be right around the football, baby. Wherever that is."

Shake said, "I'm feelin' fast, Dreamer. Feelin' fast."

And Dreamer said, "Runnin' fast ain't catchin' nothin', is it, baby?"

Shake said, "Catching a ball is where I'm at, though."

Dreamer said, "Catchin' a ball is who catches it first. Ain't that right now, baby?"

They laughed together, sort of. And Barbara Jane changed the conversation.

She said, "Dreamer, why don't you scoop up one of these little dandies around here and take her out to Disneyland and show her some of the rides?"

I said there was one called Linda he might be interested in. I said she was probably busy right now, but she seemed like the type who never particularly got tired, and she surely did think highly of athletes.

Boyce Cayce wiped his mouth off and said:

"I see one over there playin' a zone but I think I can hit her in the seams."

I frankly don't want to say much about what happened next.

All I will reveal is that Elroy and Linda came back outdoors and Elroy brought one of his footballs he had stuffed with dope. At first, we all just pitched it back and forth, sitting there on the lawn.

Then it was that crazy Elroy who got the brilliant idea

that we ought to divide up sides and play a game of two-below touch.

Since T. J. Lambert was asleep from his All-Pro fart, Elroy said the sides could be perfectly even. Me and Shake on one team, he said, and Dreamer and Boyce on the other. Giants against the Jets. Barbara Jane and Cissy on our side, and Linda the Stew along with some little old nameless debutante on the other. Two fags on our side. Two fags on their side. Elroy on our side, since he was a Giant fan. And Nancy the Nurse on their side.

Nancy the Nurse had reappeared from somewhere and she agreed to take part in the game if we would promise to wake up T. J. later so he could go up to that marble bathtub with her.

Most everybody at the party gathered around to watch the game, but before it started, Elroy announced that it was "the first annual pre-Super Bowl drunk-stoned two-below game, bringing together the gentlemanly, suave New York Giants and the fuck-head New York Jets."

Well, we played for a while. But it wasn't much of a contest since we let the fags be the passers and the receivers while me and Shake and Dreamer and Boyce just groveled around on the ground, play-blocking and falling down a lot, and ruining our clothes, and laughing and grunting and piling on each other while the fags tried in earnest to injure the girls.

We made up some truly brilliant plays, though.

One of them was Tits Go Long.

Another one was Piss to Daylight. That was for Nancy.

I think the Jets won, if you're truly interested in the outcome.

It was mainly because Linda the Stew occupied the better part of our defense—like me and Shake and Elroy —when she ran a pass route. We sure did commit some interference.

The party, by the way, is still in progress for some, even as I'm still sitting here in the living room of our palatial suite on Super Bowl morning looking at what's now left of my various remedies for headaches and remorse.

We all came home after the Super Bowl touch game, which sort of straightened out our heads. I guess I've slept about two hours.

I hope T. J. got home. We made Nancy the Nurse promise to see that he got here after he woke up and went and pissed on her all he could in the marble bathtub. When T. J. doesn't get home until daylight, Donna Lou has a tendency to worry. Of course, that's if Donna Lou's home by then.

Boyce Cayce left the party with a fairly shopworn debutante who said she lived in the Valley and would have enough money pretty soon to go straight and open up her own beauty parlor.

Dreamer Tatum left with Linda the Stew, as you might have suspected. Linda was very excited about it. She said that if she lived to be thirty or even thirty-five, she would probably never have another night when she got to have it popped in her by a famous recording artist and a famous cornerback.

Elroy told Dreamer, "You better be an All-Pro in the rack, son, because you done got hold of yourself a po-ran-ah fish."

I hope filthy little Linda has worn Dreamer's ass full out by now. I really hope so.

And I guess with that thought in mind, this is as good a time as any to say that the hour of truth has finally arrived for Billy Clyde.

It's time for me to cut the bullshit and go get ready to do the thing I've been talking about all week, which is knock the dicks off the dog-ass Jets.

Yes, sir, it's time for old Billy Clyde to go get taped and go eat the team breakfast and ride out to the Los Angeles Coliseum on this beautiful Sunday in January and hook it up with my New York Giant pals and kick the pure zebra shit out of those rotten, low-life, low-rent, dog-ass motherfuckers.

Pardon the language but my game-face is some kind of *on*.

You won't be hearing from me tonight. Or even tomorrow morning. Or even for a few days, maybe even a week or two.

Win or lose in a few more hours (and I shouldn't even question it), old Billy Clyde tonight, when he's beat up and sore and whip-dog tired and mentally wrung out from the game, is gonna get himself ass-deep in so much young Scotch that this palatial suite of ours better be able to float.

Win or lose (and I don't know why I keep saying that), this is the end of the season and that means me

and Shake are going off on our annual round trip to
Dissipate City.

Our actual plans are as follows:

Marvin (Shake) Tiller has to fly back to New York
early Monday morning to be on a couple of TV shows
that night. He says he's got some other business around
town that'll take him two or three more days, although I
can't imagine what it is. Anyhow, Shake's going back
Monday for TV, mainly, and Cissy Walford says she'll
fly back with him because she needs to see her parents
for a few hours to let them know she's alive and not
pregnant.

I'm staying here while Shake and Cissy do all that.

I'm staying here to do nothing for two or three days
but drink and sleep and maybe do me a Linda and a
Sandi. Barbara Jane is staying out here, too, mainly on
business but partly to keep me company, if I want any.

What will happen toward the end of the week is that
all four of us are going to meet in a place where me and
Shake and Barbara Jane have been going every year for
about the last three years at the end of the season.

Every year the three of us—plus the young wool of
my choice—wind up at this place in the Hawaiian Islands. For about two or three weeks over there we just
lay in the sun and eat and sleep and drink and smoke
and fuck and moan a lot.

There is nothing like it after a hard season.

The place we always go to is on Kauai, and it is hidden
away from everything but semi-paradise. It doesn't have
a telephone or a television or a newspaper or any ass

holes around. All it has is an ocean, a beach, a mountain, a valley, some lagoons, some waterfalls and no police that I've ever seen.

Anyhow, this is where you'll be hearing from old Billy Clyde next.

The game will be some kind of history by then. I will have read about it in the papers and in *Sports Illustrated* and seen some pictures of it on television before I leave.

I will also have thought about it and replayed it a few thousand times. With myself and with Shake Tiller. I will probably have heard about it from Barbara Jane and Cissy, too, and since they are sitting in the Coliseum today with Big Ed and Big Barb and Elroy and Burt Danby, I'm sure I'll learn what those great critics thought about it.

Anyhow, I will be over there in semi-paradise with my little old tape recorder and my little old wool—and my two good friends for a lifetime—when I get around to telling you my side of what happened in the Super Bowl.

So has everybody got that straight? You too, Jim Tom?

Good.

Now I got to get after it. Anybody who wants to wish me luck can feel perfectly free to do so, and anybody who don't want to wish me luck can jump up an armadillo's ass.

This is Billy Clyde Puckett, number twenty-three, the captain of the New York Giants, the humminist sumbitch that ever carried a football, going off to do a day's work.

And what I'd like to say to the world right now is fuck those lousy, shit-heel, piss-turd, nigger-wop, rat-cunt, baby-sucking, jew-Aggie, spick-cock, dog-ass Jets.

Fuck 'em, goddamn it. I mean *fuck 'em.*

Just, uh, edit that any way you see fit, Jim Tom.

When I think of all the men you must have killed
With those looks that you go lookin' at 'em with,
When I think of all the good homes that you've broke
With those promises you've whispered and you've spoke,
I wonder why the Lord has gone and willed
That a Hard-hittin' Woman ain't no myth.

When I think of all the victims that you've known,
And I think of all that whisky, love and mirth,
All I hear is lonely beggin' and some cryin'
For the wives they left behind 'em with their lyin'
And I wonder why the Lord has gone and sown
A Hard-hittin' Woman on this earth.

Hard-hittin' Woman, let me be.
Hard-hittin' Woman, it's just me.
Take your body from my kind,
Take your sweet words from our wine.
Hit it hard, Hard-hittin' Woman,
Get on gone.
Get on gone, Hard-hittin' Woman,
From my mind.

Now you've gone and wrecked another life; guess who?
I'm drunk, divorced, been fired, and headed down.

But I can't forget those pleasures I went stealin'
From an evil thing that looked and loved with feelin'
And I wonder if the Lord would make a few—
A few more Hard-hittin' Women for this town.

Oh yeah, a few more Hard-hittin' Women for this town.

That was a duet just then. All that nice harmony.

That was Barbi Doll Bookman and B. C. Puckett, with accompaniment by Barbi Doll Bookman on her guitar, singing "Hard-hittin' Woman," which is still in your top sixty on the country music parade.

This program is being brought to you from the semi-deserted beach of Lihililo in beautiful downtown Hanalei Bay, which is world-famous for the number of times that Ching Yung's trading post, bank, filling station and grocery store runs out of ice cream.

Excuse us a minute while we try another chorus. We're getting about half-good at it.

I didn't quite get back in sixty seconds, did I?

Well, time doesn't mean much out here in the islands when you don't have a whole lot to do. We've been here for almost three weeks now, and on a number of occasions I've thought about getting back to the book. But somehow I managed to get diverted by a waterfall or a lagoon or some kind of urge to snorkel.

Out here in semi-paradise we don't worry a great deal about wars or strikes or writing books.

It hasn't been my usual end-of-the-season vacation by a

long shot, and there are a couple of very good reasons. One reason is Shake Tiller. And the other reason is Cissy Walford.

They never did show up, is what happened.

Barbara Jane and I got here on a Thursday, four days after the Super Bowl, just as planned. And it was the following day, Friday, when I got this message from the mainland at Ching Yung's store. I got a message there to call the lovely Miss Cissy Walford in Manhasset, Long Island, which is where her parents live.

I called her. And to make a long story short, since it pisses me off to think about it, Cissy Walford said she wasn't going to come out here because she had a wonderful opportunity to go to Italy with Boke Kellum and have a small part in a movie he was going to make over there.

She said she really would like to be in the movies, as I should have known, and that this could be her big break.

I reminded her that Boke Kellum was a limp wrist. But she said she knew that, of course, and it didn't matter because he was so nice and attentive and gentle and he knew so many big movie stars.

Besides, she said, she never had been to Italy.

I told Cissy she was making me a little bit hot.

She said she really was sorry and that she really had enjoyed my company for the past couple of months but that Boke Kellum had pointed out something to her that she should have realized.

She said he had pointed out to her that she didn't have much of a future hanging around with me because I was only a football player. And on top of that, he told her, it was noticeable to everybody that I was never going to like any girl as much as I liked Barbara Jane Bookman.

I told Cissy to go fuck a lot of wops.

The case of our good buddy Shake Tiller is considerably more interesting.

We didn't think anything about it when Shake wasn't here in semi-paradise on the day we arrived. We figured he'd got drunk or stoned or had run into some bonus wool, and would turn up a day or two late.

But he didn't.

So we finally decided to start calling around, which, I might add, cost me a substantial amount of whip-out on Ching Yung's telephone.

Nobody ever answered at our New York apartment. None of the other Giants, who had scattered all over the country to their homes and mistresses, had heard from him.

Burt Danby said he had seen him once in Clarke's since he got back from the game and that he seemed fine. Burt said Shake was sitting in Clarke's with the owner, Danny, and a few other familiar faces, like a couple of Greek girls and some novelists.

We tried to track down Elroy Blunt but Elroy's agent didn't know where Elroy was and the only number he had for him, currently, was five four two, eight six three one.

We called Linda the Stew and managed to disturb her in the middle of what I suppose was a pretty good audible.

Linda said she hadn't seen Shake Tiller or heard from him, darn the luck. She said Elroy had been there for a while but she had worn him so clean out that he said he had to go to Crockett Springs, to his Grandma's near Nashville, for a rest before his next concert tour.

Linda sort of cackled in laughter and said Elroy told her the title of a new song he was thinking up was "Pussy-Whipped Traveler."

She said she had a top scorer in the NBA there with her right then and we ought to see the hard-on she was looking at.

Barb and I were just about to become concerned enough about Shake to go back to New York and see if our buddy had been stabbed by a spook hooker or kidnapped by the Mastrioni brothers when we got this wire in care of Ching Yung's.

The wire was from Djakarta (I'll trust you to spell that right, Jim Tom) and it said:

Pals. Secret Agent Eighty-eight on tail of evil spies who are attempting to bring physical harm to numbers of heads of state. Not all of them are spades. Clues indicate they are en route to Sumatra but other clues indicate they are traveling toward Morocco. Those places are not close unless somebody has moved them. Am in hot pursuit and might be gone either twenty-four hours or twenty-four years. It depends on how long my masters thesis takes. Eighty-eight loves his pals but he hears of mysterious things in ocean bottoms and on mountain tops and he yearns to know what everybody loses and finds there. The future of mankind lies West but maybe it lies East. Eighty-eight trusts Billy C. to find a loaf of bread for Bookman heiress. There is something on the wind and it smells like grass. Why don't we all meet one day at the varsity picnic? Love. Eighty-eight.

I'm not entirely sure what I think about Shake's wire.

I know there isn't any great trouble that he's got into which me and Barb wouldn't know about. And I'm fairly certain he'll turn up pretty soon, probably right here on Lihililo Beach when I'm involved in telling about the Super Bowl, which neither one of us particularly starred in.

Barbara Jane, however, says there's more in the wire than I care to admit.

In fact, she even went so far yesterday as to say, "I'm afraid we've lost him for a long, long while."

Around me, Barb doesn't act like Shake's absence has torn her up but she keeps that wire laying on the dresser in her bedroom of the little house we've got rented. And she has shown a tendency to do very little but sit around on the lava rocks over here and look off at the ocean as if Shake Tiller might come swimming up from Japan.

That's what she's doing while I'm laying here on the sand with my tape recorder and my six-pack of Primo that I've got iced down.

We've talked about it a lot, of course.

I keep saying our old Buddy is full of nonsense and he'll turn up almost any hour, as stoned as a giraffe, most likely, and eager to delight us with tales of banditry and intrigue. But Barbara Jane says different. She was over here a while ago, digging herself a shallow foxhole in the sand and drinking a beer.

She said she didn't claim to know Shake better than I do but she thought she knew him in a slightly different way. She had an idea that he always talked to her more seriously than he did to me.

"Things never were as uncomplicated for him as they were for us," she said. "It's true, whether you realize that or not."

She pawed at the sand.

"He thinks deeply about things, you know. He really does. He likes to act like he doesn't but he does," she said.

I made a lazy, sighing noise which came out something like, "Ohhhh, eeeee, ahhhh, gawba."

I looked out at a point on Hanalei Bay where the ocean disappears behind a high cliff. A golf course is up on top of that cliff. I idly wondered if a tidal wave would ever come that would be big enough to wash out some low scores.

"Religion," said Barb. "He's always tried to make sense out of religion."

Barb slid into her hole in the sand and propped her head up on a couple of folded towels. She spread her legs out and up, onto the beach. And she talked to the sky.

"Did he ever go into any detail about the time he was

dragged to that fundamentalist church by his grandmother? When he was six or seven? And what he felt?"
she said.

"He laughed," I said. "That would make any sane
person laugh."

Barb said, "Sure he laughed. He had to laugh at some
idiot screaming and threatening people who had to sit in
hard-back chairs in a place with lousy air conditioning."

"God's partial to noise and sweat," I said. "That's what
Shake decided. I guess he was right or we wouldn't have
so many Baptists."

"He used to say that God sure must have had a grudge
against Texas to put so many Baptists down there. Remember those lines?" Barb said.

I said, "It filled him with a real fondness for Baylor."

Neither of us said anything for a minute. I pushed an
empty bottle of Primo into the sand and covered it over.

"Couldn't put the Catholics together, either," Barb
said.

"What'd he say? The Catholics were Baptists in drag?
Something like that. Or the Catholics were Baptists with
their game uniforms on, calling audibles? I don't know,"
she said. "Something heartfelt and sentimental as always."

I smiled to myself.

Barb said, "How could God, he'd say, turn loose a
thing like the Catholics or Baptists, who could give so
many people so much torment and guilt and so many
stupid rules to live by that didn't have anything to do with
love?"

"Still a good question." I yawned. "Is God love or is

God Notre Dame? Help us out, Old Skipper."

Barb said, "I'm telling you it bothers Shake Tiller, luv.
He's still hung up. He truly is."

She was still talking to the sky.

"He has it worked out," I said. "The Old Skipper is
personal. He believes that. If a whole bunch of fools want
to use the church for social or business reasons, and if
they need all that guilt to cleanse themselves for lying
and stealing and fucking somebody else's wife, that's
their own deal. He has his."

Barb said, "But don't you see? He wonders how a real
God could let it come to that. Shake Tiller believes the
world is shit and don't forget it. That's what he thinks.
The world is shit and it doesn't work and his cynicism
helps him cope with it."

She rolled her head over toward me.

"He doesn't *like* feeling that way and he never has,"
she said.

I thought about it for a minute and said, "Well, he's
not going to find the answer to anything over in Su-
fuckin'-matra. That's all I know."

"Home is where the head is, luv," she said. "If I may
quote Shake Tiller on you."

I sat forward and took a swig of beer.

"Look, I know we're not the same person, me and him.
I know he likes things I don't like, and I know he's a lot
more restless," I said. "But how can he go off somewhere without you? I couldn't do that."

Barb didn't reply.

"I don't give a damn how much he thinks he knows

about books and paintings and all that," I said. "I don't care how worldly he is, or how tortured he is, deep down, as they say. Love to me is you. And he's gone off somewhere and that's owl shit."

"Paintings and books," said Barb, curling up on her side in her foxhole, facing me. And smiling. "Dangerous things, right?"

I lit a cigarette and said, "Books are words that somebody wrote about something that nobody usually cares what they think. Except for my book, of course."

"And paintings?" Barb said.

"Big fake," I said.

She grinned.

"Painting is what people do when they don't know how to play gin or bridge. It all started with some Italians and Frenchmen and Dutchmen. They painted a lot of shit on some ceilings and walls, mostly of women with babies," I said.

"Little Jesus babies," she said.

"Yeah," I said. "And then they started painting farmhouses and bowls of flowers and ballet dancers on pieces of cloth and paper. And one day a bunch of dumb-ass millionaires said good God-a-mighty this is really great. So they bought them all up."

"I guess that takes care of painting," Barb said. "Now, sir, would you sum up sculpture for me."

I laughed.

"No such thing," I said. "Sculpture is interior decorating by another name. It's what a fag does who can't hold down a steady job. Anybody can be a sculptor. All you have to do is go out and find some driftwood. When you get the driftwood, you take it and stick it down in some wet cement. Preferably a big, round block of wet cement. When it dries out, you go tell a rich widow about it. She has it moved over to the Guggenheim Museum and you're a sculptor."

Barbara Jane said, "I love *you*. Hand me a beer."

We sat for a long while and just looked out at the ocean and the cliff, where the tidal wave would drown the golfers.

Barb finally said, "Did he ever tell you that he thought you and I would make a better twosome, lovewise, than he and I?"

"Get out of here," I said.

"He used to talk about it with me sometimes," she said. "He said you and I would make a perfect item. He said you would adore me, and that's what a woman really wanted. He said he personally would never have the capacity to adore anything."

"Wonderful," I said.

"You don't adore me?" Barb said.

I said, "You're aces high with me, Duke."

"It's probably a pretty good deal to be adored," she said. "What have you heard about it? Do you get meals and everything with it?"

I smiled at her.

"I wonder if we could possibly make love to each other, *physically,* after all these years?" she said. "It's interesting."

"Not very," I said.

"Too many laughs, right?" she said.

"Something like that," I said.

She crawled out of her foxhole and folded her legs and reached for the pack of cigarettes and my Dunhill.

"What if we wore disguises?" she said. "You could put on a business suit and a tie and carry a briefcase. I could put on a wig and pick you up in a bar. I'd ask you for fifty or a hundred, and you could try to ferret out my heart of gold. Get me to give up the mercenary life."

I nodded a yeah, swell.

"Better still," Barb said, "when we get back to New York I'll call you up to come over and fix my refrigerator. You can dress up like a repairman and I'll be a horny old Stove with a martini in my hand when I answer the door."

Fine, I said.

"Hey, I know," she said. "We could pretend we were making a stag movie. Get a motel room and keep the lights on bright. I could wear long black stockings and a garter belt—and a sailor hat. You could roll down your socks and put on a mask and a baseball cap."

"We'd need another girl to come out of the closet, halfway through the script," I said. "Or maybe a St. Bernard."

"It just might have a chance," she said. "It wouldn't be easy, but then nobody ever said love was easy, did they?"

"It's not really a problem," I said. "When we get back to New York, Shake Tiller will be there."

Barb said, "Shake who? Who's that? Oh, you mean the

football player? He's a pain in the ass."

And Barb got up and wandered off to sit on the lava rocks and stare out at Japan.

One thing I know for sure is that nothing happened in the old Super Bowl to make Shake Tiller haul off and disappear. Although I'll say the way the game got under way made a number of us want to go dig a hole in the dirt and become a radish.

I guess it's time for me to settle down and talk about the big extravaganza, even though it is semi-painful in parts.

I still can't believe how nervous we were and how over-eager we were at the start. Whatever the record was for tight ass holes, the Giants broke it.

Shake tried to make some jokes just before we came out of the dressing room for the opening kickoff but nobody laughed too hard.

"Remember this, gang," he said. "No matter what happens out there today, at least six hundred million Chinese don't give a shit."

The dog-ass Jets won the coin flip and got to kickoff, which is what we wanted to do. In a big game you'd rather kick than receive. That's to get in some licks on defense and let the other side know you've come to stack asses.

Everybody who was there or watching on television knows how fired up the Giants were just before the kickoff. That wasn't any act, the way we were jumping up and down and beating on each other.

The guys on our sideline said later that everybody on our bench was hollering, "Come get your dinners" at the dog-ass Jets and pointing down at their crotches. And those standing next to T. J. Lambert said that he was bent over and farting at the dog-ass Jets in tones they'd never come close to hearing before.

They said he timed his best one so that it exploded just as the Jets' kickoff man put his foot into the ball. They said T. J. cut one that was so loud and prolonged that a couple of dog-ass Jets going down on the kick turned their heads toward our bench in astonishment.

The last thing I said to our kick return unit as we huddled out there on the field was, "All right now. This is what we've been waitin' for. Let's get a cunt on a cunt."

Randy Juan Llanez and me are always the two deep backs on kick returns. I want to mention that in case you might have read some foolishness in *Sports Illustrated* about Shoat Cooper making a grievous mistake by using me on the opening kickoff.

I've only been returning kickoffs my whole life. Hell, I broke three all the way during the regular season. Against the Eagles and the Cowboys and the Cardinals.

It was unfortunate that the kick was a sorry one and scooted along on the ground, bouncing sort of goofy. Because Randy Juan Llanez never actually got hold of it before he was dough-popped by two or three green shirts on our ten-yard line.

I remember thinking instinctively, "Uh-oh, Jesus shit a nail." And I knew damn well I would get hit as soon as I retrieved the ball on our goal line.

Well, as you might know if you saw it, that lick
Dreamer Tatum put on me from my blind side didn't
feel so great. It's true, as *Sports Illustrated* wrote, that
"the jolting blow momentarily separated Puckett from all
that made intellectual sense—as well as the football."

Dreamer rang my hat when he busted me, all right,
and then went on to recover the ball for a dog-ass touchdown on the very first play of the game. But I can't help
laughing now at what he said to me after he came over
and helped me up and patted me on the ass.

Old Dreamer said, "Stick *that* in your fucking book."

Throughout the whole first quarter, even the first half,
I guess it would be fair to say that we were in some kind
of a daze.

For a long time I didn't think Hose Manning would be
able to draw back and hit the ground with the football
if you held the turf up in front of his face-guard.

Shake got as open as Linda the Stew's wool three or
four times but Hose only threw the ball about twenty
feet over his head, as if Hose was afraid an interception
would give him syphilis.

After Hose had missed on his first eight passes, Shake
trotted back to the huddle and said, "It's sure nice out
there today, Hose. Can I order you anything from room
service?"

Old Hose ignored him. He just spit and said, "Let's
go, bunch. Lets strike a match now. Here we go."

Hose wasn't getting very good protection, I've got to
say.

Our line was trying to zone-block or scramble-block or

some idiot thing that wasn't working. On situations where I had to stay back and protect, it looked like a junior high school recess coming at me.

"Sumbitch," said Hose once, trying to get up after the whistle. "I thought you could only have eleven fuckers on a side."

What got us was, they were playing us normal, just like Shake and me felt they would. Dreamer played the wide part of the field, like any rover, even when Shake would split out toward the near sideline.

Obviously they were guessing that a good pass rush on Hose was the best defense against Shake Tiller.

Their defense jumped around a lot, trying to confuse us, when Hose would be up at the line calling signals. Dreamer would move up on the line of scrimmage, like he might be intending to come on a blitz, but he would back off.

It caused a couple of bad snaps and one or two delay penalties when Hose would try to call an audible. Once Hose called an audible for Booger Sanders to follow me through right guard, but Booger couldn't hear the play.

It was actually kind of funny.

Hose started his cadence at the line and then changed his play.

When he was calling out the new play, Booger hollered, "Check," meaning he couldn't hear the play.

Hose called out the signals again, and Booger shouted, "Check," again.

So old Hose raised up from behind the center and turned around to Booger Sanders and pointed at Puddin

Patterson's butt and said, *"Right* fuckin' through here, you country cocksucker."

The dog-ass Jets broke up laughing, and so did the rest of us, and we got a five-yard penalty for delay of the game.

For a while, it was a little bit unsettling to have Dreamer Tatum talking to us on the line of scrimmage.

Dreamer would say things like, "Hey, Billy Puckett, run at me, baby."

Or he would say to Hose Manning, "Watch it now, Mr. Quarterback. Dream Street comin' this time. Dream Street comin'."

You have to be a stud athlete that everybody expects miracles from to know what it's like to get as humiliated as we were in the early part of the game.

Especially in something like a Super Bowl before ninety-two thousand people and about a hundred million on television.

I'll grant you that we looked rotten, all of us, but I want to point out that it just isn't true what all of the newspapers and *Sports Illustrated* said about Shake Tiller —that he might have been suffering a slight case of over-confidence.

Some people have reasoned that this is why Shake dropped a couple of balls that Hose finally threw in his vicinity. And the reason why he fumbled the one ball he did catch in the first quarter. Which resulted in another touchdown for the dog-ass Jets.

The truth is, Shake dropped one ball because he was so wide open he was overeager to put some white stripes behind him. He knew there wasn't anything but six points in front of him if he could spin around and get going.

He just started too soon.

Shake unfastened his chin strap and walked slowly back to the huddle after the play. He winked at me and then looked at Hose and said, "Shit, it's no fun if you're gonna hit me in the hands."

Hose said, "Let's go, bunch. Let's pop the cork now and start pourin'."

I can testify also that Shake dropped the other ball because Hose threw it about five feet over his head and my buddy had to leap up, twist around, stretch out and grunt, and even then he only got one hand on it just as two dog-ass Jets high-lowed him.

But I guess the great sports writers think that if you're Shake Tiller you're supposed to be able to catch every flea that ever ran up a dog's ass.

When Shake fumbled that ball he caught in the first quarter, for what would have been our initial first down of the game, it was frankly because Dreamer Tatum knocked his eyelids off.

Shake grabbed it over his shoulder—it was a just little old quick-out—but just as he stopped to throw an inside fake, Dreamer, who was steaming up on him, caught him a lick that Barbara Jane said she could even hear.

The ball squirted straight up in the air, on our forty-five, and here came one of their dog-ass linebackers, Hoover Buford from Baylor of all places, to pick off the ball in mid-air and practically trot to the end zone.

The Baptist sumbitch could have stopped to take a

leak and nobody could have caught him. I'd hit into the line and was too far away, and Hose, of course, is not exactly what you'd call your Metroliner.

Al (Abort) Goodwin would have had a chance, provided he knows how to tackle, but Al had sprinted his usual fifty yards down the sideline.

Barbara Jane says that up in the stands after we fell behind by fourteen—even though it was obviously the work of fate and not the dog-ass Jets—there were some fairly despondent souls among the Giant fans.

She said Big Ed couldn't decide who to cuss the most, Dreamer Tatum or Shoat Cooper.

She said Big Ed kept hollering: "Big toe! Big toe! Somebody kick that nigger in the big toe or he's gonna beat us by himself."

Barbara Jane said Burt Danby just kept shaking his head and saying: "We just wanted it too much, I guess. You shouldn't want something as badly as this. You *really* shouldn't."

Barbara Jane said Elroy Blunt apparently hadn't been to bed at all—not for any sleep, at least—and that he was so tired and hung over and wool-whipped from his party that he couldn't even get excited about the game.

She said Elroy's eyes were the color of beets and he looked like he'd shrunk about two sizes.

She said that after the dog-ass Jets had us down by twenty-one in the middle of the second quarter—which was after Boyce Cayce had hit Jessie Luker on that seventy-yard bomb because Jimmy Keith Joy slipped down—that Elroy just looked up in the sky.

She said he just looked up at God and said:

"It's me again, ain't it? I got me ten large on it but you ain't gonna let me steal *nuthin'*, are you?"

She said Elroy turned to her with his floppy-brimmed suede hat halfway covering up his face and said quietly, "How come it's always my turn now instead of niggers?"

Well, of course, if anybody thinks it was semi-dreary up in the stands, they should have been down on the field.

Until T. J. Lambert smothered Boyce Cayce that time and got us a fumble on their thirty-five, we were on the brink of give-up because nothing would go right for us.

That fumble T. J. captured, which I think he got because he farted so viciously that no dog-ass Jet wanted to go near the ball, enabled us to get a field goal and at least get something on the scoreboard.

I didn't want us to take the three when we only had fourth-and-one on their two-yard line, especially when we were down by twenty-one, but Shoat Cooper wanted any points he could get.

That was Shoat's play and not Hose Manning's, so all of those Giant fans who threw all of those cushions and garbage at Hose when he came off the field ought to feel pretty apologetic about it.

I know it was Shoat's decision because Shake and me were in on the conversation when we called time out and went to the sideline to talk it over.

I wanted to try to stick in there myself, but Shoat said, "Stud hoss, if we was to line up tight, you'd get hit by ever-body in Queens."

Hose wanted to throw, but Shoat said we didn't have any passing room.

"If they stop us here without no points at all," said

Shoat, "it'll give them piss ants too much of an emotional boost."

This was when Shake Tiller said, "Hell, they're tellin' jokes out there now."

I still think I could have stuck it in there for six, but we did what Shoat ordered. Shake Tiller held the ball and Hose Manning kicked it through there and we got our three.

I was all set to block Dreamer when he rushed, but he didn't rush. He faked like he would, and then raised up and laughed. And before he jogged off the field, you may not have noticed how he patted Shake on top of the hat and shook Hose's hand to congratulate him. Would that piss you off at all?

Anyhow, that was the score, twenty-one to three, when we went in for the strangest halftime I've ever encountered.

I'm afraid that for about the first ten minutes we were in the dressing room we acted like a crowd of convicts who didn't like their fat meat. Just about everybody kicked something and slung his helmet against the wall or on the floor. It was T. J. Lambert of course who made the most noise.

"Tootie fruities!" he hollered. "We're all a bunch of goddamned tootie fruities."

T. J. snarled and puffed and built up to a roar and called out, *"We're through takin' shit!"*

There was general movement through the room, with guys going to get a Coke out of a drink box, or going to take a dump or a leak.

"Hose Manning!" T. J. yelled. "You know what your

fuckin' old offense looks like out there? It looks like a barrel of hog shit!"

Hose was over opening his locker and getting out a clipboard with pages of plays in it. He sat down quietly on the bench and started looking through the plays, and smoking a cigar.

T. J. carried on.

"By God, my defense ain't give 'em nothin' but one diddywaddle pass and they don't get that if my nigger don't slip down back there," he said. "Jimmy Keith Joy, you Aferkin sumbitch, where are you?"

From across the room you could hear Jimmy Keith's voice.

"Yo, Daddy," Jimmy Keith hollered.

"Jimmy Keith, get your ass up here in front of everybody and take a fuckin' oath that there ain't no other tootie fruitie gonna get behind you the rest of the day," T. J. said.

Jimmy Keith Joy hobbled over into the center of the dressing room.

"I got 'em, Daddy, I got 'em," he said. "Everything's groovin'."

"We ain't takin' no more *shit!*" T. J. Lambert hollered, a lot louder than he can fart.

"Giants has got one more half to be *men,*" T. J. said. "Them fuckers ain't won nothin' *yet.*"

A group of us around Hose Manning's locker got a mite testy. I guess Shake Tiller started it.

"How much did you bet on the Jets?" Shake needled Hose.

Hose only looked up at him.

"Why don't you try throwin' balls in the same stadium the rest of us are in?" Shake asked.

Hose drew on his cigar and squinted and said, "And when did you forget how to run your routes, playboy?"

Shake said, "I can't run 'em in the stadium tunnels. They call that out of bounds, where the ball's been going."

Puddin Patterson interrupted.

"Let's stay together, babies," he said. "We can move it on them cats. I can feel it. We gonna sail like a big boat this half."

Shake said, "Bite my ass, Puddin. You haven't been off your belly all day. Sixty-four's all over you like the crabs."

Puddin said, "We gonna move it this half. We gonna fly like a big balloon."

"Yeah, and I'm gonna be the first nigger on the moon," Shake said, spitting on the floor.

I said for everybody to cut the crap and let's talk about what might work.

"A runnin' back wouldn't hurt us any," Hose said, calmly. "You haven't showed me a lot of Jim Brown out there."

"Line gonna move them cats this half," said Puddin. "We gonna spin like a big record."

"Nothing wrong with us that a Namath or a Jurgensen couldn't fix," said Shake.

We had to get together, I said. "We got two quarters to play football and that's plenty. We only need three sixes if the defense can shut 'em down," I said.

Hose said, "I think the counter will give us something

if Puddin and Euger can start gettin' a piece of somebody."

"Fuck Euger," said Shake. "Seventy-one's spittin' his
ass out like watermelon seeds."

"We gonna stuff 'em like groceries," said Puddin.

It was from the other side of the room that we all heard
T. J. cut one that sounded like a drum roll and then heard
him call out: "Where the hell are the goddamn coaches?
Shit, I wouldn't blame 'em for not wantin' to hang around
this bunch of tootie fruities."

It must have occurred to all of us at the same time.

The coaches weren't there. Shoat Cooper wasn't there.
The star-spangled Polack wasn't there. None of the
coaches were in the dressing room at the halftime of the
Super Bowl.

The only indication that a coach of some kind had
even *been* there was on a big blackboard at the far end
of the room.

Written in big chalk numbers was a message of en-
couragement, I think you could call it.

The blackboard said: 24 to 21.

None of us saw it when we first got to the dressing
room because we were too busy throwing our hats and
cussing each other. And who would have thought that the
Giants' coaches would have sent us a simple message instead of their own selves?

We never did get around to discussing among ourselves what we ought to try to do. Speaking for myself, I
think I just sort of thought I'd try to run harder. And I
hoped Hose would discover something important on his
clipboard.

Football studs, by the way, get a considerable laugh out of the things they read in the newspapers and magazines after a game.

We're always reading about our strategy and adjustments, and invariably it's wrong.

For instance, the New York *Daily News* said that during the first half of the Super Bowl the big problem of the Giants was trying to "shut off the concealed rush" of the Jets.

Well, I'll read you what the *Daily News* says. I clipped it out and saved it for the book.

The halftime was devoted to a serious discussion of the options the Giants had. Shoat Cooper and his war counsel of Hose Manning, Billy Clyde Puckett and Shake Tiller calmly agreed to go with less deception in the last two periods.

In the first half, Manning had not been able to throw effectively into the seams of the Jets' sliding zone. Thus, the Jets had taken away Manning's favorite weapons—the double zig-out, the hitch-and-fly, and the post-and-go, all to Shake Tiller.

The different look of the Jets' defensive line, which shuffled in and out of a five-two, a four-three, four-four and a gap six, created disorder among the Giants' blockers.

"Our stutter rush, or what we call Foxtrot Green, gave 'em plenty of trouble," said Dreamer Tatum.

The rush not only stifled the Giants' passing game, it kept guessing exactly right on where Billy Clyde

Puckett wanted to run. He had no room. He was virtually shut down, and you could see the frustration written on his square jaw as he came to the sideline, time after time.

Wisely, however, Shoat Cooper went to Plan B. After halftime consultation with his war counsel—Manning, Puckett and Tiller—the Giants switched to Man blocking from their linemen and decided to employ basic muscle.

Although their lucky white jerseys with the blue and red trim were now soiled and tattered, and their proud blue helmets were dented and smudged by the relentless thudding of the Jets' defense, the Giant attack came alive in the second half and prevented no less than an outrageous embarrassment.

Now is that some cheap crap or isn't it?

Do you know when we finally saw Shoat Cooper?

The halftime festivities were practically over and we were getting ready to take the field when Shoat stuck his head in our door.

The door opened incidentally just as we all were yelling and rushing toward it. The door hit Al (Abort) Goodwin in the head and knocked him cold. That's the real story of why he never played the last two quarters.

"Awright, quiet down," Shoat said. "Al will be O.K. You can't hurt a sprinter unless you tweak him on the tendon. If Al ain't O.K., we'll go with Randy Juan, and that's that. Now I only got one thing to say to you pine knots. You got thirty more minutes of football to play and you can do one of two things. You can play football the way you're capable of playin' football, or you can go back out there and keep on lookin' like a bunch of turds what dropped out of a tall cow's ass."

And Shoat Cooper spit and left.

THERE'S NO POINT IN ME TRYING TO ARGUE THAT WE weren't lucky right after the second half started. They kicked off out of our end zone and we got the ball on our twenty, and it was important for us to show the Jets that we had come back with some spunk.

What we needed to do was get a good drive going, and more than anything we needed to get us six.

In the huddle on first down at our twenty, Hose said:

"O.K., ladies, let's tend to our knittin'. Lots of time now. Plenty of time. Let's block now, bunch. Everybody blocks. Ain't that right? O.K., bunch. Here we go. Gotta be smooth now, bunch."

Shake Tiller finally said, "Why don't you call a fuckin' play so we can get on with it?"

Hose called an inside belly and I got four yards. It was the longest run I'd made. And Puddin got a block.

"They all mine now, babies," said Puddin, back in the huddle. "We gonna stick like a big knife."

As everybody knows, the drive was not exactly semi-perfection.

An interference call on Shake Tiller didn't hurt us any, and neither did another one on Thacker Hubbard. Something else that didn't hurt was the quick whistle which saved us the ball at midfield after Booger Sanders fumbled.

"We got a little luck goin'," said Hose. "A little luck, bunch. A little luck's out here with us now. O.K., bunch. It's all there to be had. It's all there waitin' for us. Just a stroll in the country, bunch. That's all it is. Just pickin' up flowers."

Shake said, "Hose, you want to can the shit and call the game? We know why we're here."

That was a hell of a catch Shake made on a wobbly pass that Hose threw which got us down to their thirty-one. Just a typical one-hander from the repertoire of old Eighty-eight.

I guess this was the first time that we felt like we had moved the ball, and we were sure in sniffing distance.

I made a little yardage on a sweep, thanks to Euger Franklin's blocking, and Hose scrambled for about ten, and now we were down on their seven, and Hose called time out.

Me and Hose went to the sideline to chat with Shoat, and this was the first time that I actually think I heard the crowd. It was almost as if I had just woke up. Say what you want to, but a big old thing like the Super Bowl causes nerves and numbness.

"What's workin'?" Shoat asked Hose.

"That interference play ain't bad," Hose said, winded but grinning slightly.

Shoat looked down at his feet.

He said, "One way or another, we got to get in that end

zone. I'd sure like to stick that sumbitch right up their neck."

He said, "They's men down in the trenches and if we could score down in there it would let 'em know they's men on both sides."

Shoat took the toothpick out of his mouth and said, "Try old stud hoss here and see if you get anything. You may have to throw. We ain't goin' for no more threes."

I got two yards on a slant and I got four more on a wide pitch, and we had third down at the one. Actually, Dreamer tackled me on the three but I crawled to the one and the zebras let me have it.

"Good lick," I told Dreamer, getting up.

He patted me on the butt.

Hose called me on a quick hitter on third down, and I knew when I took the handoff that I wasn't going any-where. It was like trying to run over the Davis Mountains. I just hugged the ball and hit in there, and it was fourth down at the one-foot line.

Shoat called time out again, the dumb-ass, wasting one we might have needed. And over on the sideline, he chose to recite some coaching wisdom for us.

"They's one thing you always do when you're down to the nut-cuttin'. I never knowed anybody from Bryant to Royal to Lombardi who didn't say to go with your best back on his best play. Let's stick stud hoss here in there behind Puddin and see if we can get just enough of a crease. Is the Pope blockin' anybody? Tell that toothless Catholic sumbitch to give you a good snap. We got to have this sumbitch, Hose. You hear what I'm sayin'?"

Some people will probably always look back on this play as the biggest of the game, but there were a lot of those. This one was sure the play which caused the most fuss, of course.

It's always a close call when a back tries to leap up and dive over the line, and then gets shoved back. Was he over or wasn't he? I climbed right up Puddin's ass, and I remember hearing a lot of grunts, and I surely remember the lick that Dreamer and Hoover Buford put on me, up there in the air, on top of the heap.

The question that the head linesman had to decide was whether I had crossed over the goal before the ball jarred loose, and I was thrown back, and there was that scramble and fist fight for the football.

One zebra signaled a touchdown. Another one signaled a fumble and a Jet recovery. Another one signaled time out. And, meanwhile, six or eight Giants and six or eight Jets got into what you call your melee.

Both benches emptied out onto the field, and whistles were blowing, and guys were cussing, but the one thing I could hear above all of it was guess what? You got it. T. J. Lambert cut some that really and truly belonged in a zoo.

As much as anything, I think, it was the odor that broke it all up.

I didn't get into the fisticuffs because all you do in something like that is get injured. Neither did Dreamer. What we actually did was sink to our knees, off to one side, and laugh.

When the fight stopped, the zebras talked a long time

and finally decided to give us a touchdown. I don't like to think that their decision was swayed by the fact that T. J. stood right in the midst of them, snarling and cutting some short sweet ones. But it might have been.

I understand that even on slow motion instant replay nobody could tell whether I scored or not before the fumble, but we got to count it, anyhow. That's the main thing.

It was twenty-one to ten, after Hose made the conversion, and we were back in the ball game.

Barbara Jane said that up in the stands, some of our friends, for the first time, had started to sense a glimmer of hope for a miracle.

She said Big Ed was furious at Shoat Cooper's goal-line calls but the touchdown calmed him down.

Barb said that Big Ed said, "We're almost back in the goddamn contest. I just don't know how much character our niggers have got."

I know there'll probably always be an argument about whether I scored on fourth down at their one-foot line but I truly believe I got over before Dreamer and the others knocked me and Puddin back to the five, and the ball back to the ten.

It was surely that drive to start the second half which made us a lot more eager to do battle. In pro football, being down by twenty-one to ten is not nearly so bad as it seems, particularly when there's still a quarter and a half to go and you've suddenly got some momentum.

Of course, it took a little of the juice out of us when they came right back and drove eighty yards to our one-inch line and had a first down. And I'll never know how T. J. Lambert got back there and took the ball away from Boyce Cayce just as he was handing it to Gruver Allgood without being called for offsides.

That was certainly one of the biggest plays of the game, even though *Sports Illustrated* failed to mention it. If the dog-ass Jets had scored then, it would have been twenty-eight to ten and we might have been deader than a Jew at River Crest.

When T. J. came off the field you might have noticed that he brought the football with him and refused to give it back to the referee because he wanted it as a keepsake.

"I sucked this sumbitch up from them tootie fruities and I'm gone keep it," he sneered.

Of course, in so far as big plays go, you can't say enough about Jimmy Keith Joy redeeming himself by recovering the punt they fumbled on the following play. Hose Manning really got into a good punt and it didn't hurt any that the ball took a crazy bounce past their twin safeties and rolled damn near the length of the field, or all the way to their twelve-yard line.

Old Jimmy Keith Joy was chasing that sumbitch all the way, you might remember, as if a carload of red necks were after him. And even though Jimmy Keith and Jessie Luker sort of wound up in a tie for the ball, I think the referee made a good decision when he awarded it to us on their fifteen.

I knew with two successive breaks like that we would score quick.

In the huddle Hose Manning called for Shake Tiller to

split out by Dreamer Tatum, fake a hook and then beat
him to the flag.

"Drill it on the break," said Shake, "and my numbers'll
be there."

It was really a pretty play. Shake put his move on
Dreamer and left him hollering, "Aaaaah, shit!" and
Hose blew it right in there at Shake's numbers and we had
us another six.

When the fourth quarter started and it was some kind of
a ball game, twenty-one to seventeen, Barbara Jane said
that some of our Giant fans were bordering on insanity.

She said Burt Danby had run over a couple of box seats
away and was hugging Strooby McMackin and slapping
people on the back and shaking his fist at the whole stadium behind him.

She said Burt was shouting, "Guts! Courage! Class!
Never say die! Giants forever! *God,* I love our city!"

Barbara Jane said that Big Ed said, "We've got 'em
now. They're on the ropes. You can see it. It's all over. The
moment of stress has come and their goddamn niggers'll
quit. Watch what I'm telling you."

She said it was just about then that Dreamer Tatum in-
tercepted Hose's screen pass and went fifty-five yards for
his second touchdown of the game.

I don't mind saying that this gave us a sick feeling, to
be on the verge of catching up, and then to have something like that happen. To pull up to within four points
of somebody and then suddenly to have something terrible like that occur and fall back by eleven was almost
enough to make us want to vomit.

We probably would have, too. We probably would have just sat down and thrown up and cried pretty soon if Randy Juan Llanez hadn't taken that kickoff and run it right up their ears.

Some things I've read say television clearly showed he stepped out of bounds twice, at our forty and at their twenty-two, but all I know is that Randy Juan Llanez got credit for going ninety-eight steps to their alumni stripe, and it was six more for our side.

And if he's not the greatest little spook-spick I've ever known then you can go browse through your taco huts and find one to top him.

I'm embarrassed that I made such a spectacle of myself when Randy crossed the goal line. I was running right behind him all the way. And I was so happy when he scored that I guess I must have looked like a dress designer the way I wrestled him down to the ground and hugged on him, celebrating.

All I remember is that I was overcome with joy and Randy Juan was squirming and squealing underneath me. He said his ankle was pinching.

Barbara Jane said that Big Ed was in some kind of shock by what Randy Juan Llanez had done.

She said Big Ed just shook his head and said, "Goddamn if you'd have asked me about it, I'd have said the little spick wasn't good at anything but driving the team bus."

Barb said that Elroy Blunt looked at the scoreboard and then looked up at God and said:

"Twenty-eight to twenty-four, Skipper, and you know

I'm a sinner. What kind of fuckin' is it gonna be?"

Barb said Burt Danby was screaming tears, standing up on his seat, purple in the face, shouting back at the stadium behind him:

"It's *class!* It's *guts!* It's *courage!* It's *Manhattan,* by Christ!"

I really wish I could tell you that we knew what we were doing there at the last.

I'd like to be able to divulge that we said a lot of dramatic things to each other in the huddle. I wish I could say that every time we went in the huddle on that eighty-five yard drive, which was against both the dog-ass Jets and the dog-ass clock, that we were fresh enough to be witty or clear-thinking or exceptionally heroic in one way or another.

I've thought about it a lot over here on Lihililo Beach, where I can look out at the old Pacific or up at the rain clouds and the high waterfalls on the mountains, or at the fairly distracting sight of Barbara Jane in a bikini over on the lava rocks.

All I can truthfully remember is that I was so whip-dog tired and bruised up that I was just going along on what you call your instinct.

Over and over in the huddles, Hose Manning would be panting and jabbering things like, "Gotta have it, bunch, gotta have it. Let's get it, let's get it. Guts up time now. This is a gut check. Gotta have it."

I recall hearing Hose calling an audible at the line, now and then, like, "Blue, curfew, eighty-three," and at the same time I recall hearing Dreamer Tatum yelling defensive signals, like, "Brown, bruin, foxtrot," and then the Pope would snap the ball and I'd run somewhere and take another lick.

I guess I ran where I was supposed to run.

Somewhere along the way, Shake asked me, "You tired, Billy C.?" I remember that. And I remember Hose saying, "I'll tell him when he's tired."

That was a hell of a call Hose came up with when we had fourth fucking down on our own thirty-seven and two to go. I knew we had to go for it, because of the clock. If we punted, we might never see the ball again.

I didn't know what Hose would do. Run me, maybe. Try to hit Shake on a quick sideline, maybe. Just something to get the first down. I didn't expect what he invented and obviously the dog-ass Jets didn't either.

In the huddle Hose said, "Bunch, I got to suck it up and pick a number. This might be the ball game so everybody give me their best shot."

Hose didn't make up a play so much as he made up a change of positions. He put Shake Tiller at tight end and he put Thacker Hubbard into a full-house backfield with me and Booger Sanders. The only guy he split out wide was Randy Juan.

Then he called tight end deep, only man down. This meant that it was going to be a deep pass for Shake Tiller, out of a run formation. It was going to be that or nothing.

"I got to have good boards on this one," Hose told Shake.

"Just throw that sumbitch. I'll get there," said Shake.

If Hose had thrown a real good pass, of course, it would have been a touchdown because the play had everybody fooled, including Shoat Cooper. Nobody was within ten yards of Shake.

As it was, we only got thirty-five yards after Shake jumped up and caught the ball over his head and came down off-balance and toppled out of bounds. Instead of semi-dead, we were down on their twenty-eight.

He caught the ball near our bench, and you would have thought he had just been elected Roman emperor, the way our bunch mobbed him.

I want everybody to know that I was fairly astounded later on when I found out that I carried the ball six straight times from there.

I don't at all remember the ten-yard sweep where they tell me I flat ran over Dreamer Tatum, cunt on cunt. And he had to be helped off the field for the first time in his career.

That last carry wasn't Twenty-three Blast, by the way, like *Sports Illustrated* said. It was what we call Student Body Left, which is a play where everybody pulls left and I run a slant or a sweep, depending on how the blockers clear a path.

We called time out before that last play but I didn't go to the sideline. I just sat down and tried to breathe. I did look up at the clock on the scoreboard behind the goal post and saw that there were only four seconds left in the game.

I sat there and looked all around the stadium at those ninety-two thousand people and although there must have been a lot of roaring, I couldn't hear anything. It was weird. Really eerie. It was like I was swallowed up by this great movie, all around me, but it was a silent movie.

They say I cut inside on the play and pretty much ran over Puddin Patterson's big ass again. All I can say is that I was so tired and numb that those three yards were the longest I ever tried to make.

They say I climbed right up Puddin's big ass and then dived, headfirst like a silly damn swan, over the alumni stripe, and came down on my face-guard to win the game.

What happened for the next few minutes is also pretty much of a blur. Let's see now. They carried me off the field, of course, and I damn near got stripped naked from little kids clawing at me.

I can still hear Elroy Blunt rapping on my helmet and saying, "We done fucked 'em. We done fucked 'em."

T. J. Lambert lifted me up in the air and said, "Remind me to buy you a sody pop."

Burt Danby had tears streaming down his face and went so far as to kiss me on the goddamn lips.

Shoat Cooper managed the one and only grin of his whole lifetime and said, "What I call what you done out there is *football.*"

Big Ed Bookman shook my hand and put ten one hundred dollar bills in it and said, "Spread this around among some of your blockers and tell 'em I don't just appreciate it by myself but the whole goddamned country does."

It was pretty much after all the celebrating had died down in the dressing room—after everybody had stuck their heads under bottles of Scotch and champagne—that Shake Tiller came over and quietly shook my hand.

"Ate their ass up is all you did, Billy C.," he said.

Well, as happy as I am to be on the winning side in the Super Bowl, I can't brag that thirty-one to twenty-eight is much of a whipping. I think if we played them again it wouldn't be so close. And I surely don't agree with *Sports Illustrated* that it was "beyond question the most memorable sporting event of the century, apart from the most recent America's Cup."

I'll say this. I think the sports writers made a good choice when they voted Dreamer Tatum the Player of the Game. I'd like to have had that trophy as well as the cabin cruiser and the year's supply of bubble bath. But Dreamer deserved the award.

There wasn't anything in the newspapers about Dreamer coming over to our dressing room to congratulate us. After he had showered and got dolled up, and after the crowd had thinned out, he came over.

It was semi-big of him, I thought.

Dreamer went around and shook everybody's hand on our team.

He was wearing a leather jacket with a belt, a pair of pink velvet knickers with riding boots that had spurs on them, and a bush hat made out of fur.

"Nice goin'," he said. "Had you cats in the box but we let you out."

I thanked him for coming over.

"It could have been different real easy," I said. "A lot of things could have happened the other way."

Dreamer smiled.

"Say, I learned somethin' a long time ago about football, baby," he said. "What *could* have happened, *did*. That's what I know."

Dreamer also said that me and him ought to get to know each other better in New York. Maybe chase some wool together.

I told Dreamer that when we all got off the banquet circuit we'd sure do that.

"You the champs, baby," said Dreamer, leaving. "Scoreboard done said so."

I thought to myself that Dreamer Tatum was some kind of a stud, all right, and I hoped I could have that much class when I lost a big one.

I think I must be getting pretty close to the end of my book because there isn't much more to tell about right here. I'd like to give Shake Tiller a semi-chance to turn up before I come to Fort Worth, Jim Tom.

I hate to leave Shake hanging out there, wherever that is.

But maybe the phantom old Eighty-eight will come riding up on a wave before me and Barb run a post pattern to the mainland.

I'll be getting back to you, folks, in a few days. That'll be after I've gone to Fort Worth and met with my collaborator and tried to mend his life.

Right now I got to go stick my toe in the Pacific Ocean. The noted author seems to have worked himself up a semi-lather here in the sun.

* * *

My fellow Americans. I have come before you tonight as your Commander-in-Chief with a message of grave concern for all of us. It has been called to my attention by the head of the Federal Food and Drug Administration that certain professional football players smoke dope and drink whisky.

It has also been called to my attention that there is poverty and rioting in several of our cities. This was called to my attention by television.

I think both of these things are regrettable and I want to assure you this evening that if they don't stop, I'm going to Palm Springs and get in a few rounds of golf.

Now I'm going to dismiss the poverty and rioting issues because poverty is nothing more than a state of mind. And rioting, as I've said many times before, rioting, per se, is not a concern to any of us who don't like spade neighborhoods in the first place.

To get down to the more important subject, I'd like for all of you to meet a good friend of mine, Mr. Billy Clyde Puckett. Say hello to America, Billy.

Hidy.

Billy, you were the hero of the Super Bowl, weren't you?

Semi.

You ran real tough in there, Billy, and I want to congratulate you.

Thankee.

Now then, Billy. As an athlete worshiped by millions of youngsters around this great country of ours, I'd like for you to tell all those watching and listening whether you think it's right to drink whisky or, as they say, to turn on. Just face the camera, Billy, and tell America what's in your heart.

Is that the camera right there?

Tell it like it is, Billy.

Well, uh, this is Billy Clyde Puckett speaking, and I've got a lot of things on my heart. First of all, I don't think whisky drinking—to any excess, anyhow—is any good when you're alone.

Excuse me, Billy, but—

As for dope, I think it's the only thing you ought to use when you turn on.

Uh, Billy, just a min—

Something else is bothering me, too. I heard the other day that exposing yourself in front of little girls was against the law. I think that's a lot of shit.

Billy Puckett!

It's what I got on my heart. Also, I want to get me some pussy.

Hi, gang. It's the real me this time. I was just having a little fun there, imitating the President and my alter ego. Actually I was trying to entertain a very dear, very warm, very old, very wonderful friend of mine, the lovely and charming Miss Barbara Jane Bookman.

Take a bow, Barb.

The deal is that I'm laying here on a sofa in me and Shake's palatial apartment in New York City, New York, with a young Scotch in my hand and my little old tape recorder.

Miss Barbara Jane Bookman is sitting across the living

room from me in her traditional pair of tight, faded Levi's and a whole blouse full of dandy lungs.

Whoops. She just threw a *Sports Illustrated* at me.

Missed though. Kid never did have an arm.

Wait a second. She wants to say something.

It wasn't too funny. She said, "Good tits, no arm."

She's gone now—shopping or something—so that's good. Won't be any more interruptions while the noted author faces up to the chore of the last remaining paragraphs of one of the great books of the ages.

It's later than I thought it would be when I thought I'd get around to this. It's almost spring in New York, which I think is a pretty stud time of year, especially when a man can walk down the street as the world champion of professional football.

The trees are starting to take on a little green, and almost all the slush is gone. And all the little girlies around town have slipped out of their big old coats and slipped into not too much.

It's kind of a pleasant sight as a fellow takes himself around from bar to bar.

One or two fascinating things have happened since you last heard from me over in Hawaii.

For one thing, it looks as if Barbara Jane was right about Shake Tiller. Right about Shake staying away for quite a while.

It's been so long now that I'm beginning to think the sumbitch might make it a lifetime, but I don't really believe that.

I suppose I'll never know what he finds so stimulating about spies or ceiling fans or mountain tops, but I don't think he'll ever know, either.

Just before we left Hanalei we got another wire at Ching Yung's. This one was from Bangkok and it said:

Pals. Have met a quinine hunter who can play the banjo and an escaped murderer from Hollis, Oklahoma. Have met a rich old stove who used to be married to an Argentinian general before she had him shot. Found a mystic who promises to tell me all the secrets of the Shriners. There are spies here and counter-revolutionaries and we have exchanged chili recipes. Your new split end ought to be a spook. You know of course how fast spooks are. Don't save me any meatloaf. Love both of you more than pickin' and singin'. Love. Eighty-eight.

We weren't very amused.

Barbara Jane said, "The key sentence is, 'Don't save me any meatloaf.' That means he won't be home for supper for a long time. He's really gone, you know. What do you want in the pool? I'll take five years."

She read the wire again, standing out on the board steps of Ching Yung's, just by the road. She looked up at the big mountain with the waterfall, and then over at me.

"Some people say Shake Tiller is a rat bastard prick," she said.

I tried to get Barb to come with me to Fort Worth, and then maybe even go out on the banquet circuit with me.

She said she needed to see Big Ed and Big Barb right

then about like she needed a skin rash.

She said she had a couple of jobs in New York, if she wanted to take them.

"If I play my cards right, I think I can be the new Plus-White Pick-up Girl," she said, flashing her teeth.

Fort Worth might be kind of fun, I mentioned. See some of the old joints. Some of the people. Eat some decent Mexican food. Get drunk, of course.

"I thought we spent our life trying to get out of there?" Barb said.

"It's only a stopover," I said. "I'll go over the tapes with Jim Tom. Earlene can throw a clock radio at us. And then we'll leave. Might be able to slip in and out without even calling your folks."

Barb said it was tempting at that. But no.

"I'll do my New York number, and you do your Akrons and your Denvers. Listen, I've got plenty to keep me busy for a while. For one thing, I'm a member of an organization which plans to blow up the World Trade Center. I've got meetings to attend."

I guess I grinned.

"After that," she said, "I'm starting a campaign to get all the dead Puerto Ricans and crates of brassieres out of the Hudson River."

I took one of those overnight flights from Honolulu to Dallas, the kind where you can't sleep because you've got to get drunk twice, eat three times, see a movie, and make a run at a stewardess.

We landed at six in the morning and I rented a car. I think I was at the stew's apartment until noon. Her name was either Shirley or Connie. Stovette, Dirty Leg. Not so great.

I drove over to Fort Worth and got into a room out at the Green Oaks Hotel. I called Jim Tom and said he ought to come get the tapes so he could be transcribing them onto paper while I slept for the next day and a half.

Then we could go over them, I said, and he could compliment me on the fine job I'd done.

"Can I bring you a package?" Jim Tom asked. "I can probably scare up a friend of Crazy Iris or somebody."

I said, "If you do, you'd better bring along somebody to fuck her. I'm whipped."

It was the next morning when Jim Tom woke me up on the phone, laughing like hell.

"Hey, Stud," he said, "I want to know a little more about that waitress Carlene at that place called the Ho Chi Minh Trail. Sumbitch. She sounds like somebody who ought to be in the Dream Backfield."

I yawned and coughed and groaned.

"I'm about halfway through getting it typed. Sounds good. I guess the publishers don't mind a friendly and natural little *fuck* and *shit* now and then, do they?" he asked.

"They're just words people use," I said.

"Two people have been wanting to know when you're coming to town. Ed Bookman and your uncle. They've called a couple of times in the last few days," Jim Tom said.

I asked how much more time Jim Tom needed to type

up the book, read it, and think about some suggestions.

"With some real good luck, we could meet tomorrow noon at Reba's Lounge and go over the whole thing," he said.

I said that was good. I'd knock out Uncle Kenneth and Big Ed today and tonight, and then I'd be free. I pointed out that I had a luncheon in Akron and a dinner in Denver coming up soon.

"I don't want to have to come back here," I said.

"But Fort Worth loves you," Jim Tom said.

I met Uncle Kenneth that day at Hubert's Recreational Center, a combination pool hall and domino parlor downtown. It's been there for years. You can get a bet on most anything at Hubert's, including the up-to-the-minute price of grain. You can play gin, or moon, or bridge, or eight-ball, or six-ball-wild-snooker.

Uncle Kenneth enjoyed showing me off to his pals, some of whom I remembered, like Puny the Stroller and Circus Face and Jawbreaker.

"This here's my nephew that won me five large on the Super Bowl," Uncle Kenneth would say.

Puny the Stroller, who is still fat and walks around town a lot, never looked up from a gin game when Uncle Kenneth took me over to him.

All Puny the Stroller said was, "I don't know nuthin' about it, don't you see, but it looked to me like somebody done reached the zebras in that fuckin' game."

Uncle Kenneth and I sat over in a corner and had us a couple of beers. He was dressed just like always—in a golf shirt, a sports coat, a pair of tasseled loafers and a little Tyrolean hat. And he wore his shades.

"Billy, I want you to know that I'm real proud of you," he said. "You strapped it right on 'em there at the last."

I asked Uncle Kenneth how he liked his bet when we were way down at the half.

"Oh, hell, the damned old bet don't mean anything. You winnin' that game is all I cared about," he said. "I believe in winnin', Billy, as I've always tried to tell you about sports and things."

Uncle Kenneth's hat was cocked down over his eyes. His shades, I mean.

"It's like one of them old coaches—Bear Bryant or somebody—always said. Winnin' ain't the only thing in life but it beats the dog shit out of whatever's next."

We talked on for a while, until Uncle Kenneth decided it was time for him to go to work. At snooker.

As I was leaving, Uncle Kenneth was chalking his cue and explaining the rules of the game to two guys who looked like they sold insurance.

"This here's Call Shot," he said. "It's five dollars a man to them what beats you. The six is wild. It's call ball, call pocket, call kiss, call bank and press when you feel lucky."

He gave me a wave as I stood at the door.

"Take care, Billy," he said. "How you like these two geese I got here? Goddamned if ever day ain't a holiday and ever meal ain't a banquet."

I knew there wasn't any getting around dinner with Big Ed and Big Barb out at River Crest. I had hoped it might just be the two of them but Big Ed insisted on inviting some friends along. He brought along one of his partners, Jake Ealey, and Jake Ealey brought along his wife, Georgene. And there were two other couples who had familiar names from the dynamic world of Fort Worth money.

Their names don't matter.

They all congratulated me on the game and they said they guessed I was sure happy to be back in "God's country," if only for a few days.

"Good for you to be back where you can breathe some air you don't have to *count,*" said Jake Ealey, being humorous.

They all discussed some of their more bitter experiences with New York waiters, cab drivers, hotel clerks and shopkeepers. One of them said he understood New York was "closed until further notice," and everybody laughed. Another one said he understood New York was "for sale."

"What I do," said Jake Ealey, "is get the hell in there, conduct my bidness, and get the hell out as fast as possible."

I wish I didn't always find myself listening and smiling in conversations like that, as if I agreed.

Big Ed got me in a brief conversation about Shake Tiller.

"Marvin, Sr., hasn't heard from him since he called him after the game," Big Ed said. "Barbara Jane tells me you and she haven't either. What the hell's he up to?"

I said, "He just wanted to go off on a vacation by himself. Travel around. You know."

Big Ed said, "No, I don't know. And I'm worried. He's off over there in one of those parts of the world where a bunch of goddamn chinks and gooks can stab him and rob him and kill him and feed him opium and everything else."

Jake Ealey said, "If we'd dropped the bomb on them goddamn bugs when we had the chance, the world would be in a lot finer fix."

I had to grin.

"When you think Shake will be back?" Big Ed asked.

I said, "Well, I don't know. But I'd sure be surprised if it wasn't before training camp starts. One thing about our old buddy. He likes to find some time for himself when he wants it, and not when somebody *allows* it."

Big Ed said, "That's fine, but what the hell is Barbara Jane supposed to do?"

I thought for a minute while they all looked at me.

"Understand," I said.

There was a pause and Big Ed said, "Well, that's just goddamn great, isn't it? What do you think of that, Jake? How would you like to run your goddamn bidness that way?"

Jake Ealey said, "If I did, I'd have a goddamn dry hole bigger than Arizona."

Big Barb said, "I just wish Barbara were married and settled down to some *normal* person and lived down here over on Westover Terrace, or something, and was raising children. Honestly, when I think of how difficult you all make your lives. Living in New York. Some of the friends you have. Well, I don't know."

She gazed across the dining room into a large mirror on the wall to see if her hairdo was O.K.

Big Ed said, "Some people know the goddamned art of fine living and some people don't."

I said I sure agreed with that. And that I ought to be going.

Jake Ealey said, "You tell Barbara Jane that she's too pretty a thing to be wasting away up in that jungle. Tell her we've got some eligible young men down here with a hell of a lot of oil production and low handicaps. She can take her choice."

I wished for a second that Barb was around to reply to that.

"Enjoyed the dinner and the talk," I said, shaking hands all around. And touching my face to Big Barb's, and giving her a hug which wouldn't wrinkle her outfit.

"If any of you see Shake Tiller before I do," I said, "tell him the Giants have drafted a spook who can run the forty in four-four, uphill, and catch anything in the air that doesn't sting."

Big Ed walked out of the dining room with me, with his arm around my shoulders.

I had to stop at a couple of other tables and write something on the menus in the way of autographs.

"He's Fort Worth's own," said Big Ed to the people. "And, by God, we're proud of him, aren't we?"

We walked down the staircase to the front lobby.

Big Ed said, "You and Barbara Jane can take this for what it's worth, but I've got quite a bit of influence, you know, and if you two kids want me to, I can track Shake

Tiller down and have his butt dragged home."

I thanked Big Ed but impressed on him that it certainly wouldn't be necessary. I said Barb and I agreed that Shake had a right to do whatever he damn well pleased.

"If you hear he's in any kind of real trouble," said Big Ed, "you let me know and I'll go to the top. You understand? I mean the goddamn *top*."

I said it sure was a comfort to have friends in high places, and Big Ed said, "As high as we goddamn need to go," and I smiled and left.

Reba's Lounge was the new name of an old place out on White Settlement Road. It used to be the B-52 Grill, I remembered, in honor of all the Carswell Air Base heroes who drank there between red alerts.

It looks like every other place that Fort Worth ever called a lounge or night spot. There was a bar with stools down one side of the room. Behind it was a barmaid who had left her youth in a trailer camp and who had gone out and managed to get somebody to make her hair turn the color of a log fire.

There were tables through the middle of the room, and booths stretched along the wall opposite the bar. A juke box was up by the front door, and a puck bowling machine was down at the other end, by a piano stand and a small dance floor.

I got there ahead of Jim Tom at noon and ordered a young Scotch at the bar. It was semi-dark but nobody recognized me anyhow. Not even the barmaid, who told me her name was Edna Mae. That she'd been down on her luck. And that she hadn't seen me in there before.

Most of the tables and booths were occupied by two, three and four girls who could pass for receptionists at a bank, or Hertz clerks, whether they were or not. A few guys were scattered around, looking like they sold lumber or maybe hospital supplies. They wore white shirts, checkered ties and suits that Barbara Jane would call "Chevrolet blue."

I wasn't so sure what a couple of the guys near me at the bar thought of my leather pants and my suede bush jacket.

When Jim Tom got there we sat down in what he said was "his" booth, which was as far away as anybody could get from the juke box, the dance floor or the bowling machine.

"Nobody comes in until five," Jim Tom said, "but if you see anything you like, speak up."

"What'll we do until then?" I asked.

"Hopefully," he said, "we get drunk."

Jim Tom and I talked about the book for a little while. He said that all he would do was break it up into chapters, and maybe move a couple of anecdotes around. And maybe take out a few fucks.

"How much more will there be?" he asked.

I told him just one or two more tapes, which I would do when I go back to New York after I had been on the road for another three weeks or so.

"Shake Tiller's off jacking around somewhere, acting like he's Mr. Mysterious. I'll give him a chance to turn up, but if he doesn't, then I'll just end the book," I said.

Jim Tom asked if I knew what Shake was up to.

I said I had a suspicion or two.

"He's always had a little semi-hippie in him," I said. "And he's told me he's tired of playing ball. Now that we've won the Super Bowl, I'm about to believe he just might hang it up. He's interested in a lot of other things, you know."

Jim Tom motioned for some back-up Scotches.

"Barbara Jane know how to handle all this?" Jim Tom said.

"I think so," I said. "She's not gonna sit on her ass the rest of her life, wondering whatever happened to old Eighty-eight. She's a perky sumbitch, you know. And she's got a whole pile of pride going for her own self."

"How long will she wait?" Jim Tom said.

"In some moods, as long as it takes," I said. "But in others, about five minutes."

I said, "She's into a lot of stuff. She's working all the time, and she knows everybody in New York. When she's not with us, she's moving around town with TV people and ad guys and agency types and the show biz crowd."

Edna Mae brought two young Scotches to the table and lit Jim Tom's cigarette for him.

"You met my football hero here?" Jim Tom asked her.

"Thought you looked familiar," Edna Mae said. "Billy Clyde Puckett, ain't it?"

I smiled.

"Goddamn, wait'll I tell my sons you was in here," Edna Mae said. "They'll be so excited they'll get constipated."

I thanked Edna Mae for the compliment.

Jim Tom said to her, "If anything comes in that looks good, ask 'em if they'd like to fuck old Billy Clyde Puckett."

Edna Mae said, "I don't see why they wouldn't. They done fucked everything else that walked in here."

I told Jim Tom I wasn't all that interested in getting laid for some reason, but I said for him not to mind me. If he saw something enticing, go right ahead. I'd just drink.

He said, "Stud, I've got to confess something. Once you've had Crazy Iris, it's a close-out on anything else. I'm not lying to you. That crazy sumbitch is Babe Ruth and Jack Dempsey and the whole golden age of fucking rolled into one."

His home life sounded about normal, I mentioned.

In the three hours that followed Jim Tom told me some of the great horror tales about marriage. It seems that his wife, Earlene, had come to despise him so much over the past couple of years that she had gotten fairly inventive in displaying her hate.

At first, he said, Earlene did all the predictable things like locking him out of the house and throwing clock radios at him. Also, he said, she developed the habit of running screaming out of restaurants and bars.

Because he hadn't lit her cigarette.

"Stud," Jim Tom said, "believe me when I tell you that there's no terror in the world like being out with a group of friends and being in a conversation with somebody else and then casually looking over at Earlene Padgett—who had seemed to be having a good time, mind you—and seeing in that instant that her cigarette isn't lit and she's glaring at you."

I asked, "What's the punishment for that?"

Jim Tom said, "Oh, that can be anything from your clothes being thrown out in the yard, to all the sleeves cut off your sports coats at the elbow, to a Sunbeam hair-curler being thrown through the screen of your color Zenith."

I said, "Would you mind telling me something else? Why in the fuck don't you get divorced?"

Jim Tom Pinch grinned and lifted his young Scotch up in the manner of a toast.

"Stud," he said. "I don't have a cent to my name, but if I have to sleep in the back of my car and write my column in this booth, that's exactly what I'm about to do."

I clinked my glass against Jim Tom's.

"It took me a while to figure out that I'd rather starve to death than get bitched to death," he said.

I explained to my collaborator that I'd like to drink with him the rest of the evening but I had a lot of phone calls to make, for plane reservations here and there. And I'd promised I'd call Barb.

"Send me the book as soon as you think it looks enough like a book to give the publisher," he said.

In the parking lot of Reba's Lounge, a Volks drove up and a girl jumped out, rather hurriedly. She wriggled toward the front door, carrying an overnight bag that I thought might have had Jim Tom's undershorts in it.

She had short brown hair, a mouthful of gum, and a fairly stout body. She reminded me more than just a little bit of Earlene Padgett five years ago.

"You wouldn't be Crazy Iris, would you?" I said.

The girl stopped, turned, and squinted at me, putting her hand over her eyebrows. She had a voice that was more on the order of a yelp.

"I might be and I might not," she said. "Who the piss wants to know?"

I WOULD LIKE TO BE ABLE TO REPORT THAT I HAD A number of thrilling experiences after I left Fort Worth and went out on the green pea and fat roast beef circuit.

Unfortunately I can't.

In Akron I met a fairly cute brunette who said she worked in public relations for a tire company. I didn't learn much about tires but I got drunk and dimly remember that before the night was over she said she needed $100 for her mother's cancer treatments.

I don't often get fooled like that.

They asked me several questions in Atlanta about the attitude of the spade ball players.

The Jaycees in Charlotte made me go bowling with them.

In Denver I somehow wound up on a TV panel show with a militant fag photographer, a woman psychiatrist and the editor of a teen-age newspaper. They told me that because of football America was in her "sunset years."

In Detroit somebody named Freddie kept calling my hotel room and trying to get me to come out to a certain address in the suburbs. He said I would have a keen time if I asked for Doris, Jackie, Florence or Pam. They were all great guys, he said.

The Elks in Omaha made me go play handball with them.

And the head of the American Legion in Charleston told me all about the games he'd won for Clemson and the Hitler War he'd won for the United States.

It was in Atlanta, about a week and a half ago, when I found out about this letter from our old friend Shake Tiller. I was talking long distance to Barbara Jane and she said we had just gotten it, postmarked from Fez in Morocco.

She said the letter was addressed to both of us but it had been mailed to her New York apartment.

I have it right here, and if it pleases the court, Your Honor, I would like to read it into the record at this time.

Pals—

I am learning much about primitive arts and handicraft, and also about the guesswork of life.

Did either of you know that the Indians who killed George Custer had gone to Little Big Horn as part of a cultural exchange program? A dope peddler from Sioux Falls explained it all to me yesterday in the casbah.

Behind the veil of almost every Arab woman lies a bicuspid with a cavity. And atrocious breath.

In Casablanca I drank with an old Nazi bomber pilot whose hobby is flying over Rotterdam, London and Coventry and singing Auld Lang Syne.

He who snort coke talketh on and on.

Why don't you two get married and have me over

for Christmas dinner some year?

Whatever you do, remember: anticipating infinity is a self-canceling thought-form.

Go Giants,
A charter subscriber

After Barb had read me that letter over the phone, I said, "I just hope he doesn't get busted."

Barb said, "Yeah. You know what they say about Arab prisons, don't you?"

"I've forgotten," I said.

And Barb said:

"Well, for one thing, they say you can't get a good cheeseburger, no matter how hard you try."

JUST BEFORE MY LAST SPEAKING ENGAGEMENT, WHICH was in Columbus, Ohio, only a few days ago, I phoned Barbara Jane to tell her I could make a flight back to New York late that night.

"I've loved every minute of it," I said, "but I've got to get my ass back to America."

I asked her to meet me at Clarke's around midnight and I would cheer her up with tales of the great heartland.

It turned out that when I stepped into the terminal at La Guardia, Barb was there at my gate with a young Scotch and water in both hands.

"Here." She smiled, handing me a drink. "I promised the girl in the Admiral's Club that I'd bring these glasses back, but she told me she was a Jet fan. So fuck her, right?"

I laughed and gave her a hug and kissed her on the forehead.

"This is a celebration," said Barb. "It's a celebration and also the announcement of a grand scheme."

We began walking slowly toward the baggage claim area and Barb took my arm.

"Now don't say anything until I'm finished," she said. "I've been doing some thinking lately. About the world and the economy and the general social upheaval, and

I"ve come to a momentous decision."

"Which is," I said.

"Just hush," Barb said. "I've reached the conclusion that you and I, being so much alike, and having shared so many experiences, and having such an immense fondness for each other, are simply going to have to become lovers."

We kept on walking and I didn't respond.

"Like it?" she said. "What do you think?"

"About what?" I said.

She stopped.

"About *what?*" she said. "Oh, I don't know. About the history of the Colorado River project, I guess."

I looked at her.

"Let me put it a different way," Barb said. "Look. You probably have a perfect right to think that I would make a suggestion like this with an ulterior motive, right? Which would be to get back at Shake Tiller. You *do* remember Shake Tiller?"

I kept looking.

"That's already entered your mind. But you know me better than that, so you've dismissed it," she said.

And sipped her drink.

"It has also passed through your head very quickly that I've gotten desperately horny and maybe we could *somehow* work it out to screw and Shake Tiller, if he ever *does* come back, won't ever have to know about it. As if he'd care. But you've dismissed that, too," she went on.

I reached in my jacket pocket to make sure I had my baggage claim tags.

"Now you've had time to think about the third thing," she said. "That I'm quite serious, but it's only because I've been so hurt that I don't know what I'm doing. And I'm afraid of being lonely because you two guys are the only people I've ever known or been close to."

I said, "When do I get to vote?"

She took my arm again and we walked on. I've never had a close gate in an airline terminal in my life, by the way.

"Hell, I don't know what would happen," she said. "We might just laugh ourselves to death, I don't know. See. What we'd have to do is this: take a totally different view of each other as individuals."

"Do we get to wear costumes?" I said.

She said, "Damn it, I'm serious. You haven't got anybody else to fool around with, and I certainly don't. You don't enjoy talking to anybody but me, and I don't enjoy talking to anybody but you. Not in any length. Of course, we'd have to try very hard not to think about the seventh grade or anything."

She stopped again in the corridor.

"Aw, you know what, Billy C.? I *do* love you. I genuinely do. I was thinking the other night that all these years when the three of us have been together, that it was always old Eighty-eight for sex and smart-ass, and it was always old Twenty-three for sweetness and understanding," she said.

I sort of frowned at her and glanced down at my young Scotch.

"I wonder if my luggage has gone to Puerto Rico as usual," I said casually.

Barb continued.

"The thing about it is, you love me too," she said. "You always have. I know that. You know that. Everybody knows that. Can I tell you something? I have caught myself wondering why it was I could never really like any of those Cissy Walfords you kept bringing around. I think I know now that it wasn't just because they were empty-headed bitches, it was because they were with *you*. I never wanted anybody to be with you, except me. I always thought that you and Shake were both my own private property, and that was hardly fair to you because if the two of you were sharing me, then old Eighty-eight certainly had all the best of it in terms of getting laid."

I think two nuns were walking by in the corridor when Barb said the next thing.

"And you know what I suddenly thought this morning?" she said. "I was pining for you, I really was—for all the stuff you mean to me, in so many ways—and I thought, *Christ*-o-mighty, what if Billy C. on top of everything else is a great fuck!"

In the taxi and later on when we stopped by Clarke's to get something to eat, during all that time, I tried to explain to Barb why her grand scheme was such a bad one. And why, even if Shake Tiller did become a stoned monk—or whatever—which might detain him for a while; why, even so, her plan probably wouldn't turn out to be anything more than a waste of time.

It could even affect our friendship, I said.

But Barb kept on arguing.

"All you have to do is pretend I'm a brand new wool," she said.

"But you're Barbara Jane Bookman from Fort Worth," I said. "Your mother is planning a big debutante party and sending you off to school."

Barb pressed her leg against mine beneath the table in the back of Clarke's and whispered to me, kind of huskily:

"You can call me Miss Earthquake, fellow. Where you from? Des Moines?"

Well, I can't truthfully say that I know what my intentions were, but I finally agreed at least to play the game. Two or three days ago, we started *dating*, I guess you could call it.

It was pretty funny at first. We explored some new restaurants in some curious parts of town. She even got me to a Broadway show.

We did a lot of lines. Like I would say I'd just as soon hold T. J. Lambert's hand as hers. And she would say she knew she could never mean as much to me as Martha Nell Burch or Amelia Simcox, but if she could only have me in showers after workouts, that would be enough.

It was just last night that Barbara Jane managed to write the ending to this book, in a manner of speaking.

Are you listening close, Jim Tom?

Tell Crazy Iris to get her face out of your lap and pay attention. It's semi-touching, is what it is.

What happened was, Barb and me had decided to stay home so she could show me how she could fix one of

my favorite meals, which is the chicken-fried steak,
cream gravy and biscuits that we all know and love from
Herb's Café.

She just missed making it as good as they used to at
Herb's, but of course the meal she fixed was a whole lot
better than the food we sometimes pay a surly Frenchman
forty dollars for.

We had a few drinks before and after, and then we
plunged into some Irish coffee. And mainly we just sat
here on the sofa and kind of half-watched television and
half-read magazines.

After a while, for some reason, I found myself looking
at Barb. And after a while, she looked over at me. And
we just slouched there, looking at each other.

Finally, Barb said, "Hey, don't say anything funny,
O.K.?"

I shrugged and smiled.

She kept on looking at me like I had never quite seen
her look at me before. I can't exactly describe the look
except that it was tenderly solemn, if that makes sense.
Her lips kind of were parted and the whole thing made
my eyes blur.

I put my hand over the back of her streaked butterscotch hair and kind of caressed it. And I gently squeezed
the back of her neck. She kind of slid over nearer to me.

I almost said something then. Something smart-ass
about how subtle we both were with our indicators.

But what I did instead was, I hauled off and took it
upon myself to kiss her like I most likely have kissed a
lot of Cissy Walfords the first time out of the blocks.

And then I kissed her again the same way.

She turned around then and laid across me, facing up to me, with her legs stretched out on the sofa. She blinked at me and sort of quivered, and she softly rubbed her hand on my shoulder and my cheek and over my mouth.

We kissed again very seriously and held onto each other like we were in the back seat of a car out in the woods on a cold night and the windows were fogging up.

"Say, uh, whatever your name is," I said quietly. "I think this deal might work out."

And Barbara Jane said, "It sure as hell might. I'll be a sumbitch."

DAN JENKINS

Dan Jenkins is a native Texan who has been a writer all his life. A former reporter, sports editor and columnist in his home state, he is now a Senior Editor at *Sports Illustrated,* and his by-line appears frequently in that magazine. He lives in Manhattan with his wife and three children.